Eldenvine
The Heir
of Elvara

Emlyn Thompson

Eldenvine Book One

Dedication:

First, I dedicate this book to God. Second, to my family who have always supported me. Third, to my creative writing teachers, Ms. Hastings, and Dr. Wong.

In memory of Grampa Skaggs, Great-Grandma Lotz, Great-Grampa Thompson, and Great-Grandma Lynn, I miss you.

Contents:

Prologue: (Almost Fifteen Years Ago - Elvara)

James Elvecrown sat on the ledge of his window. In his hands, he held a scrap of paper with the face of a beautiful woman drawn on it. He traced the woman's cheek with his fingertip and his heart ached with familiar hollowness. He heard a rumble of thunder and his head jerked up to see the sky darkening. His lip curled with a smile for the first time in the year that he'd been imprisoned.

He grabbed a bag from his feet and triple-checked his supplies. With one last glance at the paper, he folded it and carefully placed it in the bag. He threw the bag onto his back and leaped through the window, crying out when his hand caught the rough wooden ledge.

The winds were strong, and he hadn't climbed the walls in a very long time. However, he'd never lost his skill. As a child, he and his sister had competitively raced across the exterior walls, he clung to those memories to guide his movements down the ancient bark.

Three years previously, his older sister Inaria had disappeared, killed by their uncle, King Sonoson of Elvara. James ran away that night. He'd traveled to Islaria, fell in love, and got married. But Sonoson caught up to him and used a cruel trap to bring him back. His mind drifted to his wife and dread filled him. Her last message had been two months ago and he had no idea what had happened to her.

James felt a surge of fury towards his uncle, the cruelest most heartless man he knew, who seemed to relish in his misery. As soon as it had appeared, his fury vanished and was replaced with regret. He should've been more careful. He'd known that Inaria was long dead, but he had been foolishly hopeful. His uncle sent him a message claiming to be from his lost sister and James fell for it.

James finally reached the ground and carefully walked through the dense woods until he found an elk wearing a soft leather saddle. He silently thanked his close friend Elrine who'd hid the animal that morning. He would miss her, but it was safer for her to stay in Elvara.

"You can't leave without saying goodbye." Her voice suddenly called out. James turned towards her, startled.

Elrine walked out from behind the trees, and he noticed her bright green eyes were wet. "Elrine, I," She cut him off.

"Go. Someday, Sonoson will be gone, and you can come back." Elrine's usual teasing voice was heavy with emotion. James gently embraced her.

"Thank you." He said softly. Elrine nodded. She'd been Inaria's best friend and practically his second sister, he would miss her. She and Max, his best friend, had helped distract Sonoson so he could escape. Elrine stepped away and wiped her tears away with the back of her hand.

"Goodbye, Elrine." James climbed onto the back of the elk and gripped the reigns tight. He nodded once more, before ridding away to the woman he loved.

"Goodbye James," Elrine whispered, but he was already gone.

James rode north, to Islaria, to his wife. "I'm coming Pearl," He whispered, "I'm coming."

Part One – An Unfamiliar World

Chapter One: What is Lost Always Finds its Way Home.

Everen Thatcher's fist slammed into the fake leather of the hanging punching bag as she let out an angry yell. "That *hag*!" She snarled and hit the bag again, grimacing in pain when she hit it at the wrong angle, straining her wrist, she'd sprained it last week.

Her day had been horrible, like most days at Red Water Middle School. She was in the eighth grade, a grade made up of arrogant, immature, and generally clueless children. She hated it.

Her day hadn't started horribly, she'd actually been looking forward to it. She had Theater that morning and was going to run lines for the school's production of Shakespeare's *Julius Caesar*.

However, her bliss could only last so long. When she'd walked into class, her stomach had dropped, seeing Trissa Smith speaking with the play's director. In just a moment, she'd lost her part, Mark Antony, and it was given to Trissa.

Since they were little girls, Trissa and Everen had despised the earth the other walked on. In recent years, Trissa had gotten worse, targeting Everen more than ever.

Afterward, Everen tried to talk to Trissa, to ask her for her part back, but the girl just smirked at her, telling her to complain to her mother about it.

Trissa's words wouldn't usually get such a rise out of her, but the girl knew that Everen's mother was a sensitive subject. Ara Thatcher had walked out on them when Everen was barely five years old.

The sound of crunching gravel under tires interrupted Everen's spiraling anger. She re-tied her thick brown hair in a ponytail, grabbed her water bottle, and paused the classical rock music that she'd been playing. Her father had raised her on Bon Jovi, Led Zeppelin, and AC/DC, so she knew all their songs by heart. She pulled the metal garage door open and walked onto the driveway barefoot.

Everen loved her home, it was painted in a shade of whiteish cream and had dark green trim and shutters. The cottage was relatively old, it had been her father's childhood home, and Everen hoped she never had to leave it.

She loved how the tall windows were divided with iron diamond shapes and she loved the lavender bushes planted around the foundation. Her grandfather had tended to the lavender himself (her grandmother wouldn't be caught dead gardening).

Everen greeted her father as he climbed out of the fire truck red Ford which crawled up the driveway and parked in front of the garage. "Hey Dad," she said, hugging him. "Welcome home."

"I'm sorry I'm late, work was a headache. I'll make it up to you with *Star Wars?*" Henry Thatcher suggested. He worked as an attorney for a local law firm, so she was used to his work ending late.

Everen grinned and hugged him again, it was Friday, and therefore family movie night.

"Sure, I'll make popcorn." She grabbed her father's navy travel coffee mug and skipped inside, dropping it off at the kitchen counter to wash later. She stood on her tiptoes to reach the popcorn kernels from the pantry and poured them into a large pot on the stove.

As she adjusted the heat on the stove, someone dropped several bags of groceries on the counter beside her, making her jump. "How's my favorite granddaughter?" A voice called and Everen rolled her eyes.

"I'm your only granddaughter, Grams." Everen teased and opened the grocery bags, she counted milk, eggs, bread, and a pack of soda. "Didn't Dad ban soda for two weeks?" Everen asked with a raised eyebrow, she and her grandmother had accidentally shaken up an entire box of Sprite, which exploded all over the backseat of the truck several days prior.

Grams winked with her bright green eyes, "What he doesn't know won't kill him, I'll hide it with the stash in the garage." Her grandmother was wearing a brown sheepskin-lined leather jacket covered in pins and her wavy greying auburn hair was pulled back in a low ponytail. Today she also wore faded skinny blue jeans and a printed white t-shirt with an old AC/DC logo.

Everen couldn't hold her laughter as she helped her grandmother put away the groceries. "When you say that it sounds like we're involved in something illegal."

"Who says we aren't?" Grams replied cheekily, her bright red lipstick stretching with her smile. "How was your day?"

"Trissa was a jerk like usual," Everen answered, pointedly ignoring the first part of her grandmother's reply. "You're late," she added. Grams was supposed to be back an hour earlier.

"Ah well, I was arguing with Miss Leaders about *Lord of the Rings* at the bar. The conversation got heated, I think I may have had one too many shots." Everen rolled her eyes at her grandmother's smirk. Grams was notorious across town for starting arguments and being able to outdrink anyone, which was odd considering the older woman was barely taller than her five-foot-two, thirteen-year-old granddaughter.

Once the popcorn finished popping, the grandmother-granddaughter duo crashed on the couch and pulled up *Star Wars A New Hope*, arguably the best movie of the original trilogy. After a few more minutes, Everen's father joined them. He'd changed out of his suit and into a set of sweats.

As the opening music played, a small dog jumped onto Everen's lap, tipping over the bowl of popcorn. Everen laughed at the light brown Labrador dog. Cinna had been the best birthday present she'd ever gotten.

As the movie played, Everen's attention drifted and she found herself looking at the large framed picture over the fireplace, it was of her parents' wedding.

In the picture, Ara wore a long white gown and rested her head on Henry's shoulder. She had bright blue eyes, glossy with happy tears, and wavy golden-brown hair that was elaborately braided over her shoulder. Her sharply featured face was broken with a massive smile and gold pearls hung from her pointed ears. The ears were a unique genetic anomaly from her mother's side of the family, but Everen had never met them.

Everen had inherited a lighter version of her father's deep brown eyes with more amber. Her skin was constantly tan, unlike her mother's pale complexion. She'd gotten it from her father and grandfather, who'd been an Indian immigrant and a successful businessman in the tech industry. He'd died shortly after Everen's birth.

Everen tore her eyes away from the photo bitterly. Her parents looked so happy in the photo. She didn't understand why that couldn't have lasted.

After the movie finished, the family of three cleaned the kitchen while Cinna ran around their legs. When Everen finally went to bed, she picked up the dog and carried her up to her room. Grams had gotten her Cinna for her seventh birthday. Everen laid back on her bed with her dog in her arms and closed her eyes. She slipped back to that day, which she remembered like yesterday.

Her mind flashed back to the moment, "Where is she? Why won't she come back!" Everen was screaming with clenched fists in the middle of the kitchen. The little girl hadn't understood that things weren't going to be fixed. She hadn't realized that the cruelties of life were permanent; she was just a child.

Grams had wrapped her in her arms, holding the shaking girl. "Sometimes, people leave our lives, and we don't know why. But we have to keep going, even though it's hard."

The girl started to cry. "I want my mom. Dad said she would come back. What if I forget her?" Grams broke away from the girl and held her shoulders tightly. Her own eyes started to water.

"You won't. My granddaughter is strong. I'm here for you. Your father is here for you. You are not alone; you *never* will be alone." The girl sniffed and nodded as she wiped her eyes. "Come here." Grams whispered and tightly hugged the girl again.

"I love you, Grams," The little girl whispered. The grandmother nodded.

"What do you think about a puppy?" Grams asked kindly, standing up and holding the girl's hand gently. The girl's face lit up.

"I love puppies!" The girl grinned, and all was forgotten.

Everen woke up with a start. It was early morning, and the rays of the sun were barely lighting the sky. Everen glanced at the analog clock beside her bed, it read some point between six and seven. She stretched as she got up and made her way downstairs, noticing that she was the first awake, which was rare. Usually, her father was up at dawn, throwing a healthy breakfast together while her grandmother usually slept in until noon.

She grabbed a muffin from the fridge and ate it as she let Cinna outside. She wiped the crumbs off her hands onto her jeans and followed her dog out. The two made their way towards the woods behind the house and Everen began to whistle the tune of a Guns n' Roses song. She broke into the jog and ran for a few minutes before slowing down and arriving at her favorite spot in the woods.

It was a small trickle of a creek that burbled as it ran over the dark grey stones. Everen crouched on the vibrant green moss and took off her teal tennis shoes, her favorite color. She stepped into the icy water and grinned. It was April, so the weather was warm enough to bear.

As she walked in the creek, she fingered a long silver chain that hung from her neck. The delicate chain had no extra decoration and was one of the few things Everen still had from her mother, it had been the last thing she'd given her daughter.

On her tenth birthday, Everen had tried to throw out everything her mother had given her. Her father had found her throwing stuffed animals into a trashcan after she'd snuck away from her birthday party.

"What are you doing?" He'd asked.

Everen hadn't looked at him, but her face took on an angry scowl. "I don't need these anymore," She'd said as she tried to throw away a particularly beloved teddy bear.

Henry had caught her wrist and gently took the poor bear away. "Why?"

Everen finally faced him with anger flushing her cheeks bright red. "Mom gave it to me, and she's not here. I don't want it."

Henry's gaze had softened, "How about you keep them for now, and we think about this tomorrow. You can go get some cake and play with your cousins; they're missing you."

Everen shook her head to clear the memories and she dropped the necklace. Her mother had been gone nearly eight years without a single word. Things were better now, and she didn't know why she was thinking so much about Ara.

Everen faintly heard the voice of her father calling her from the house and whistled for Cinna. The two ran back through the woods and reached the house.

Henry laughed when he saw her flushed cheeks and muddy shoes. "I see you went out."

"It was a beautiful morning, and you and Grams were both sleeping. I fed Cinna and ate a muffin though." He nodded and hugged her.

"I made pancakes and bacon." He moved to the kitchen and she followed. Everen pulled out a stool and joined Grams at the counter. She devoured the cinnamon and chocolate chip pancakes as her grandmother chatted about whatever gossip she'd picked up.

After eating, Grams led Everen outside, where she'd parked her 1966 convertible Mustang. The car was bright red with chrome accents and was Grams' pride and joy. Everen's grandfather had given Grams the car as her wedding present.

Grams climbed into the passenger seat and Everen frowned. "Who's driving?" She asked.

"You are!" Grams laughed. Everen looked horrified.

"Grams, I'm thirteen! I can't drive!" She protested.

"Darling, I hijacked a car and drove it across the state border when I was younger than you. This is your first lesson." Everen knew better than to keep arguing with her grandmother, so she sighed and climbed into the driver's seat.

"Alright, I know you know which pedal does what and how to start the car. Put it into reverse and press down on the gas." Everen nervously followed her grandmother's instructions. The car rumbled underneath her and jerked backward. Everen's eyes widened. The car moved unsteadily, but Everen eventually smoothed it out. Grams directed her down the driveway and they parked it at the end.

"Dad is going to kill us," Everen mumbled when her grandmother climbed into the driver's seat.

"Nonsense," Grams replied, "I taught your father how to drive, I will teach you too." Everen briefly wondered how her grandfather had reacted to that.

They returned home three hours later and thankfully Grams didn't force her to drive again. The two laughed as they walked inside the door.

"Now that wasn't too bad, for your first try." Grams laughed, clapping Everen's shoulder.

"Remind me not to climb into a car with you," Everen teased and Grams cackled.

Her father met them in the hallway, "Grams was that bad?" He commented.

"Not really," Everen replied to her grandmother's wild laughter.

"You know? I don't even want to know what you did." He sighed, "Then I won't have a legal headache on my head." Everen and Grams shared a look before bursting out with laughter.

That night Everen was plagued with strange nightmares. She was chasing a woman she didn't know through a beautiful forest. Sunlight slipped through the leaves and the world became darker the longer she chased.

Suddenly the woman stopped and Everen got a good look at her. She had waves of golden-brown hair that went to her knees with a crown of golden leaves resting on her head. Her long green dress pooled in the grass and the gold embroidery glowed ethereally in the faint light.

"Who are you?" Everen demanded, but the woman was silent.

Everen stepped forward and repeated her question. The woman turned around to face her. Everen's eyes widened in recognition, but before she knew who she saw, she woke up.

Everen jerked upright, drenched in sweat, and breathing heavily. That dream hadn't felt like a dream, it felt more real and vivid, like a memory. A memory that she couldn't remember.

Chapter Two: When Secrets Should Stay Buried.

Everen heard the faint sound of running water from downstairs as she climbed out of bed and slipped on her pale blue nightrobe. She cautiously opened her door, grateful that it didn't scream on the hinges like when she opened it wrong. She stepped down the stairs silently like a cat.

Her father sat on one of the wooden stools at the kitchen counter. He wore his long dark blue nightrobe and in his hands was a maroon mug filled with warm milk. The warm milk was her father's specialty. He would whisk an egg with milk and spices, and then simmer it on the stove. Ara had taught him how to make it. The result was a warm comforting drink. He turned towards Everen, not seeming at all surprised to see her.

"Everen, it's quite late, what are you doing up?" He asked.

"Nightmare. What about you? It's the middle of the night." She responded.

"I've just been thinking." He drifted off glancing away from his daughter.

"What about?" She asked, taking a seat beside him and setting her chin on her palms. Her fingertips tapped against her cheek and her feet swung gently under the chair. She was a lot like Grams in that way, constantly moving.

"Your mother." He replied, taking another drink of the milk.

Everen immediately scowled and sat up stiffly, "What about her?"

"The truth." Her father replied with a sigh. "I'll get you something to drink." He pulled a second mug out of the cabinets, filled it, and handed it to her. She thanked him and took a sip, it was hot, but not bad enough to burn her tongue.

After he sat beside her again, he began. "You need to stop holding this grudge against her. It's not healthy and she doesn't deserve your anger."

"Excuse me?" Everen was taken aback, "She left you to raise a five-year-old daughter for no reason. Are you forgetting that?"

"No. But I never was able to tell you why, Ara didn't want you to know until you were older, she wanted you to have a normal childhood." He attempted to explain.

"What do you mean?" Everen asked, her voice raising.

Henry sighed, "Ara wasn't from Earth. She called herself an Elve, from a place called Eldenvine."

Everen choked on her warm milk and wiped her mouth with a napkin. "That doesn't make any sense. Mom was an adventurous hiker and a paramedic, not an alien."

Henry shook his head. "I found her in the forest. She was wearing a silver dress made of crystals. I helped her get into medical school and find a stable job. Don't you wonder why you don't know any family on her side?"

At his words, Everen's mind flashed to her odd dream, but she ignored it.

"I thought we cut off contact after she left," Everen replied. Also, she had plenty of family on her dad's side. Her grandfather had three brothers and Everen got to see the extended family constantly.

He shook his head. "That's not why, your mother was alone here, she didn't have anyone."

"This is ridiculous," Everen muttered under her breath.

"No, it's not. This is the truth. She left us to return to her home, where she belonged!" Henry now raised his voice.

Everen stood up. "I can't believe you're making up a story to try and make me forgive her! Goodnight Dad!"

She stormed upstairs, absolutely furious. She slammed her bedroom door and sorted through her drawers in an angry haze.

She changed into a pair of black jeans and a green shirt. She ran a brush through her tangled hair, tied it back, and put on her black leather jacket. She straightened the collar of the jacket with a snap of her wrists, Grams gave it to her for her thirteenth birthday. She found an old backpack buried in her closet and packed it with snacks, a flashlight, a blanket, and her water bottle. She filled it up in her bathroom sink. Everen laced up her maroon combat boots and opened her bedroom window.

About to climb through, she hesitated and glanced back at her jewelry box. With a quiet sigh, she went back to open it and grab her mother's necklace, then she returned to the window.

The window was barely a foot above the roof, and she easily climbed onto it. She felt her neck prickle and turned to see Grams leaning on the doorway. Her eyes widened comically in surprise.

"You know, I did the exact same thing once, several times actually." Grams commented in the silence.

Everen flushed with anger and guilt. "I'm just going out for a walk." She said defensively.

"Yes, on the roof, at night, carrying a bag, which I assume is not full of bird feed for the wildlife. But I've seen stranger." Her grandmother winked.

"Don't tell Dad," Everen mumbled.

Grams let out a laugh. "Darling, if was going to tell my son I already would have, and if I did tell him I would be quite the hypocrite. I'm just here to give advice."

"Thanks, Grams." Everen walked over to hug her. Grams squeezed surprisingly tight for an older woman.

"You're welcome. I only have three things I think need to be said. Use common sense, don't get yourself killed, and when you get the feeling, telling you to come back, do." Grams' tone was more serious than usual and Everen nodded at her grandmother. "I love you, now go and cool off."

"I love you too, Grams. I'll be back by morning." Everen whispered, before climbing back onto the roof and over to the edge. She dropped down onto the porch railing and then down into the grass.

Everen turned on her flashlight and walked into the woods, wiping her eyes with the back of her hands as she went. She was more than just angry, she was hurt. It was bad enough to be abandoned by your mother, but to have it lied about just made everything worse.

Everen didn't believe the nonsense her father had said. She didn't know why he'd said it, but she knew it wasn't true, it couldn't be.

Everen collapsed at the roots of one of the trees and started to cry, mentally cursing her parents for this mess.

As her tears made their way onto the bark, they began to glow gold. Everen noticed the light and she sat back, staring in shock at the strange energy that was spreading through the tree. "What?" She said aloud.

The golden glow spread through the roots of the tree at an increasing speed. Everen stumbled to her feet and backed away. The gold energy rose into the trunk of the tree and a large doorway grew out of it.

Everen gasped and started to run away. Vines made of golden energy lurched out of the hole to grab her from behind and pull her into the tunnel.

The last thing Everen remembered was screaming for her father as the darkness consumed her.

Everen awoke lying in a bed of moss in the shade of a tree that reminded her of the one in the woods. Except this one seemed more unreal and brighter, with leaves like raw jade and golden bark on branches that twisted high. Pale pink blossoms nestled between the leaves and the warm summer breeze sent falling petals onto her face. Everen wiped off the layer of petals that had already formed on her face and carefully sat up, taking note of her surroundings.

It was mid-morning, judging by the faint heat of the sun and she was in a clearing, outlined by six weathered stone pillars. Behind which was a dark pine forest, so tall it pierced the sky.

Everen breathed in and smelled the combination of flowers, earth, and breeze, a smell characteristic of late spring. She also caught a more distant scent carried by the wind. It was the smell of the ocean, salty and exciting.

She rose to her feet, "Dad?" She called. "Dad!" She yelled louder. She felt as though she'd awakened from one nightmare into another. "What's going on? Where am I?" She wondered what had happened, she didn't recognize the place from the woods around her house.

Her hand flew to her head at her sudden throbbing headache. She remembered the fight with her father and running away. "Dad!" She yelled louder, with a tone of guilt. This had to be a sort of twisted dream, or she'd traveled farther than she'd thought in the night.

She took deep breaths between screaming for help and noticed the air was unusually clear. A cold feeling sank into her chest. Clear air meant no nearby city, her family lived near the country, but not nearly far enough for that.

"Dad!" She screamed again with panicked desperation.

Suddenly a teenage girl leapt out of the trees right in front of her. She held a broadsword casually, like someone who knew how to wield it dangerously and effectively. Everen froze in surprise, and admittedly, fear. The girl lunged and held her blade to Everen's throat. She inhaled sharply and tilted her chin up, away from the lethal sharp silver.

The stranger faintly smirked at her reaction, "Hello stranger, my name is Blood Blade. Prepare to taste my steel, it is the last thing you will remember." Her tone was casual and cheerful, like she was saying "Good morning."

Chapter Three: Friends In Strange Places.

Everen held her breath in terror as she looked at Blood Blade. The girl looked around fifteen, two years older than Everen. She was wearing ripped light blue pants that looked like jeans, with a scabbard on her belt and a loose cream-white blouse covered with a black sleeveless corset. She wore black leather boots trimmed with gold and a leather eyepatch over her right eye. Underneath the eyepatch was a pale scar that went from her lower cheek to the middle of the side of her forehead. She had shoulder-length jagged brown hair that looked like she'd cut it herself and her other eye was piercing blue. Her ears were slightly pointy and her skin was a creamy pale with a light tan. Out of the corner of her eye, a boy of about fourteen walked into the grove, with pointy ears and dusty pale bronze-colored hair that accented his rich brown eyes. He grasped an elegant bow in one hand and a quiver of dark green fletched arrows hung over his back.

"Aldyn! Every time we meet people do you have to threaten to kill them?" He asked with exasperation. The boy was handsome, he wore a dark green cloak and light brown pants. He had a pale collared shirt, which was unbuttoned at the top, and brown leather fingerless gloves. His eyes were compassionate and intelligent, and the way he held his bow told Everen that he knew how to use it.

"It's called intimidation, Nathan." She snapped, but her tone wasn't very mean. "I've been doing this a lot longer than you." However, she lowered her sword from Everen's neck and stepped back.

The boy stepped forward, "I'm sorry about that, Miss. My name is Nathan Willowsar, it's good to meet you." He set out his hand and Everen tentatively shook it. He grinned disarmingly. "But you can call me Nathan, the rude person who almost killed you is Aldyn, she does that to everyone."

Aldyn rolled her eyes and sheathed her sword, but her body remained tense, prepared to fight.

"Who are you, and why are you in the Dark Woods alone?" Nathan asked, frowning with a mix of worry and suspicion.

"I don't know what you're talking about. My name is Everen Thatcher, and I have no idea how I got here. Where are we?" She asked.

"To be specific, we are in the Golden Grove. It's in south-eastern Wryrom, in the middle of the Dark Woods."

"Am I dreaming?" Everen whispered to herself, making Nathan look concerned.

"No, this is Eldenvine. How could you not know that? Did you get hit in the head?" He asked gently.

Everen immediately paled and felt nauseous. Nathan reached out and steadied her. "Are you okay?"

"No, no I'm not! I don't belong here!" She exclaimed, turning away from him and throwing her hands into her hair.

"What do you mean?" Aldyn asked sharply.

Everen looked at her with wide eyes and took a deep breath. "I'm from Earth."

Nathan immediately tensed and Aldyn paled. "That's impossible." Aldyn breathed, for the first time showing an emotion other than irritation. "Earth doesn't have magic, and the Elders forbade the use of the Lost Path."

"You're wrong. My mother was from here and I grew up there." She insisted.

"This is incredible!" Nathan commented and both Everen and Aldyn scowled at him.

"How can I get home?" Everen demanded.

Nathan shared a glance with Aldyn, "I promise we will help you as soon as we can, but right now we're kind of in the middle of a mission."

"What?" Aldyn interjected stiffly, "We don't have time!"

"We can bring her along!" He argued and she glared at him. Finally, she relented.

"Fine. The Earthborn can come with us." She growled. Nathan laughed and smiled at Everen, who smiled gratefully back.

"Thank you," Everen said to them both.

Nathan's smile turned sweet. "Don't worry about it, Miss Thatcher."

"Just call me Everen." She shook her head.

"Alright, Everen."

Aldyn led the way out of the Golden Grove and into the Dark Woods. The light drastically faded, and the trees turned a dark grey hue. The undergrowth became thick with thorn bushes and dark green ferns, so Aldyn used her sword to cut a path through it.

"So, you're really Earthborn?" Nathan commented after a little while. "No one has encountered someone from Earth in a very long time."

"Why is that?"

"Well, Earth doesn't have magic, not like Eldenvine. The two worlds are connected by the most ancient of magic, but the Elders forbade travel between the worlds and built magical barriers between them. Aldyn knows some people who keep an eye on it all, and last I heard the barriers were strong, they are considered impenetrable."

"Could they be weakening?" She asked and Nathan shook his head.

"No, you must have accidentally fallen through the Lost Path, it's a way through the barriers but is supposed to be blocked. No one in the last two thousand years would be strong enough to get through. The entire Elder Ring holds it together." He explained.

Everen nodded, although she didn't fully understand. "Why did you separate from Earth?" She asked.

Nathan shrugged, "Probably because humanity became jealous of our magic and tried to steal it." Everen flinched, she wasn't surprised. "But we do still keep an eye on your planet, especially your technology."

"Why would you, if you had magic?"

Nathan grinned, "We use it to inspire our own technology, which runs on magic instead of electricity. Although we don't have much, unlike Earth, Eldenvine never industrialized."

Everen nodded, she had questions about that, but wasn't going to press at the moment, "If we find the Lost Path, theoretically could I use it to get home?"

"Theoretically. But I'm not sure. We can talk to some people who know about magic, they can help you." Everen nodded. "You said that your mother is from here?" He asked.

"Yes, her name is Ara Thatcher. She came to my world eighteen years ago and returned about eight. She's an Elve." Everen explained.

"I don't know any Elves named Ara who are old enough to be your mother, that's a rare name. When I get back to Elvara I can ask around, if you'd like." He offered.

Everen shook her head. "She left. I don't need her forced to come back." Her tone was colored with bitterness. "Anyway," She changed the subject, "What's the mission you and Aldyn are on?" she asked, remembering the comment from earlier.

Nathan replied without hesitation. "There is a group that has been killing lone dragons on Mytharica, the main continent of Eldenvine, Agatha, Aldyn's mentor, thinks this is more than just random terrorism, so she sent us to track them and gather information. Once we gather enough evidence, we can send it to the Council. The Council then will be forced to listen to us and do something about it." Nathan answered. At Everen's confused expression, he elaborated. "Dragons are from the war-torn land of Dragaria, constantly fighting for dominance and territory, so some dragons chose to escape the bloodshed and hide in Mytharica. The dragons committed treason by abandoning Dragaria, so the dragon rulers didn't care about it. I met Aldyn a couple of months ago on a different mission and we became friends. So when Agatha asked Aldyn to look into this, she reached out and I agreed."

"How did you meet her?"

"I was on a mission and we were after the same old map, a few mercenaries were also after it so we teamed up to fight them off."

"Sounds fun," Everen commented and he laughed.

"I got a cool scar out of it," He lifted one of his sleeves to reveal a pale curve on his arm.

Everen's eyes widened and he grinned, "Never pick a fight with a pirate, they play dirty."

The two continued talking and Everen remembered his comment from earlier, "When will you drop me off with your friends who know magic?" She asked.

"We can go to Agatha's when we pass by, she's Aldyn's magic contact. If I didn't have to follow the mission, I would personally help you return to Earth. We should be able to drop you off in a couple of days." Everen felt a tinge of sadness that they would be leaving her so quickly. Aldyn and Nathan seemed like people she would be able to rely on as friends. She had her friends back on Earth, but Trissa had made things tense with them.

"Aldyn, I was just telling Everen about the time we met," Nathan called as Aldyn walked over to them. He was taller than her, but her intimidating glare made his grin fade, if only slightly, "Remember how you got captured and I saved you?"

"Shut up Sharp-ears." Aldyn punched him gently in the shoulder and he cackled. Everen smiled but tried to hide it behind her hand.

"Funny, that's the same thing you said after I saved you, Swords." Nathan grinned. The nicknames were a memory of that first mission. They hadn't known each other's names, so they had made them up.

Everen noticed that the Dark Woods seemed to fade in darkness the further they got from the Golden Grove, it was as though the forest was guarding the secret place. Aldyn told them she was going to scout ahead and walked off.

"So, can you tell me about Eldenvine?" Everen asked, turning to Nathan now that he wasn't talking with Aldyn. She wanted to know as much about the world she was trapped in, hoping it would help her get home sooner.

"Sure. Eldenvine currently has eleven lands. Eight are part of Mytharica which is the main continent. The eight lands on Mytharica are Calestia, Islaria, Ralaji, Wryrom, Mistica, Eldersa, Elvara, and Mythea. Six of those lands are magic lands. There are seven lands of magic. Calestia is the land of Calestic, Islaria is Oceanic, Elvara is Elvic, and Ralaji is Featheric although all the Featherens are dead, so it is mostly uninhabited. Mistica is Mistic, but Mistic magic is outlawed, so Mistica is forbidden territory, Eldersa is Elderic, the main ruling magic of Eldenvine. Dragaria is a massive island east of Mytharica, it is the land of Dragic. The other four lands of Eldenvine are the Gleamaric lands. They are Vlarcia, the land of Vikings, Wryrom, the region of the Dark Woods, Klondor, the Sea of Pirates, and Mythea, the land of the Kingdoms and the states. The planetary capital is Elden, it's in between Mistica and Eldersa. The Eldenvine Council meets there." Nathan lectured.

"What is the Eldenvine council?" Everen asked.

"The Eldenvine Council is composed of the rulers of every land, spare Ralaji and Mistica. Historically, the seven Alpharics, magic leaders, also were part of the council. Also, whenever our world is in critical danger, Eldenvine herself sends a representative." Nathan explained.

"What do you mean *herself?*" Everen asked.

"Eldenvine. She is the land we're on, the planet itself. Our stories describe her as a giant tortoise walking across the cosmos." Nathan answered casually.

"You cannot be serious!" Everen's eyes were wide in shock, of course, she knew Eldenvine would have their mythology, but it sounded ridiculous.

Nathan shook his head. "In a world with *magic,* is it really that impossible?"

Everen was quiet. She'd already seen and heard so much proving her understanding was wrong, but she didn't want to admit it.

The three continued through the forest, with Everen and Nathan talking. Suddenly, a roar broke out nearby. Aldyn immediately froze and gripped her sword with white knuckles. Nathan sent her a worried glance and drew his bow.

"Come on, we have to follow it." He yelled, running after the sound. Everen glanced at Aldyn, who was practically shaking. Aldyn recovered herself and the girls ran after him.

Nathan led the charge through the trees. "We found the Hunters! We can't lose them again!" He hollered.

As they ran, Everen tried to dodge branches, but even years of running through the forest around her house hadn't given her the ability to weave through them. Nathan, however, slipped through the brambles like snow melting into the ground. Aldyn had similar grace, however, she didn't care much about getting hit by the branches, so she spent less effort dodging.

It took them several minutes to reach the origin of the roars, and when they did, they were already silenced. Aldyn found the slain dragon first, in the middle of a clearing. Evern had to cover her lower face with her hand in an attempt to block the metallic scent of blood.

The dragon's massive body sprawled on the ground and thick, vibrant blood pooled around the corpse. Dragon blood was unique, the red was flecked with specks of gold. The dragon was a beautiful creature, with jewel-like purple scales, long navy horns, pale purple wings, and large black eyes.

The massive wing of the dead dragon lay over an upturned nest. Two eggs were shattered on the soil, with the green yolk spilling out. The bodies of the dragonettes weren't fully formed and stabbed through.

"Who could do this?" Everen asked with a flash of anger. The scene horrified and disturbed her.

Nathan shook his head slightly. "We've found a series of similar attacks, absolute massacres. Many of them were also dragonesses with eggs."

Suddenly, a shrill cry, like a young child's rang out. Aldyn tensed. "We're not alone." She whispered and drew her blade.

The girl with the eyepatch crouched near a fallen bush and threw back the branches with the flat of her sword, revealing a small dark blue creature.

The dragonette had scales of shimmering iridescent blues and purples, with deep blue horns and eyes, she was no taller than Everen's knees.

The baby dragon yelped and crawled back, limping on their front talon. Aldyn raised her sword, but Nathan stopped her by setting his hand on her arm.

He moved in towards the creature. "It's all right. We're not going to hurt you." He said gently. Everen watched in awe as the dragonette stopped backing away and let Nathan scoop them into his arms. The dragonette immediately curled into Nathan's chest and wrapped their wings around him.

Nathan slowly walked back to the girls as he carefully held the dragonette. "What are you doing Nathan?" Aldyn asked with an edge. "We don't have time to take in another stray."

Nathan met her eyes. "She's an early hatcher and has no one to care for her. Her mother is dead. Did you see the nest? Two eggs are missing. The Hunters stole them." Aldyn's breath sucked in sharply. "This is the same as two of the other sites, I wonder if they all had missing eggs that we didn't see."

"Why would the Hunters take dragon eggs?" Everen asked.

Aldyn answered with a grave expression. "Many reasons, and each one is worse. We have to go to Agatha with this." Nathan nodded in agreement.

"Yes, and we're taking this one with us."

Aldyn crossed her arms and glared viciously at him. "By Oceana we are!" She swore. "I will not travel with that *creature!* You know what dragons are like!" Everen hadn't yet seen Aldyn so angry, so far the girl had been rather controlled with her emotions.

Nathan tensed, "Aldyn,"

She cut him off. "No! I was fine with the girl, but I am not willing to be near a dragon, no matter how big they are!"

"I know!" Nathan snapped. "I know." He repeated softly. "But we can't leave her. Even though she's a dragon, you can't leave her to die." He set the dragonette on the ground and gently grabbed one of her hands. "You're not like that."

Aldyn glared at him, and glanced once more at the dragonette, before looking back at him. "Fine. But we're leaving her with Agatha." Nathan nodded.

"Thank you." He whispered and she nodded.

Aldyn stepped away from Nathan and looked at Everen. "We're not going to keep following the Hunters, we're going to Agatha. She can help you find a way back to Earth, and we need to tell her about this development."

Everen nodded, and the girl turned away to scout the area. Nathan picked up the dragonette and walked over to her. "What was that about?" She asked.

Nathan glanced at Aldyn's retreating form. "That's a story I don't think I should share." His tone was sorrowful.

"I'm sorry for asking. What do we do now?"

Nathan shook his head, "You're good. Now, Aldyn's off to gather our horses. I want to honor the dragoness."

"How do we do that?" Everen asked.

She helped Nathan cover the dragon's body with branches and flowers. Afterward, they placed a ring of stones around the body. Throughout the process, they were silent. As Aldyn returned, with the horses, Nathan said a few words. He kneeled on one leg in front of the dragoness' head. "Your sacrifice is honored. We will care for your child and bring justice to those who have taken your young. Your spirit is free to fly the eternal skies."

Aldyn coughed and waved the horses' reins. "Let's get going, we're burning daylight." Nathan nodded and took the light brown horse. Aldyn climbed onto her own, horse with a straw-colored coat.

"Everen, you can ride with me. The dragonette stays with Nathan." Aldyn ordered. Aldyn helped Everen climb onto the horses' back.

The three rode east without stopping. Eventually, the light faded, and Aldyn slowed the pace. "We need to make camp." She announced.

Nathan made a fire as Aldyn hunted. Everen didn't know how Aldyn hunted in the dark with only one eye, and she didn't dare ask. Aldyn came back with four fish skewered on her sword that Nathan began to roast. Everen had left her bag on Earth, so Aldyn gave her a spare navy blue blanket.

Everen quickly wrapped it around her shoulders, the spring night was cold, and the warmth was welcome. "Thank you." She said.

"You're welcome. You can freeze to death in Wryrom at night." Aldyn replied. Everen's eyes widened.

"Seriously, thank you," Everen repeated. Aldyn laughed.

"You might take that back when you are stuck with us for the next few days," Aldyn replied. "Here." She handed Everen a sweet roll from her bag. "It's a bit stale, but it should be fine."

Everen thanked her again and ate the roll, noticing only afterward that Aldyn didn't have a second one for herself.

Nathan whistled for their attention from the fire, "Fish is done!" He announced. He handed a fish to each girl on a small metal plate. He'd already gutted the fish, but Everen had to be careful of the small bones.

The seasoning was spicy, but bland compared to her father's cooking. Overall it was good. After taking a bite, Nathan coughed. "Sorry about that. I accidentally used Aldyn's seasoning. She mixes dried peppers and intense spices and called it good." Aldyn crossed her arms.

"I can handle it." She said grumpily.

He rolled his eyes. "I'm pretty sure my mouth is on fire." Everen tried to cover her snicker and was unsuccessful.

The three were sitting close to the fire as they enjoyed the meal. After they finished, Nathan looked at Everen. "I bet you've had a crazy day.

"Maybe a bit." She answered with a smile. He grinned. She yawned and felt her eyes begin to fall.

"You can go to bed. I'll take the first watch." Everen didn't answer, she was already asleep.

Aldyn woke Everen up when the sky was barely a pale purple. "Wake up. We have to go." Everen forced herself to open her eyes and stretch. Nathan and Aldyn were already awake and packing up to leave.

Everen dragged herself to her feet and still felt half asleep. She rolled her blanket and walked over to Nathan who was feeding the dragonette an apple.

"Good morning." He greeted.

"I don't think this qualifies as morning," Everen grumbled. He laughed. Everen handed Aldyn her blanket and Nathan helped her onto the horse. Before long they had continued their race to Agatha's.

Everen watched as the forest became brighter the further they went from the Dark Woods. The thick trees also thinned, and the environment became an elegant and beautiful forest.

This time, she was riding with Nathan. Aldyn was taking all the gear, so Everen held the dragonette tightly in her arms. As they rode, the two got onto the topic of Aldyn. "She once drank a whole bottle of Liquid Burn on a dare." He told her.

Everen laughed. "I knew a girl like that. No one could take more spice than her. I can handle a lot, but I couldn't beat her."

Nathan was quiet for a bit, "About your mother, she's probably still alive, I could ask Queen Inaria to find her."

Everen immediately tensed. "I know."

Nathan continued. "Don't you want to ask at least why she left?"

"I don't care," Everen snapped, "Can we talk about something else?" She asked. Nathan didn't bring it up again. She knew she did want to see her mother if only to yell at her and demand answers. Everen was grateful Nathan couldn't see her because a stubborn tear was falling down her cheek.

After a little while, Everen called up to Aldyn, "Where are we headed?"

Aldyn sent a wide grin back at her. "We're going home to Pine Village."

Chapter Four: Magic Doesn't Have All the Answers.

Pine was a large village in Mythea near the border of Wryrom. It took them half the day to reach it. As they rode, Everen and Nathan continued to talk, staying carefully away from the topic of her mother. He told her a bit about his family, but mostly he listened to her stories from Earth.

Even though Pine was technically outside of Wryrom and the Dark Woods, the village still had the darker trees that were characteristic of it. When they reached the outskirts of the village, the group of three dismounted their horses and continued on foot. The stone streets were wide and dipped in the center to organize water runoff. Grasses grew in the center of the roads along with blooming dandelions.

As they walked, the three were almost run over by six children on bicycles. Luckily, the children swerved and missed them. Everen noticed that none of the children were wearing helmets and at least half of them were barefoot. She asked Nathan about it, and he shrugged, saying magic would easily heal them if they got injured.

Aldyn led them to the center of the small city where there was a well. Around it was a group of children who were being shooed away by their mothers. Aldyn drew some water and she and Nathan helped the horses drink. As the horses rested, Everen looked around. She noticed that most of the houses were two stories tall and had potted plants on the windowsills. In between the houses were small, dense gardens, and the architecture was reminiscent of an old rural Dutch town. The entire place had a busy but tranquil air thanks to the bustling shopkeepers and shoppers.

Another group of children came near and Everen saw about five kids running around with a ball made of pale leather strips.

"Throw it to me!" One girl yelled to the boy holding the ball. He threw it to her but overshot and it fell in the well. The kids groaned because they wouldn't be able to get it back easily. Aldyn noticed them and kindly used the bucket she was still holding to scoop them out of the water.

"Next time don't play that close to the well." She scolded kindly. Both kids nodded and thanked her before running off back to their friends. Aldyn looked after them with a bittersweet smile, then sighed softly as she came over.

Everen lingered, looking at the kids for a bit before realizing her new friends had disappeared. Everen looked around, spotted Nathan waving to her at a street corner, and ran to catch up with him.

The house they eventually stopped at was a small pale cottage on the edge of the village. In front was an unruly garden with oddly colored pumpkins, surrounded by a short metal fence. Aldyn opened the iron gate and the three walked up to the door. The cottage had purple curtains pulled over every window and dark purple vines with lilac-colored flowers grew on the walls.

The three walked up to the house and Nathan held the dragonette. "Who is she?" Everen asked Aldyn who stood before the dark purple door. The place was making her feel strangely nervous.

"Agatha took me in. She is one of few people I trust in the entire world to have my back, and she has earned that trust." The one-eyed teen knocked sharply on the door and was answered after several seconds.

"Leave me alone Elder Pine!" A woman snapped as she opened the door. Her green eyes widened in surprise at the three teenagers on her doorstep. The woman wore dark purple robes. Her raven black hair was streaked with silver and fishtailed down her spine. Her pale skin had crow's feet at the corners of her hard eyes, and she spoke with a thick accent that sounded Russian. "Aldyn. It's been a little while."

"Hello, Agatha. We have an important update on our mission." Agatha held the door open for them to enter and locked it behind them.

"What happened?" She asked once they were inside. "And why is Nathan holding a dragonette?"

"We found her at the site of an attack, she's a survivor," Nathan answered. Agatha reached out her hands and Nathan passed her the dragonette. Agatha carefully held the orphaned dragon and stroked the blue horns.

Meanwhile, Everen looked around the cottage. It was clean and cozy with a basket of red apples on the table in the entry room. The house smelled of lavender, explained by the flowers and herbs hanging on the wood beams on the low ceiling. There was a dark purple door at the far end of the first room and a loaded bookshelf beside it.

"Now who is this girl?" Agatha asked, drawing Everen's attention.

"We found her a bit before the dragonette. She claims to be Earthborn." Aldyn answered.

"Earthborn?" Agatha repeated with amazement. "Now that is interesting. You must tell me about it."

"After I give my report." Aldyn interjected, "The mission is the most important."

Agatha nodded reluctantly, "I understand. Let's speak to the others." Agatha led them into a larger adjacent room. It had a large fireplace in the back with flickering purple flames. Before the hearth was a black cat with emerald eyes.

In the center of the second room was a round table surrounded by arguing women. There were two older women and three young adults in the heated discussion.

"You brainless idiots don't see the problem! We must act now and break into Alderen!" one of the older women yelled. She wore high-heeled black boots, a red dress, a black pointed hat, and a brown leather bomber jacket. Her eyes were bright green and most of her greying auburn hair was pulled into a loose bun at the nape of her neck.

"Quiet Less!" One of the younger women hissed. She looked to be eighteen and had shoulder-length black hair with red irises. Her nails were painted blood red, matching her red lips, and she had reddish-black horns on her head. She wore high-heeled black boots even taller than Less', a sleeveless red leather corset top, and ripped black jeans. On one of her shoulders was a colored tattoo of a flame.

Beside her were the two other younger women. They looked around the same age. One had long purple hair and wore a lilac dress shaped like an upside-down flower. Around her waist were white flowers made of pearls. The other girl had white hair in a pixie cut and had ice-blue eyes. She wore a black leather jacket over a shirt with white at the bottom that shifted to blue at the top.

The last person at the table was a beautiful and calm woman who was the obvious leader of the group. She had chocolate-colored skin, much darker than Everen's father's, and ebony braided hair. Her eyes were vibrant green, and her lush green robes kissed the ground. A dark green cape hung from her neck.

Agatha coughed loudly to stop the argument. The women all turned to stare at them. "Ladies, we have company." She announced. "You remember Aldyn?"

Less laughed loudly, "Heck, we remember Aldyn! We practically raised her."

"This is Nathan. He is an Elve and I have mentioned him several times." Agatha introduced. "And she is Earthborn. What is your name child?" She asked gently.

"Everen. But my mother was an Elve from here." As Everen spoke, Less choked on her drink and the girl with horns slapped her on the back, harder than necessary.

Once she recovered herself, Less asked, "How did you get here?"

"I ran away," Everen replied. "When I was out in the forest, some sort of golden portal opened and dragged me here. I need to get back home."

"Mother Mistic." Less groaned. "You shouldn't be here!"

"Who are you?" Everen's eyes widened in recognition. "No way! Grams!" She yelled. The five other women all glared at Less, who shrank back.

"I'm sorry Ev." She muttered.

"I can't believe this! Dad lied about Mom, and you kept this from me too?" Everen's face was hot with anger as she snapped at her grandmother.

"Pause for a moment and let us explain." Agatha interrupted, "Sit down." She ordered. Everen glared but sat down in the extra seat next to the women with green robes. Aldyn sat next to the girl with horns and Nathan joined Everen.

"Explain," Everen demanded, glaring at Less, who flinched.

"We will. But first, we should introduce ourselves. Wistra Windhorn is our leader." Agatha gestured to Wistra who was the chocolate-skinned woman wearing green. "And we are some of the last Mistrys on Eldenvine."

"Mistrys have been in hiding since our magic was outlawed." The girl with horns cut in. "My name is Hecktra. My sisters are Sace and Krissa." The girl with white hair, Sace, nodded and the other girl, Krissa, waved.

"Our magic is unique to all of Eldenvine," Krissa explained.

"I was born with horns and highly enhanced senses. Sace can freeze almost any liquid and Krissa can create illusions, she's half-Cestry." Hecktra explained. "Aldyn is also one of my honorary sisters."

"But I'm the better swordswoman," Aldyn boasted.

"In your dreams. I taught you everything you know." Hecktra snorted. The girls grinned at each other.

"Grams," Everen asked, she had cooled down a bit, "What happened?" Less turned to her granddaughter with a gentle expression.

"When you ran away, your magic activated, taking you here," Less explained.

"What do you mean 'my magic?'" Everen asked.

Less sighed. "Real magic. You are a mix of Eldenvine and Earth, so your magic is unique."

"Less, do you mean-" Hecktra started.

"Yes." Less shot a warning glare at Hecktra who paled.

"What are you doing here?" Everen asked.

"Eldenvine is my home. When I was a little girl, I discovered my magic. Wistra found me and taught me to control my power. I have a faint connection to Gleamaric because I am a direct descendant of Mistic. When I was eleven, I found a way through the barriers between Eldenvine and Earth, I consistently visited your world and had many adventures. When I was in my thirties, I met your grandfather and we married. Wistra was furious, but she couldn't stop me." Less grinned.

Everen's shock had faded, and she could never be mad at Grams for long. She had always told Everen she was saving some of her stories for when she was older. "So, both my mother and grandmother are from Eldenvine, did you know?" Everen asked.

"About your mother?" Everen nodded. "The second I saw her I knew. However, I was never able to talk to her about it. She was very tight-lipped, and I didn't want your father to find out about me if I confronted her."

"How is dad?" Everen asked, feeling a sudden surge of guilt.

"He's very worried. I didn't know what had happened when you didn't come back. We thought you had gotten kidnapped." Less explained and Everen winced.

"I'm sorry." She said softly. Less stood and wrapped her granddaughter in her arms.

"It's not your fault. It's mine, I'm sorry."

"When can I go home?"

Less hesitated, "I know you want me to take you back, but I can't. I'm not strong enough to take someone with me through the path. You might be able to take someone along, but first, you have to learn how. It takes a long time to develop your magic skill to that point."

"So, I'm not going to get home," Everen whispered, her eyes began to wet, and she stubbornly blinked away the tears.

Grams sighed. "I will go and explain everything to him. In the meanwhile, I recommend getting comfortable, you're stuck here for a while." Everen looked down and Grams looked away.

"I am sorry. But we have other matters to address." Agatha apologized, "Aldyn, what have you learned?" She asked.

Aldyn stood up from beside Hecktra. "We believe that the Hunters are targeting nests. We found smashed eggs at multiple sites, but realized that those were to cover up the eggs that were taken." She summarized.

"The Hunters could be taking the dragonettes to harvest magical power, or to experiment on them. We don't know." Nathan explained as Hecktra twirled a black dagger on her knuckles.

Hecktra suddenly stabbed her blade into the table. "Vile rats!" She exclaimed. "Why do we have to suffer the foolishness of the Council?" Agatha had warned the council months before about the Hunters, but the threat hadn't been taken seriously.

"This is up to us. The Council is weak and won't do anything before it's too late." Wistra's voice was grave. "Hecktra take Sace and Krissa and find out the history of the Hunters' attacks. If they have been targeting eggs like we believe, learn why. Agatha, continue monitoring the Alderen situation. Aldyn, you and Nathan will go back out and follow the Hunters directly. Take a few days to rest though, I know you have been going hard for a while."

"What?" Aldyn snapped loudly. "We'll lose them if we don't go back out now. They're in Wryrom, that's a day's travel!"

"Aldyn!" Wistra's tone was cold and silenced her. "I understand you wish to continue, but please take a rest, for once." Aldyn scowled furiously, but she dropped it.

Less rolled up her jacket sleeve and checked her antique watch. "I have to go."

"What?" Everen asked, jumping to her feet. "You're just leaving me here alone?"

Less sighed. "I'm going back to Earth; I will talk to your father. I will be back, I promise."

Everen nodded, holding back her panic, "When?" She asked.

Less hesitated, "As soon as I can." Less walked to the corner of the room and closed her eyes. Her expression was tense in concentration and suddenly a crackling, sparking gold portal appeared behind her. "I love you." With one last glance at her granddaughter, Less disappeared, back to earth.

The room was silent. "Would anyone like something to eat? I made soup." Agatha asked kindly.

Everen nodded numbly and the older woman returned with a large tray covered in bread bowls loaded with soup. Agatha handed one to Nathan, Aldyn, Everen, Sace, and Krissa. Hecktra shook her head at the offer, so Agatha left the last bowl in the kitchen. The soup was warm, delicious, and comforting, but it couldn't take Everen's mind off of her mess.

After eating, Aldyn set her spoon down and cleared her throat. "When can we go back out?" She asked.

Agatha shot her a sharp glare. "When I say so. The way you handled the Hunters earlier was incredibly irresponsible. You and Nathan could have been killed if you'd been able to confront them."

"You know I can handle myself, and anyone who tried to hurt Nathan would do it over my dead body." Aldyn snapped.

"I'm not arguing about this. Be more careful next time." Agatha ordered sharply. "I promised Sharine her son would be safe."

Aldyn glanced at Nathan and then looked away. "Fine. I'll be in my room." She stood up and left the room.

Agatha sighed. "This meeting is adjourned." She announced. Wistra stood regally and shifted into green mist and glitter.

"We know our orders," Hecktra said, before taking her sisters' hands and transporting them away with dark red smoke and sparks.

Now, only Agatha, Nathan, and Everen remained. "Everen, I wish to teach you how to use your magic. Only then will you be able to return home."

"How long will that take?" Everen asked.

Agatha sighed, "That's up to you."

"Fine." Everen sighed, "I just want to go home." Agatha nodded approvingly, and a hint of a smile graced her lips for the first time.

"You will." The woman promised.

Chapter Five: Heist.

Agatha let them borrow rooms upstairs to sleep. Nathan took one and Everen took another. She passed out the second she hit the bed, not knowing that Aldyn had gone back downstairs to speak with Agatha.

"I knew you'd come back," Agatha said. "You should be pleased to know that I took care of the little dragonette."

"You know I don't care." Aldyn snapped back. "And I'm not here to discuss the monster spawn Nathan saved, I'm here to talk about Everen."

"What about her?" Agatha asked.

"How did her mother get through the path, Less is the only one in *centuries* who's able to manipulate Gleamaric enough to use the Lost Path."

"You are right. Everen's mother didn't have magic to take her through. However, I believe I know why." She paused, "Are you familiar with recent Elven history?"

"Of course." Aldyn snorted.

"Then you know the reign of Sonoson. During his time, he found a powerful enchantress, who knew of the Lost Path. There were rumors that he used her magic to banish political threats to Earth." Agatha explained.

"Why not just kill them?"

"Because he needed them alive. I believe Everen's mother was one of these political threats, probably a close ally of the princess."

"So why couldn't you just banish Everen to Earth? That would reunite her with her father." Aldyn asked.

"Because I won't risk damaging her magic. Everen inherited Less' magic, but it is much stronger." Aldyn sucked in her breath sharply. "Her magical power is raw. Banishing her would damage it, and that could hurt her."

"You think she can wield Gleamaric?" Aldyn asked quietly.

"I'd be a fool to not even suspect it. But now is not the time to discuss this, you need to sleep."

"I'm fine," Aldyn brushed her off.

"You're lying Aldyn, I practically raised you, I know when you aren't honest."

"I'm still alive, aren't I?" Aldyn asked bitterly.

"When was the last time you let yourself mourn? Or cry? Or love?" Agatha's voice was layered with sadness.

"You know I can't." Aldyn's reply was quiet and barely louder than a whisper.

Everen awoke feeling rested, which was a surprise. She walked down the wooden steps and sat at the table beside Nathan. Aldyn walked in from the kitchen and handed her a plate of fresh fruit with warm bread covered in butter, brown sugar, and cinnamon.

"Morning." She greeted, taking a seat beside her.

"Thanks," Everen replied and began to eat.

"Morning Aldyn!" Nathan said cheerfully. "Did you sleep well; you were up late."

Aldyn shrugged, which wasn't an answer, but he let it go. Agatha came over, "Today you need to resupply, tomorrow you will go after the Hunters."

"Do you have a lead on location?" Aldyn asked, forgetting about her meal.

"Wolfmoon region." Agatha's tone was tense and Everen saw Aldyn grip her fork tightly.

"Agatha, could you send a message to my parents? They thought I would be home already, and I don't want them to worry." Nathan asked.

Agatha nodded, "Of course." The three teenagers were finished with their breakfast at that point, so Agatha took the dishes into the kitchen. When she returned, she told Everen to join her, before leaving. Everen sent Nathan a nervous glance and he shrugged, she only hesitated another second before following Agatha.

Everen followed Agatha out into the forest behind the cottage. "Magic is powerful, but it is limited." Agatha began when they reached the tree line. "It is the force and blood of our world. It is the constant energy that keeps this planet alive. It is simply a part of our way of life, like the scientific rules that define how reality functions."

"How do you know I can use it, maybe coming here was just a fluke," Everen asked.

Agatha laughed, "You are speaking Elden, the vernacular, the common language of Eldenvine. That is your instinctive use of magic."

Everen was stunned for a moment before asking, "How am I doing that?"

"If you are sensitive to magic, you can manipulate it and therefore manipulate the world. The more sensitive you are, the more potential you have. When we subconsciously wield magic, it is usually in self-preservation. Your instincts recognized the danger of not being able to communicate, and your magic addressed it. Magic in its purest form is called Gleamaric, meaning all magic. It is unrefined and practically limitless in function. Gleamaric is refined into seven different branches, each with different specializations and strengths. These branches are Mistic, Elderic, Dragic, Calestic, Featheric, Oceanic, and Elvic. Although your mother is Elvic, your magic came from Less and you are sensitive to Mistic.

'Mistic magic is a secondary branch. So is Elderic. This is because they were created after the other five. Mistic comes from Lady Mistic; she and her brother Alder were from the early age of Eldenvine. The two were incredibly talented and made it their life goal to master Gleamaric. Mistic unlocked it first, and she created her branch devoted to it. Her followers couldn't access full Gleamaric, but they were able to master the diluted and refined branch that she created. Her brother Alder saw her success and attempted to mimic it, he generally succeeded, although he was unable to manipulate true Gleamaric like his sister. This is why the Elderic and Mistic branches are so similar.

'The other five branches are the primary branches. They are extremely specialized and much more limited. Dragic is the magic of the Dragons, Calestic is the magic of the Cestrys, Elvic is the magic of the Elves, Oceanic is the magic of the Pearlings, and Featheric is the magic of the Featherens. These five branches come from the seven daughters of Eldenvine, Awkra, Vinegress, Calcia, Fayra, Draesa, Oceana, and Elvira. The younger five daughters created the five primary branches and they are known as the Alpharics. Awkra and Vinegress, the eldest daughters, did not create branches. Vinegress in fact was the mother of Mistic and Alder, and maybe a second sister who was forgotten in history.

"What happened to the daughters of Eldenvine?" Everen asked.

"The Alpharics are still alive, but deeply hidden in their lands. Except, Fayra, of Featheric, is presumed dead. Since their birth, Oceana and Fayra despised each other. During the Great War, the sisters engaged in battle and Fayra was grievously injured. She hasn't been seen since. The eldest sisters, Awkra and Vinegress, died during the War of Magic, which was the first true war in our history. The war was started by Lady Mistic and Alder who were struggling for domination of magic, their fight for power drew all Eldenvine into their fight. They killed each other before the war's conclusion. Vinegress, seeing the deaths of her children, was devastated and sacrificed herself. Vinegress' death ended the war. Awkra, seeing the death of her beloved sister, died of heartbreak." Agatha explained.

Everen nodded slowly, trying to keep track of all the information Agatha had thrown on her, "Earlier, you said that Mistic magic was outlawed, why is this?"

"At the end of the War of Magic, the Elders took power. They outlawed Mistic and confiscated books on the study. This was two thousand years ago." Everen choked.

"Two thousand years? Mistrys have been in hiding for two thousand years!" She exclaimed. Agatha nodded.

"Yes, we have dwindled over the centuries, thanks to the Elders' efforts." Agatha's voice turned solemn and mournful.

"I'm sorry," Everen said softly.

"Do not be. Sorrow is pointless. Fighting is a much better option."
Agatha was quiet for a few seconds before speaking again. "You must learn
to feel magic, it is everywhere, especially here in Mythea. Only then will I be
able to teach you further. Touch the ground and close your eyes."

Everen sank to her knees and touched the ground with her fingertips.
"Now what?" She asked with her eyes closed.

"Stop asking pointless questions. I will tell you when I do." Everen
sighed. "Take command of your power. Feel its presence. Chose to be strong,
or you will always be powerless."

"I don't feel anything!" Everen protested.

"Do you *want* to see your father? Do you *want* to be weak?" Agatha's
voice grew in volume. "Take control! You have the highest potential power
since Mistic herself! Do not waste it!"

"I don't know what I'm looking for!" Everen yelled.

"Sense it, focus! Notice how it feels!" Agatha was shouting at this point.
"Stop resisting it!"

Everen yelled in annoyance and suddenly she felt something. It was
like static electricity or gravity. Something present but hard to define. The
energy surged beneath her touch, and she heard Agatha scream.

Everen opened her eyes and jumped to her feet. She gasped when she
saw what she had done. Agatha was tangled in the branches of a new tree.

Small pink flowers fell over her face and thick grass concealed her feet. Everen paled and stared in shock when the older women began to laugh.

"Congratulations." She said between breaths. "You are a Mistry."

"You are quite powerful; it was almost easy for you to awaken your magic." She continued, "This confirms my suspicions."

"What suspicions?" Everen asked.

"Do you remember what I told you about Gleamaric?"

"You said it was pure, unrefined magic, and no one alive can use it," Everen replied.

"But it is so much more. All magic comes from Gleamaric, and therefore all magic is Gleamaric. The refined branches are limited but have their uses. Mistic and Elderic are weak but versatile. Calestic is peaceful and keeps balance on Eldenvine. Dragic is powerful, but unpredictable and dangerous. Elvic is stable but slow and worthless in a fight. Featheric is aggressive and unable to be subtle. Oceanic is vicious and strategic but doesn't know mercy. Each magic is strongest in their land, here in Mythea, they are all about equal. It is why magic wielders are so much less powerful outside of their native lands." Agatha explained.

"But what does that have to do with me?" Everen asked. "Aren't I a Mistry?"

Agatha shook her head, "No, Everen, you are more. You can fully access Gleamaric," Agatha said.

"What does that mean?" Everen asked.

"You can manipulate *all* magic in Eldenvine, you are not limited to just Mistic," Agatha replied. "There are reasons why magic is divided, raw magic is too powerful to be used lightly."

"What could happen?" Everen asked nervously.

"Usually, instinctual magic does not hurt us. However, due to the sheer strength of yours, instead of you controlling your magic, the magic could control you. It has happened several times in history, where a magic wielder lost control. I do not want that to happen to you, Everen."

"I will be careful," Everen promised.

Agatha just smiled sadly. "I hope so, for more than just your sake. But now, we have more important things to do." With a wave of her hand, the tree surrounding her aged and crumbled to ash. The older woman dusted off her robes and stepped past Everen, forcing the girl to turn, "I can teach you how to create unbreakable shields, colored fire that can heal injuries, castles of glass, and other amazing things. These are spells, they are written in the ancient languages of Eldenvine. Spells are accompanied by actions, which will perform magic in preset ways."

"Is there any limit to magic?"Everen asked.

Agatha hesitated, "Magic is a part of this world, and we cannot wield magic outside of Eldenvine. We also cannot mess with time, the lines of reality, or the permanent nature of death. These things are not ours to mess with, so do not try." Everen nodded quickly, but her curiosity was awoken.

"What would happen if I tried to change any of that?" She asked, at Agatha's glare she added, "I'm not intending to, just wondering what would happen."

Agatha sighed and closed her eyes. "Magic is like a muscle, when we use it we can exhaust it. Using it too much can injure it. The sheer amount of power required to mess with the fundamental laws would kill you, and if you somehow survived the process, your life would be cursed forever as punishment for attempting to become a God." Everen shivered.

"I got it. Don't mess with time, reality, or death."

Agatha's nod was harsh, "Nothing is worth it." The woman was oddly quiet after that and Everen had to jog to keep up with her.

Agatha spent the next few hours simultaneously lecturing Everen about magic and drilling her in spells, it was difficult and exhausting, but she thought she'd successfully memorized several of them.

After training, Agatha took Everen inside where she gave her a new set of clothes, her old ones were ripped and muddied from the Dark Woods. Everen's black jeans were replaced with a new set and her green top was

replaced with a short green tunic. Everen thanked the woman and went to
the washroom to take a bath and change. Afterward, she put on her new
clothes, tied a golden brown belt around her waist, and with a wave of her
hand, her jacket was cleaned. Everen grinned at her reflection in the mirror,
she loved magic.

As she looked in the mirror, she was struck by the realization of how
different things were compared to Earth. Here, she was happy, without
Trissa and the headache of her school's drama. Here, she didn't try to hide
her oddly shaped ears to escape the teasing. This world was full of magic
and wonder, she admitted to herself she wished she could stay.

Everen felt a surge of guilt. She couldn't leave her father behind, no
matter how amazing Eldenvine was. Everen pulled her mother's necklace out
from under her shirt and ran her thumb on the delicate metal. She left it to
rest on her collarbone, instead of hiding it and turned to leave.

As she walked out, she accidentally ran into Nathan. She tripped
backward and if it wasn't for his quick reflexes, she would've bashed her
head into the door.

"Careful." He teased and she scowled at him.

"Where's Aldyn and Agatha?" She asked as he pulled her up.

"Agatha's making lunch, and Aldyn is practicing sword forms, she'll
come in when it's time to eat." He replied.

"Thanks," Everen said as she walked past him towards the kitchen. She took a seat at the table and caught the tail end of Aldyn's conversation, who was already inside and was speaking with Agatha.

"I don't like being near Wolfmoon, it's too close."

"Is the death warrant still out?" Agatha asked.

"I will be fine, that warrant isn't out for me," Aldyn replied as she noticed Everen. Nathan also walked in and took his seat beside her. Agatha didn't respond and Aldyn turned to the two, "You look different."

Everen raised her brow, "A good different or a bad different?"

"We will have to see," Aldyn replied, she turned back to Agatha. "We will be fine; Sharp-ears and I can handle it." Agatha sighed.

"Everen, I would like to share with you more of the history of Mistic Magic. Learning something is not just understanding how it works, but also where it came from." Agatha informed her.

Aldyn joined them and Agatha passed out plates of salad and roasted chicken for lunch. The three ate quickly, Nathan finished first with Aldyn right after him.

"We will be back in a few hours, don't die," Aldyn told them and Everen rolled her eyes. Aldyn grabbed Nathan's arm, leading him out. As they left, Everen heard him laughing at something the one-eyed girl said.

Agatha began her lecture right after the others left. "Eldenvine herself is the source of magic. It is her blood. Her seven daughters began the process of refining magic, and it was continued with the work of Mistic and Alder. The five Alpharics were the first rulers of their lands. The other lands are the Gleamaric lands because they do not herald from a specific branch. Mistic and Alder started different territories and legacies. Mistic trained women in her art, and Alder trained men. It was a perfect balance.

'However, the balance did not last forever. When Mistic and Alder were older, they became bitter and struggled for power, instead of accepting the balance. The struggle broke into a war that consumed the land. None were allowed to remain neutral. When Vinegress ended the war, the Elders took power. Lady Mistic's granddaughter, Mikayla, led the Mistrys into hiding. Under her reign, we were able to survive the Elders' attempt to purge us.

'Mikayla was powerful, but she couldn't live forever. She passed of old age and gave her leadership over to her granddaughter Victoria. Victoria passed the title on to her grandniece, who gave it to her great-granddaughter. The Mistry throne continued to pass and now Wistra holds it."

"So are the Mistrys going to die out?" Everen asked.

Agatha hesitated. "It is a possibility. Our society will crumble if we can't train more Mistrys, and the Elders have made that rather impossible of late. But we are hopeful."

"How?" Everen asked, and Agatha grinned.

"You," Agatha replied, "You are proof that the Mistrys will survive."

"But I'm not going to stay, I have to go home," Everen argued.

Agatha hesitated, "You won't be able to go to Earth until you master your magic, that will take years. Less will teach you what she can, but learning to walk the Lost Path is something you must learn yourself."

Everen frowned and her heart sank, "I don't want to be a Mistry. I just want my father." Agatha gently set a hand on Everen's shoulder.

"Sometimes we must do things we don't wish to in order to reach our goals. You want to go home, I want the Mistrys to survive. Train under me, become a Mistry, help our cause, and I will help you."

Everen's shoulders slumped, "Fine. Where do I start?"

Agatha smiled, "By learning everything you can. Nathan told me he explained the lands of Eldenvine, but he did not explain to you the current state of our world. Eldenvine is at a point of collapse, the Council is weak and divided, the Pearlings are beginning to expand into Ralaji, the Elders are losing control, and the Dragon Hunters are gaining power. If the Hunters are not stopped, they will increase tensions with the Dragons, and Dragaria may declare war. Eldenvine won't survive a conflict of such magnitude, especially without the Featherens."

"Why isn't the Council dealing with this?" Everen asked.

"Because the Council is controlled by the Elders, who desire power more than the good of our world," Agatha explained bitterly.

"How did the Elders even gain power, how were they able to outlaw Mistic?" Everen asked.

"In the aftermath of the War of Magic, the land was so severely damaged that the other nations chose to focus on their recovery instead of justice. The Elders set the narrative that they were victorious and in the right, and used their new authority to hunt down surviving Mistrys, confiscate our books of magic, and imprison our remaining leaders. Before the Mistrys and Elders worked together, but the power balance was lost. They have too much power and are spread too thin to utilize it. Instead, they hide in Alderen, the capital of Eldersa, surrounded by impenetrable mountains, and watch as our world crumbles."

"Is there any way to fix that?" Everen asked quietly.

Agatha shrugged, "They hold our books of magic, without them, the Mistrys will remain weak."

A hint of a smile twitched onto Everen's face, "What if we stole them back?"

Agatha grinned widely, "I knew you'd be an amazing Mistry."

Agatha led her to the middle of the town, where there was a large house surrounded by trees. The house was significantly nicer than any other in the village and Everen wondered who lived in it.

"This is the house of Elder Pine. Convince him to bring you to Alderen, the Elders love to show young people around their capital. Once you are there, search the library. There you will find the confiscated books. Be selective in using your magic, you do not want to get exposed as a Mistry." Agatha told her.

"What if I get caught?" Everen asked.

"Then escape by any means necessary. This is incredibly dangerous, but the reward will be worth it. Take this." Agatha set an emerald necklace over her head. "It should keep you safe. Remember, Elders are not to be trusted." Agatha's aging face contorted with pain at that last line. "Today, you are a Mistry."

The older woman nodded once at her, before turning and disappearing in the crowds, leaving Everen alone on her mission.

Everen took a deep breath and knocked on the door exactly three times. It was opened by a man wearing gold wire spectacles who appeared to be several years older than Agatha. The man was wearing green velvet robes with a gold pine branch clasp and gold embroidery. He had a freshly trimmed beard hanging barely below his chin and his silver hair hung just over his ears.

"Hello, I didn't expect a visit today, are you from the academy?" He asked.

Everen latched onto the lie. "Yes. My name is Everen, I was wondering if you could show me Alderen?"

He smiled kindly. "Of course. Come in." He held the door open for her and Everen came in. The entry room was large with tall glass windows partly concealed by evergreen curtains. The room was filled with natural sunlight and smelled faintly of pine trees. In the corners of the room stood the trunks of trees, still with their bark, supporting the ceiling.

Elder Pine was a kind man who loved to share his stories. He told Everen about magical history from the Elders' perspective and it was interesting to hear, even if it was quite repetitive.

He told her about Alder and how he'd taken eleven apprentices. The twelve became powerful sorcerers who worked wonders across the lands. They built wells, crafted protection spells for small villages, healed diseases, and more. They were good people who brought good to Eldenvine. However, they were still human. Elder Pine admitted that the War of Magic was horrific, bloody, and terrible. Everen asked him about the outlawing of Mistic magic, and he told her that Mistrys were dangerous. She privately thought the whole matter was stupid but wisely held her tongue.

"Mistic founded the sister magic of Elderic. Her fame started after she defeated the greatest threat ever seen by Eldenvine, but the details are lost.

She gathered dozens of apprentices and trained each in her skill and power. Over time she grew jealous of her brother, Alder, and incited the War of Magic. The siblings fought for dominance and dragged the rest of our world into the conflict, making it the bloodiest war of all history. Featherens aligned with the Mistrys, and Pearlings aligned with the Elders against them. It was one of the few moments in history when the dragons were united, they allied with the Mistrys. The Cestrys joined the Elders, and the Elves joined the Mistrys. The Mistrys bribed the Pirates' allegiance and the Elders convinced the Vikings to help. Even Mythea was divided. Everyone in the war had their own agenda. The war lasted for over a century and ended shortly after Mistic and Alder killed each other. In the ruins, the Elders stood superior and the Mistrys were defeated. We confiscated all books on Mistic magic and have worked to eliminate the study." Everen's attention perked at those words.

"The Mistrys and Elders have a long and intense relationship. After the war, the Elders became the leading force of magic in Eldenvine, replacing the Mistrys. Villages are now led by an Elder, and both Wolfmoon and Crowthorne have an Elder advisor. Elders run the Council and ensure peace throughout the lands." He finished.

The two had reached a decorative garden at the backside of his house. The garden was beautiful with intricate pots holding plants and small juniper bushes growing along the path.

"Why are we here?" Everen asked.

Elder Pine smiled. "Here is the portal to Alderen." He pointed to a round, green door embedded in thick branches.

The doorway was covered in small carvings of leaves and painted gold. A large golden handle was on the right side of the door, it was shaped like a branch from a pine tree.

"I have one question," Everen asked as she thought of it, "Is your name actually Elder Pine? Or do you have a different one?"

Elder Pine laughed, but his eyes became sad. "No. I have not always been Elder Pine. Long ago, I was Clemment Asper. However, when my ability with magic showed itself, the Elders took me in. They trained me, and when the opportunity arose, they sent me back to my childhood village, to watch over it. But now," he trailed off and shook his head, "The village changed, and my friends were different."

"I'm sorry," Everen said, not knowing what else she could say.

"Thank you. Now, I believe I promised to show you the capital." His smile was contagious, and he opened the door to the portal. Everen's eyes went wide.

The door opened into a spiral of green and gold glitter. It was mesmerizing the way the colors swirled and twisted. "How does it work?" Everen asked.

"Magic." He replied with a grin. "It connects two distant points and creates a tunnel between them. Some portals are like tears in reality, others, like this one, are points that will instantly transport you."

"What can't magic do?" Everen murmured under her breath, barely pausing before walking through the swirling portal after him.

Everen's jaw dropped as she looked around Alderen. She stepped out onto a large walkway which was near the center of a large city.

Unlike most cities she was used to, this city was incredibly spacious with thick stretches of forest in between impressive white stone buildings. It was full of elaborate gardens and open-air pavilions with man-made rivers winding through the streets.

"Alderen is named after Alder, the first Elder. Since its creation, the city has remained impenetrable and unconquerable." Elder Pine explained. Everen looked around with wide eyes and a gaping mouth. She realized that the abandoned land of Mistica had once been equally beautiful before the Elders forced the Mistrys into hiding.

"You mentioned the library earlier?" Elder Pine asked.

"Yes! I wanted to see the books on magic." Everen answered quickly.

Elder Pine smiled kindly. He lectured as he led her to a massive structure supported by marble pillars. The doors were guarded by men with long green capes. They held gold staffs and had an air of power that only worsened Everen's nervousness.

The interior of the library was split into collections of texts, and quiet halls for studying. Elder Pine explained in detail the organization and the available information. Everen had to admit it was pretty amazing. She enjoyed reading but preferred fiction books.

Elder Pine led her into another room full of books. "Here is a copy of every spell book from the last twenty-five centuries." He explained.

"Even the ones from other magical branches?" Everen asked. He nodded.

"All of the confiscated Mistic books are here. Occasionally, Elders will look through them to try and adapt the magic, but we have been largely unsuccessful." Elder Pine elaborated.

"Really? Where are they?" Everen asked she knew that she was pushing a bit too much, but she was excited.

Elder Pine stopped walking and looked at her, his face tightened with confusion and suspicion. "At the end of these shelves, it's marked in dark purple. Why would you need to know?"

Everen swallowed thickly, "I'm just curious." She said weakly. Elder Pine frowned and Everen backed away. "I really should get going, I've learned a lot! Thanks!"

Before he could ask further she turned around and bolted. Everen was immediately grateful for casually joining her school's soccer team. She was easily able to outpace the old man. She reached the end of the shelves, took a sharp turn, and leaned straight against the wooden shelf.

She tried to stifle her breathing and stayed perfectly still as Elder Pine passed, looking incredibly worried. She felt a bit guilty for deceiving him, but not too much. She carefully made her way back to the end of the row that Elder Pine had shown her.

She leaned down and checked the rows searching for the purple markings. "Where are you?" She murmured aloud.

"What *are* you doing? Girls aren't allowed to study Elderic." A boy said. Everen jumped to her feet with a hot blush on her face. The boy was handsome and a bit older than her. He had very short black hair, pale skin, and almond-shaped chestnut eyes. He wore a simple but high-quality brown leather tunic and a dark green sash around his waist. He had tan pants and brown boots. Everen recognized him as an Elder apprentice.

"What are *you* doing? Last I checked Elders weren't supposed to be stupid." Everen crossed her arms stubbornly.

He looked confused, and even a bit embarrassed. "I'm not sure what you're talking about." He admitted.

Everen rolled her eyes. "Well, I'm not surprised. You should leave." His jaw dropped at her audacity.

"No, you're not allowed here." He insisted.

Everen tried to conceal her cringe and scrambled for ideas. "My father works here." She blurted, "he sent me to pick up some books." She added. Everen was usually a better liar but at the moment she was stressed and nervous.

"Who is your father?" The boy asked, suspicious.

Everen racked her brain, "Elder Rose." She decided, using her grandmother's middle name, she internally thanked Theater class for teaching so much improvisation. The boy's eyebrows raised.

"You mean Elder Black Rose? Only the apprentices call him Rose, and that's when he's not around." The boy asked.

Everen nodded aggressively, "That's him. Now can you please leave?"

Thankfully, the boy decided to leave her alone. Everen turned back to the bookshelf and grinned when she found the purple markings around a set of books. There weren't very many, only twenty-nine in total. Everen removed three of them and then pushed the other books in, so it wasn't very noticeable.

Everen held the stolen books of magic to her chest and covered it with the cloak, making her look like a frumpily dressed villager. She climbed out a side window of the library and hid by bushes before blending into the crowds near the library.

It took her a little while to reach the courtyard full of portals, and even longer to figure out which one was Elder Pine's but eventually, she was able to sneak back to Pine. Elder Pine must've thought she'd returned home, and she was lucky that he hadn't caught her. With a deep breath, Everen made her way to Agatha's.

Chapter Six: The Daughter Of Wolfmoon.

When she had reached Agatha's house, the older woman grinned immediately. "I'm impressed! We've never had a successful heist."

"The trick was to outrun Elder Pine, then everything went practically perfectly," Everen explained, as she handed the three stolen books to Agatha. "There weren't many, but these looked interesting."

Agatha smiled kindly, "You've been immensely helpful. I'll look through these and see what I can teach you." Everen nodded, "Oh and feel free to keep that necklace, you deserve it." Everen grinned.

The necklace with the emerald pendant matched her mother's chain and Everen remembered it was enchanted with some protection magic. She made her way to the kitchen, where she joined Aldyn and Nathan for dinner.

They enjoyed roast and warm sourdough bread. Agatha had also made a salad, but there were strange-looking orange berries in it which Everen didn't like much. As they ate, Everen told her story. She had fun talking and answering her friends' questions.

After eating, Agatha sent them off to bed. Everen said she wasn't very tired but ruined her point by yawning. Nathan laughed and the three teenagers went off.

Morning came, and Aldyn dragged Everen out of bed, Everen was not a morning person. Agatha gave her a mug of strong tea, which woke her up in a jolt.

They spent the morning working through the books. Agatha taught Everen about portals and shields, which were two simple, but exhausting works of magic. "Remember, you only have so much magical strength. It's like a muscle, you have to build it up and right now you won't last long." Agatha reminded her.

Everen scowled and went back to working on her shield, which was a flimsy layer of gold stardust.

Finally, the two went inside. As Everen came in, she saw Aldyn packing a bag beside the front door.

"Where are you going?" Everen asked.

Aldyn stood up. "Nathan and I have a mission. We are going out to finish it." Everen's face fell, she didn't want her new friends to leave her life as quickly as they had come into it.

"Could I come?" Everen asked. "I know how to use magic and I can help." She added.

"Well, you already tagged along with us to come here. I'm fine with it, and I know Nathan with love it." Aldyn shrugged.

"If Everen goes, I need your word she will be safe." Agatha interrupted, who had snuck up on the girls. "You must promise not to directly attack the Dragon Hunters. You are doing reconnaissance and sabotage. I do not want to deal with dead teenagers."

"Whether she goes or not is her decision." Aldyn snapped.

Agatha raised her brow, "Everen is the first new Mistry in over a decade. You will protect her."

"Fine. You have my word we will all come back alive."

"Swear on the shell of Eldenvine." Agatha's tone was cold and insistent, and her accent was thicker than usual.

"I swear on the shell of Eldenvine herself, all three of us will come back alive." A hum rang through Everen's ears at Aldyn's words.

"What's that?" Everen asked Aldyn after Agatha had left.

"Swearing on the shell of Eldenvine is a magical oath, breaking it brings a curse onto you, and your family, and can even kill you." Aldyn explained, "That's why people don't usually make it, they can die if they aren't careful."

Everen raised her eyebrows, "So if I die, you die?" She clarified.

Aldyn sent her a sharp look. "If you're dumb enough to get yourself killed, I will haunt you for eternity."

"With that lovely thought, what's going on?" Nathan asked, entering the conversation.

"Everen is coming with us," Aldyn explained.

Nathan grinned, "Awesome! Oh, and Agatha made lunch. She told me to get you."

The girls joined him in the kitchen, where Agatha handed out plates of chicken lemon salad. While they ate, Aldyn and Nathan discussed tactics and strategies for dealing with the hunters.

"No, the Hunters aren't stupid enough to go to Dragaria, even for non-terrorists, that's a death sentence," Aldyn argued.

"Think about it, so far they've apparently only killed dragons hiding in Mytharica and Northern Klondor, they are running out of targets." Nathan countered.

Aldyn shook her head, "I disagree. Dragaria is a bloodbath. The Hunters most likely are heading north, to hit nests on the cost of Mistia."

"Aldyn, Nathan, no matter where the hunters are, you need to stay safe. Nothing is worth losing your life." Agatha said sternly.

"Scales and bones, I already swore to keep us alive." Aldyn snapped. Nathan sent her a sharp look. "*What?*" She said.

"I swear, you curse worse than a half-dead pirate."

"How do you know what a half-dead pirate sounds like?" Everen interjected. Nathan grinned at her.

Before he was able to answer, probably with a witty comeback, the door to Agatha's cottage was knocked. Agatha shushed them and cautiously walked over to the door, Everen noticed her fingers twitching. Agatha opened the door, and a small green hummingbird flew in and landed on the table between Everen and Nathan. The bird had a letter tied to its ankle. Agatha frowned and untied the letter. The bird flew away with its message delivered.

Agatha opened the note and read it swiftly. "It's a message from Hecktra, the hunters are leaving Wolfmoon, you have to hurry if you want to catch up to them." Aldyn cursed.

"Well then, we will leave sooner than expected." Aldyn shrugged, "Goodbye Agatha." Agatha nodded at her, and Aldyn and Nathan went to gather their packs. Nathan handed a bag to Everen, who swung it onto her shoulder. Agatha gave them all cloaks; it would provide some identity protection and warmth.

"Aldyn, I recommend going to a traveler's stable, you will be faster with a third horse." Agatha reminded her. "Everen, make sure you avoid the Elders, eventually someone will come after you."

"I thought they were just going to keep it quiet?" Everen said.

"They won't set up a bounty, but their highest operatives will be looking for you. I will set a false trail and work to keep them off your back." Agatha promised. Everen nodded her thanks.

The three were out of Pine and in the wild of Eldenvine within the hour. Everen had changed her outfit underneath her dark indigo cloak into brown pants and a cream shirt with a leather breastplate.

"Do you think we will have to worry about the Elders?" Everen asked Nathan.

"I trust Agatha will distract them for a while, and if they get past her, Aldyn and I have a bit of a reputation for mild destruction." He grinned.

"Thanks." She said.

"Yeah, you're welcome," Aldyn called up. "Picking a fight with the Elders is always entertaining."

"True. But I prefer pirates." Nathan called.

"That is where we disagree, I hate pirates."

"Really?" Everen asked, with genuine surprise.

"Pirates are ruthless." Aldyn turned away and walked faster. Everen watched her, before turning to continue talking to Nathan.

A little while later, Everen asked Aldyn. "Where are we going?"

"Wolfmoon, it's north of here, but still in Mythea. It's where Hecktra said the hunters were last. Hopefully, we can catch up to them; if not we will keep chasing them around Mytharica."

"Can you tell me about Wolfmoon?" Everen asked Nathan.

"Sure." He replied. "It's one of the two kingdoms in Mythea. Wolfmoon is ruled by King Howlett and Queen Lupine, they have two daughters, Princess Erica, and Princess Aronna. Erica was assassinated almost eight years ago, so Aronna is the heir. Crowthorne is the other kingdom. It is ruled by King Ravenbone and Queen Bramble. Their son is Prince Thorne. The two have a tense history and are currently at war." Nathan explained briefly.

"Who are the other royal families?" Everen asked.

Nathan hesitated. "Queen Inaria of Elvara has no children, and she is unmarried. If she died, the strongest claim to the throne would be Prince James, but he disappeared several years before she became queen. The Queen's closest friend is Elrine, she is the legal heir in case something happens to the Queen. But Queen Inaria doesn't have to worry about heirs for a few decades. In Islaria, King Sharkir and Aquanda co-rule. They have two children, Jazon and Lana. Calestia is ruled by Queen Monartha, her husband Aazon the First died almost twenty years ago. She has three daughters and two sons. Ralaji has no royal family because all the Featherens were killed, it's probably ruled by the Sky-giants, as some of them definitely survived. Eldersa is ruled by a council of Elders, and Mistia is in ruins. Cat's Eye is the King of Klondor, which is mostly merchants and pirates. And Dragaria has a different ruler per tribe." Nathan listed with a shrug.

"That is significantly less complicated than on Earth. We have almost two hundred separate countries with separate governments and leaders." Everen said and Nathan whistled lowly.

"Yeah, Mythea is split into a ton of little city-states, like Pine and Wolfmoon, but nowhere near that many. If I had to learn all those different countries, school would take at least fifty years."

Everen laughed. "Fifty years is a long time, over half your life."

Nathan looked surprised, "That's not even middle-aged for Elves. How long do Earthborns live?"

"About eighty years, longer if you're healthy." She answered. "Why, how long do Elves live?"

"Two hundred years. Which is nothing compared to Dragons, who can live up to a thousand. Cestrys live about a hundred and eighty. Featherens and Pearlings both live about a hundred and fifty. Regular Mytharicans live a hundred years." Nathan explained.

"How old are you?" Everen asked with concern.

"One hundred." He deadpanned. Everen's jaw dropped, and he burst out laughing.

"Na, I'm fourteen. We age at the same speed." He explained. She smacked him.

"Idiot." She snapped.

"We're here," Aldyn called, silencing their bickering.

The three were in the forest, near the fields of crops and animals that surrounded the walled city of Wolfmoon. Aldyn led them under branches into a protected hollow.

The hidden camp was surrounded by thick brambles and trees that provided storm cover. There were ferns around the small hollow and an old firepit that hadn't been lit in years.

"This is an old camp of mine. We can set up here and scout the area until we find the trail. It's a bit overgrown but still good." Aldyn explained.

Suddenly the sound of galloping horses came near them. A voice shouted, "Find her. You know who she is."

"Yes, Captain Hound." Voices answered and the horses continued.

Behind the three, snapping twigs attracted their attention. Everen turned to see a girl scramble down the tree. She wore brown leather armor over a knee-length sapphire blue dress. She had a scarlet cloak which partially covered her long, thick black hair.

The young woman faced the three and glared with intelligent green eyes. "What was that about this being *your* camp, Aldyn? I vividly remember doing all the work building it."

"What are you doing here?" Aldyn demanded, ignoring her comment.

"This is free land. I can go wherever I want." Aldyn growled and Nathan stepped between them.

"Care to introduce yourself?" Nathan asked.

"Erica Wolfcrown." The girl answered boldly, making Nathan breathe in sharply with surprise.

"You're supposed to be dead."

"Then why is the Royal Guard after me?" Erica asked, "Queen Lupine tried to have me killed. My friend and handmaiden looked nearly identical to me. She learned of the plot, and we switched roles. The assassin mistook us and killed her. My dear mother figured out that I wasn't dead, and framed me, disguised as my friend, for my own murder."

"Why?" Nathan asked tensely, he couldn't imagine his mother betraying him like that.

Erica grinned disturbingly. "Because I blatantly refused the betrothal arrangement with Prince Thorne. Mother realized she wouldn't be able to control me, unlike my perfect little sister Aronna, and decided to deal with it." Erica's voice dripped with fake sweetness as she described her sister.

"Why don't you just tell people the truth?" Nathan asked.

"Even if people did believe me, which would never happen, I would be forced to return to the palace and eventually marry that horrible prince. I do not want to be a political puppet. All Wolfmoon have hunted me for years, and they will keep hunting me as long as they believe that I killed Erica Wolfcrown." Erica laughed hollowly. "It's ironic, chasing a woman responsible for her own death."

"Enough about your tragic life Erica, why are you here?" Aldyn snapped, refusing to listen to the old story any longer.

Erica sighed dramatically, "I thought that was obvious. I'm on the run."

"You're always running."

"Yeah, and I'm alive." Erica snapped back. She turned towards Nathan and Everen. "What are you doing with Aldyn of all people?" She asked.

"We are following the Dragon Hunters so that we can hopefully sabotage their organization," Nathan replied.

"Aldyn helping dragons, maybe she can change," Erica commented. "Knowing her, she would join them for the sake of revenge." Nathan glanced at Aldyn who looked livid. He turned back to Erica.

"How do you know Aldyn?" He asked.

Erica snorted. "We spent a year adventuring around Eldenvine together. I had just escaped my mother and Aldyn seemed like a friend. Oh, was I wrong." She growled. Aldyn opened her mouth to argue but her words changed into a question.

"Do you know where the Dragon Hunters are now? If you are not going to be helpful, leave us alone." Aldyn said.

"Oh, I know where the hunters are, they traveled out of Wolfmoon early yesterday," Erica said in a bored tone.

"Where are they now?" Aldyn demanded.

"If I tell you, let me join your mission."

"Absolutely not!" Aldyn shouted, "I wouldn't do another mission with you if my life depended on it!"

"Then you won't have a mission. You need my information." Erica replied.

"Why do you want to come with us?" Everen asked.

Erica looked at her with a wide grin. "Because I know how much Aldyn will hate it."

"Fine. We don't have time to wander around aimlessly. You can come with us, what do you know?" Aldyn said.

"Ralaji," Erica replied simply.

"Why are the Dragon Hunters there?" Aldyn asked, she was pale. "It's far away from Dragaria and practically barren!"

Erica shrugged. "Supposedly there are several hidden Fire Flight nests on the eastern coast." Nathan and Aldyn shared a solemn look.

"We learned that the hunters are stealing eggs," Nathan informed Erica, who frowned.

"Maybe the hunters seek to have power over the tribes by threatening to kill their children. But all these children are traitors, so who knows."

"Maybe, but I fear there is something worse at play," Nathan said, and she shrugged.

"We won't learn by speculation. Let's go to Ralaji." Erica said.

"Ralaji is a wasteland because of the last war. The survivors would be dangerous scavengers, it's a death sentence to go there." Nathan warned her.

Aldyn shifted uncomfortably. "If we're careful we should be able to avoid any confrontation with the Firens, Sky-Giants, Northbirds, and Boneflyers. The Northbirds and Boneflyers haven't been seen since the war, the Sky-Giants keep to the mountains and the Firens despise confrontation."

Everen's eyes widened as Aldyn spoke. The Great War which had wiped out the Featherens had happened over two hundred years prior, and the nation was still weak and divided. The Featherens had made up nearly eighty percent of the Ralaji population, with the four other species forming the other twenty percent. The Pearlings, determined to eradicate them, had left Ralaji sparsely populated and a far cry from their earlier glory.

Erica shrugged again. "Agreed. The survivors would try to kill us if they could catch us." She turned to Aldyn. "We have no reason to stay in Wolfmoon, I'll lead you out of Mythea tonight."

Chapter Seven: The Exiled.

They left Wolfmoon and traveled northeast across the continent. What was left of Ralaji was a large peninsula of the north-eastern coast. Before leaving, Erica retrieved her horse, called White-Whistle. Everen rode with Aldyn.

Aldyn led them to a stable on the side of the road, somewhere in Eldersa. They had to pass through the edges of Eldersa because it was directly between Mythea and Ralaji. The stable was surrounded by fenced green pastures sparsely filled with horses. Aldyn tied her horse's reins to a post and led the way to the main barn. The others followed her example and walked after her.

Inside the barn was a handsome boy who looked a few years older than Aldyn. He had spiky blond hair and dark blue eyes.

"Hello Aldyn, what are you visiting Star Path stables for?" He asked politely.

"I'm here for a horse." She answered briskly, as though she had done it a hundred times.

"What kind?" He asked.

"Thunderon, I'm assuming you have a good selection." She raised her brow. The boy just laughed.

"You know it, Aldyn. You can take your pick." He turned to the rest of them. "My name is Jack, by the way. What are yours?" He asked.

"Nathan, Everen, and the hag is Erica," Aldyn answered, she jerked her hand to each person as she named them. Erica rolled her eyes.

"Pleased to meet you." He said, shaking each of their hands. "Come I'll show you our best."

He led them out into the pastures. "So what adventure are you on now?" He laughed. Aldyn crossed her arms. "Renting or buying?"

"Renting. I don't have enough to pay in full. And no, I won't tell you the mission details." Aldyn replied.

"Disappointing. Anyway, you know the drill. If you keep the horse longer than you paid for, I will charge extra. If you lose them, they are trained to return but if they do not, you owe me another horse." Jack said.

"What do you mean another horse?" Everen asked.

"Aldyn lost one of my horses three years ago. It was one of my best." Jack shot her a glare, but there wasn't much strength in it. Everen could tell he had forgiven her.

"I paid you back, *more* than paid you back. Triple the regular in gold!" Aldyn crossed her arms.

"Agree to disagree." Jack waved his hand.

Aldyn led Everen through the pastures, Erica decided to stay behind at the barn. Everen picked out a horse with a deep brown coat and a black mane. His name was Vince. Jack helped her saddle the horse. Everen rarely rode on Earth, but the horse was well-trained so she would be fine.

"You have an eye for horses," Jack commented to Everen. "Aldyn," He addressed her, "That will be ten dayz. I'll give you three weeks before I start charging extra, an additional dayz per sunset." He warned her. Aldyn rolled her eyes and handed him twenty gold coins, paying extra just in case. The coins were round with a sunset engraved on each face. Jack set the coins in a satchel that hung across his chest. Aldyn then handed him an extra coin for a tip.

"What's a dayz?" Everen whispered to Nathan.

"Basic Eldenvine currency. Twenty lefz is a dayz, fifty dayz is a roze. However, there is also a lot of jewel trade and bargaining in Eldenvine, especially Klondor. I once saw Aldyn bargain for a full meal with half a dayz." He explained.

The group of four waved goodbye to Jack as they rode away on their four horses, continuing their way towards Ralaji.

Ralaji was dense with mountain ranges and had a wide range of elevation. It was rocky and bare except for grass and wildflowers which had grown in the ashes of the trees. The capital, called Featherwind, had been built on the peaks of three tall mountains, and at its center was the palace.

According to the stories, Featherwind was adorned with gold and rubies, so it glowed like a fire during sunset.

Ralaji was the land of Featheric, home to the powerful Featherens. Before the war, it had been known for its herds of winged horses, flocks of giant birds, and incredible artists. Now, it was remembered as the land of blood and fire.

Featherens were warriors, trained since birth, and they had been exterminated. Everen shivered, trying to stop the mental calculations of deaths. At the moment, Erica was explaining the history and culture of Ralaji. Aldyn and Nathan were already familiar with it, so it was kind of her to explain.

"Featheren artistry was a statement of wealth and connections in the time before the war, my family owns a tapestry and some jewelry, which is incredibly rare. Mother kept it in the treasury and brought it out to show off." Erica said, and Everen nodded. "One time, I purposely wore a Featheren necklace to a banquet with a Pearling ambassador. Mother was livid." Erica grinned and Aldyn rolled her eyes. Erica's favorite pastime seemed to be finding ways to infuriate her parents, it was no wonder things escalated.

Nathan spoke up, "Did you ever see the ruins?" Erica hesitated just a moment before shaking her head.

"They're considered cursed, no one's actually seen them." Erica elaborated, and then her eyes widened and took on a wicked glint. She turned to Everen and said in a low voice, "It's said that the spirits of the fallen warriors rise when the sun falls in Ralaji."

Everen accidentally yanked on the reins of her horse, and the animal neighed in surprise. "Erica!" Aldyn snapped, "Cut it out with the ghost stories."

Erica scowled and Everen glared viciously at her. Although, she had to admit it was a good one. Everen loved to tell ghost stories to her younger cousins. She'd actually gotten in trouble multiple times for it.

It took them a total of seven days to reach Ralaji. Seven days of riding where Aldyn and Erica almost ripped each other to shreds. In the evenings, the four would sit around the campfire and tell stories. Erica and Aldyn were barely able to remain civil, so Everen and Nathan worked to diffuse the tension.

When they reached Ralaji, Everen was surprised to see tall forests at the border. "I thought it was burned to the ground?" She said.

Erica shook her head, "Featherwind and the surrounding area were destroyed, but the edges of the land escaped the flames. This forest is at least a thousand years old."

Everen's eyes widened. A thousand years was a long time. These trees were older than the Great War, they had lived through more history than she could ever dream of.

The four made their way through the forest, and Aldyn led them to a place not far inside the border. "We'll camp here tonight and scout out the southern coast tomorrow." Aldyn decided, unmounting, and beginning to unpack. Everen climbed off her horse as well and tied the reigns to a low-hanging branch.

Everen's neck prickled oddly, and she glanced behind them. She thought back to Erica's story from earlier, about the fallen warriors whose spirits rose during the night. She shivered and forced the thought out of her head, before going to help Nathan set up camp.

It didn't take them long to pitch the three tents and start a small fire. Aldyn was off hunting, and Erica was standing guard beside them.

After a little while, Erica relaxed and pulled out a worn book to read. The girl sat in the roots of a tree and leafed through the yellowed pages.

"What are you reading?" Everen asked if she hadn't seen Erica read before and she didn't recognize the book's cover.

Erica glanced at the page number before closing her book. "*Edible and Medicinal Plants of Eldenvine Updated and Expanded Edition Volume Seven.*" She answered. "You never know when it could come in handy. Before leaving Wolfmoon, I stole several books from my father's library. After finishing a book, I'll trade it for another. I got this one last week. I don't need to reread it; I have a good memory."

"That's impressive," Everen commented, and Erica gave her a real smile.

"Thank you."

At that moment Aldyn returned. She had three medium-sized fish hung over her shoulder on a thin chain with hooks.

"Dinner has arrived." She announced, dropping the fish into a pot beside the fire.

Nathan frowned at the fish, "Aldyn, there are only three here." He said warningly, knowing she was picking a fight.

"Yes. Just because I'm allowing Erica to travel with us, doesn't mean I have to feed her." Aldyn snapped and kneeled to begin cooking.

The kinder side of Erica that had begun to show was buried with a scowl. She stood up, grabbed her bow and arrows, and walked into the forest, bumping into Aldyn as she passed.

"Aldyn." Nathan sighed.

"Don't." She ordered and Nathan shut his mouth.

When Erica returned, they decided who would take the first watch, Nathan volunteered and Everen would go second. Erica would go third and Aldyn last.

Everen got to sleep for several hours before Nathan woke her up to hand it off. She yawned and sat up next to the fading fire, poking it with a charred branch. She almost fell asleep several times before her turn was up and she passed it to Erica. The second she hit the ground she fell back asleep soundly.

Everen awoke to sunlight dancing above her eyes. She instantly knew something was wrong and she practically jumped up. There was a young woman in front of her. She looked almost eighteen and had dark brown hair with orangish eyes. She held three daggers before Everen's throat. The daggers were white bone with amber veins engraved on the side. Out of her back grew massive wings covered in feathers the color of pale wood. Everen presumed she was a Featheren, apparently, they weren't as dead as everyone thought.

Everen looked around the camp. Nathan, Erica, and Aldyn were all tied up and surrounded by other Featherens. Nathan looked very irritated, but somehow Erica kept her stoic expression. Aldyn's face was furious, but she didn't appear surprised.

"What are you doing in Ralaji?" The Featheren demanded.

"We are following the Dragon Hunters, we're on a mission to stop them," Everen answered quickly. She heard Aldyn groan from where she was held captive.

"So, you're telling me that an assorted group of Mythean children is tracking a group of terrorists." She scoffed. "The more likely story is you were bored and wanted to loot the ruins of Featherwind. I smell your magic blood, *Mistry.*" The Featheren growled.

Everen flinched when the Featheren announced her secret. She saw Erica's mask slip with surprise and cursed internally.

"We were never going to enter Featherwind. You don't need to take us prisoner." Everen argued. The Featheren hesitated, and Aldyn used the distraction to break free from her bonds and grab her sword which was abandoned on the ground.

"We didn't come here to fight you, but we will if you make us." Aldyn stood in a stance ready to attack.

"I find it ironic that a sea-blood is the one to claim peace." The Featheren snarled. Aldyn's stance loosened and she looked surprised.

"What are you talking about?" Aldyn asked.

"You know *exactly* what I'm talking about, *Pearling.*" The Featheren spat, she said Pearling as though it was a disgusting disease. "Obviously you are in your walking form, so you can hide among us."

"You don't know anything about me," Aldyn growled and the Featheren laughed.

"Don't I? I'm a Featheren, I have better senses than you could ever hope for. I'm also not stupid."

Aldyn lunged at the Featheren, who turned to her side to block the blade with her daggers, revealing they were not daggers, but claws of bone coming from between her knuckles.

Aldyn attacked with an overhead strike and the Featheren blocked it with her claws, making a faint ringing sound. Aldyn feinted to the side; she was amazing with the blade. The Featheren slashed Aldyn dodged, the Featheren's claws raking against her shoulder.

Aldyn grimaced with pain and spun, slashing deep across the Featheren's arm. The Featheren snarled and batted Aldyn's second blow away with her bare forearm, leaving another bleeding cut. With her other arm, she lunged forward to grab Aldyn's neck. Aldyn's sword clattered to the ground, staining the grass red.

Aldyn struggled in the Featheren's grip, but the Featheren was angry. Her injury throbbed and she raised her claws to Aldyn's face. "How would you like a matching scar?" She asked. For a second, fear flashed across Aldyn's face.

"Aldyn!" Everen yelled, attracting the girl's attention, and raising her hands to attack with magic. She had never fought like this, but she had to help her friend.

"Stay out of it!" Aldyn yelled, kicking the Featheren's chest. The Featheren grunted and dropped Aldyn to the ground.

Everen kicked Aldyn's sword to her, right before her arms were grabbed by a second Featheren warrior.

Aldyn caught the spinning hilt and twisted over to block the claws which stabbed toward her exposed collarbone.

"Yield." The Featheren ordered, her orangish eyes flashing.

"Never." Aldyn spat. The Featheren brought her other claws to Aldyn's eye, centimeters away from scratching her iris. Aldyn flinched. The Featheren got to her feet and dragged Aldyn up, before shoving her towards two Featherens, who immediately grabbed her arms tightly.

"A tragedy for bravery like yours to waste away in a cell." The Featheren commented, and Aldyn attempted to lunge for her but was held back by the other Featherens. "You shouldn't have come here."

Aldyn glared at her furiously but managed to hold her tongue. Even she couldn't fight her way out of this one. Everen tried to struggle with the Featheren holding her. If she used her magic, escaping would be easier, but she didn't want to risk the others getting caught in the crossfire.

The Featherens marched them through the forest with their horses held in the back. The trees they passed were taller than any on Earth, and Everen wondered if it was even possible for trees to be as large. Brightly colored birds in red, yellow, and orange themes flew through the branches with chorusing songs.

Then, the beauty ended abruptly. Everen couldn't stop herself from gasping sharply. The gorgeous trees and greenery changed into scorched earth. Black husks of dead trees still dotted the land. The soil was black from charcoal and burned foliage which had slowly decayed over time. The only signs of life were the occasional specks of thin green grass and peaking red flowers. The Pearlings had literally burned Ralaji to the ground, making ash so deep, that it choked the plant life that tried to return. Even the rivers and streams were damaged, the ash made the water toxic and the fires had dried up many smaller waterbodies.

"The Pearlings burned these forests two hundred years ago, only now are they starting to recover." The Featheren's voice had a hint of sadness underneath her anger. "My great-grandfather used to tell stories of the land before the war, I'm glad he doesn't have to see it now."

"Someday they will pay for it." Another Featheren said, the one holding Everen. He had dark wings and pale grey eyes which flashed with vengeful determination at his words.

They walked in silence after that. Everen looked over to her friends, Aldyn was baring her teeth at her guard and glaring with her good eye at the Featherens. Erica was analyzing the surrounding area, memorizing it as she worked to untie her ropes discreetly. The Featherens had taken her cloak, which was revealed to be lined with daggers, throwing knives, and ninja stars. Everen thought that Erica looked incredibly different without her cloak, her long braided black hair hung down her spine on her leather armor and her face was lighter and less shadowed. The runaway Wolfmoon princess was slightly taller than Aldyn, a fact Everen had not realized previously. Erica was also incredibly beautiful, but it was a cold beauty like the tundra of the north.

Everen turned her attention to Nathan. He had hidden a spare arrow in his shirt and was currently using the arrowhead to cut through his ropes. He saw Everen and sent her a mischievous grin. He tried to move closer so they could talk, but Featheren smacked him with their wing.

A little while later, a Featheren flew out of the trees and landed in a bow on his knee before the young Featheren woman.

"Captain Firex, you are needed at the palace; the Queen is waiting." He stood up. He looked like he was Firex's age, with dark skin and black hair. His wings and eyes were a dark grey and he wore more armor than the other Featherens. The other Featherens who had captured them wore a breastplate, leather skirt, and metal boots. But he had metal plates on his wings and skirt, with a silver helmet under one arm. Everen noticed that all his armor was engraved with spirals, and she wondered what it meant.

"Tell my Aunt I am busy transporting prisoners," Firex replied, waving her hand dismissively.

"Drop them off at the nearest outpost, they can be held there until you can deal with them." He ordered and Firex sighed, she hated that he was her superior.

"Fine, Commander Gull." She snapped, and he leaped into the air with a single beat of his wings before flying off.

Firex led them to a wooden outpost. It was built of pointed logs and had around a dozen cells. It was only guarded by four Featherens, three were gambling with a deck of cards and a stack of metal feathers. The fourth guard wore armor unlike any other Featheren Everen had seen so far. She wore as much armor as Gull had, but hers was white with golden diamond shapes. Her leather skirt was paler, and her helmet had golden feathers on the sides. The elaborate long spear she held was especially unique; none of the other Featherens carried weapons, as they relied on their claws. She had long pale blond hair and grey eyes with pale wings.

Firex walked over to her. "Eventide! What is a member of the Featherwind High Guard doing out here?" She asked. Everen noticed that Firex's wings twitched and moved as she spoke like she was speaking with them as well.

The Featheren smiled and lifted and rustled her wins. Everen guessed her age to be at least four years older than Firex. "Pearlings. They have always wanted our territory, and we fear they may take it now that the land is beginning to recover, and they believe we are dead. I will return to Featherwind tomorrow after I finish scouting our border." She answered.

"I wish I could join you, but Aunt wants me back at the palace." Firex sighed.

"Do not speak of the Queen in a disrespectful tone! Even if you are an heir to the throne." Eventide scolded.

"You know I wish to be Peakatroir, Phinx can have the throne. I want to command the armies of Ralaji." Firex retorted with a laugh.

"Well, *Peakatroir* I will take your prisoners so that you can return to the palace, your soldiers can return with you." Eventide nodded her head at the Featherens gambling beside her and they moved to take Everen, Nathan, Erica, and Aldyn.

Everen could still hear Firex laughing as she took to the skies, followed by her warriors, heading north.

Everen and the others were marched to a large group cell. The walls were made of logs, as though the outpost had been built quickly and ignored. Iron bars kept them in their cell, and it was held with a locked iron chain. After they dumped the prisoners, the Featherens walked away, probably to continue their game of cards.

After the Featherens left, Everen turned to Aldyn. "How did you know?" She asked.

"What did Aldyn know?" Nathan asked, looking confused.

"She knew about the Featherens, she wasn't surprised when they captured us," Everen explained.

Nathan rolled his eyes, "That's ridiculous! We all thought the Featherens were gone."

Aldyn set her hand on his shoulder, "Thank you for defending me, but I will do it myself." She turned to face Everen, "You're right. I did know that the Featherens were alive and in hiding. Erica and I both knew, why do you think I wanted to avoid coming?"

"How did you know? They're supposed to be extinct." Nathan asked.

Aldyn hesitated, unsure how to answer, and surprisingly Erica came to her rescue. "We came here when we were about ten years old. We wanted to see the ruins of Featherwind, not knowing that the Featherens were alive and in hiding. They captured us to keep their survival a secret, as they have now done to us. After being captured, we befriended a young Featheren who was close to the royal family. She convinced them to free us if we vowed on Eldenvine's shell to keep it a secret." Erica met Aldyn's gaze for a long moment before turning back to Nathan and Everen.

"What happened in the past doesn't matter anymore, we have to escape before the Featherens recognize us, and so we can finish our mission."

Chapter Eight: Sacrifice.

"The simplest way to escape the prison would be by magic." Aldyn decided, "Everen, can you use a spell to break the bars?" Everen nodded.

"Good. Nathan," He turned towards her. "You will get our horses, the Featherens are probably holding them outside the fort, with the few Featherens here, I doubt they are guarded." Nathan nodded in understanding. Aldyn turned to Erica, and they met each other's gaze.

"Erica, find and retrieve our gear. I trust you can handle something that simple?" She asked. Erica stood up and glared at her.

"I can handle it. But what will you do? Hide in the background like a coward." Erica snapped. Aldyn stood up and faced off with Erica.

If Nathan wasn't there, it probably would've dissolved into a fistfight immediately. However, he set his hand on Erica's arm and sent Aldyn a pleading look.

Aldyn stepped back. "The only coward here is you." She hissed coldly.

"You led her to her death!" Erica shouted with balled fists, jerking away from Nathan.

"And you left her to die!"

Nathan stepped between them. "Now is not the time to fight! You can murder each other once we are all out of here."

"Nathan's right," Aldyn sighed, stepping back, "We can finish this later." She turned to Everen. "Break us out tomorrow morning, we wasted most of the day walking to our prison."

"Fine. Do you know what the Featheren was talking about, about you being a Pearling?" Everen asked.

"I'm clearly not a Pearling." Aldyn's voice had a tone of finality and she went to lean against the wall of the cell.

Erica moved to the opposite corner of Aldyn and leaned against the wall as well. Several hours later, one of the Featheren guards came and delivered dinner.

"At least the prison treatment is decent." Everen joked drily. Nathan laughed.

"This is definitely better than Captain Bloodskulll, remember Aldyn?" He said, turning to her.

Aldyn snorted. "Of course, I remember, you idiot."

Nathan raised his eyebrow. "I had to rescue you; I think that means you are the idiot."

Aldyn scowled, "Because you dropped the map, I had to go back for it."

Nathan's grin faltered, "In my defense, we had several dozen pirates after us."

"Correction, all of Klondor was after us. Bloodskull's one of Cat's Eye's lower lieutenants." Aldyn informed him.

Erica looked up, "Could the Featherens have been talking about your birth parents?" She asked.

"I don't know," Aldyn replied, her voice becoming cautious.

"It could be though; you are only half Elve." Erica reasoned.

"Leave it alone Erica." Aldyn snapped.

"Then what do you want to talk about? We are stuck in a Featheren prison, we have nothing to do except talk."

"We do have something better to do, escape." Aldyn shot back.

"That's in the morning," Erica said dismissively.

Nathan interjected before Aldyn got even more annoyed. "Let's all go to bed before anyone does something they'll regret." The other three agreed and lay down on the wooden floor.

Everen awoke hours later after the middle of the night with a gasp. She couldn't remember her dream, but it had been terrible.

The prison cell was black. Everen heard the soft sounds of her friends' breathing. Aldyn tossed and turned restlessly, and Erica was as still as a grave.

"Everen?" Nathan said sleepily. "What are you doing awake?" He asked.

"Just woke up. What about you?" She replied.

"I haven't been able to sleep, I'm thinking about my family." He admitted.

"Tell me about them," Everen suggested.

"Well, my mom, Sharine, is worrying about me because I haven't sent any messages in a while. My father knows I can handle myself, his name is Oliver and he works in the royal records. I have three brothers, Archer, Lance, and Leo. And two sisters, Gendevia and Lizzian."

"I wish I had siblings, it's just me, Dad, and Grams," Everen said.

"Sometimes our friends become our family. We haven't known each other very long, but Aldyn is like another sister to me." Nathan said softly.

"When Erica mentioned her birth parents earlier, what did she mean?" Everen asked.

"Aldyn was left by her birth parents in a river when she was less than a year old. She was taken in by a fisherman and his wife. They raised her as their own, until the burning of Cedar."

"What was it?"

Nathan hesitated, "Nearly nine years ago Cedar City was burned to the ground by a rouge dragon, Aldyn lived in Cedar. She'd the only survivor." Nathan explained.

"That's horrible," Everen whispered and stared at the sleeping teen. "Why?"

"No one knows. The dragon died in the fire."

Everen shuddered, "How did you meet her?"

Nathan's sad look was replaced with a half-smile. "Aldyn and I were both after the same map in Klondor, Bloodskull's actually. I was on a mission for the Queen's Bow. Aldyn was after it to try and find Cat's Eye's camp, he's the current Pirate King. I got the map first and she challenged me to for it. The pirates surrounded us, and we were captured. Before they could kill us, Aldyn distracted them, and I stole the map back. Then I dropped it while we were running, and she went back for it. We barely made it out." He grinned.

"How long ago was that?" Everen asked.

"Six months ago. Afterward, we kept in touch, and a month ago she asked if I wanted to help her on this mission." Nathan replied. Everen yawned. "You should get back to sleep." He said.

Everen shook her head. "Only if you do."

"Alright." He agreed and the two laid back down. Everen closed her eyes and fell into the gentle embrace of sleep.

Nathan shook Everen awake. Her eyelids felt extremely heavy, but she forced herself to wake up. As her vision came into focus, she realized that Aldyn was arguing heatedly with three Featherens, one of them was Firex and the other two Everen didn't recognize. The girl had soft brown hair and golden-brown wings and the boy had raven black hair and sleek ebony wings. Nathan pulled her to her feet, and they moved over.

"DON'T TOUCH ME!" Aldyn yelled at the two Featherens who grabbed her wrists.

"Shut up sea-blood!" The black-winged Featheren yelled.

"Let her go!" Nathan yelled.

"We are taking you to Featherwind for trial. Arguing will only cause you more problems!" Firex said angrily, "Wren, Raverick secure her." Firex ordered. The Featherens attached thick metal cuffs to Aldyn's wrists. The cuffs were connected to strong chains that the Featherens used to pull Aldyn out of the cell.

"We have to do something!" Everen said, panicking.

Nathan whirled towards her. "Use your magic! Now!" Everen paled and turned to Aldyn.

A golden blast knocked the Featherens back hard against the walls. Raverick smacked his head on the wood, and he slumped to the ground and passed out. Wren hit the wall on her back and fell to the ground with a groan of pain.

Firex crossed her arms in front of her face to protect herself. But the blast still pushed her back against the wall.

Aldyn spun towards Everen, "How did you do that?" She demanded.

"It doesn't matter! Run!" Everen yelled. Aldyn nodded and led the way down the corridor. Erica followed her with Everen and Nathan right behind.

They deviated from the original plan and split into two groups, Nathan and Aldyn went after the horses and Everen went with Erica to find their weapons and gear.

They found a large storage room that was guarded by a Featheren. He looked bored and miserable. He was tall but skinny for a Featheren. His wings were reddish-brown, and he had brown eyes, red hair, and freckles. His armor was the basic silver and leather. His face was shaped like Wren's, and Everen wondered if they were related.

"Great. How are we going to get past him?" Erica grumbled.

"We might be able to convince him to help us," Everen said sarcastically.

"After your blast of magic, we might as well try, you need time to recover." Erica snapped and Everen scowled.

Erica led the way to confront the Featheren warrior. She hid a small knife behind her back. Everen wondered how she'd managed to keep it.

The Featheren didn't even look surprised to see them. "I knew you were there." He informed them.

"Why didn't you attack?" Everen asked, and he shrugged.

"I don't think you deserve to be thrown in prison for life just for wandering into Ralaji, no matter what Firex says." He answered, "I'm Robin Quickflight."

"Everen Thatcher." Everen introduced herself.

"Erica Wolf." Erica added, "Can you help us?" She asked. "We are trying to find our gear."

Robin nodded, "Just don't tell anyone I helped, I'm in enough trouble with Captain Firex. I'll pretend I didn't see you." He glanced once more at them before walking down the hall away from them.

After he left, Everen turned to Erica, "That was strange."

"So, we found the one Featheren who doesn't want to fight. Whatever, we have to hurry."

The two girls worked quickly and gathered their weapons and supplies within several minutes. Erica pulled on her cloak and lined it with her daggers. Everen found a long knife that looked like it was carved bone. She looped it through her belt, hoping it wouldn't stab her while she ran.

Everen and Erica found the others on the lower floor of the outpost. The guards who they'd knocked out were missing, probably searching for them.

"Where are they?" Everen asked Erica, as they ran down the empty corridor. She heard the clash of claws on metal. "Never mind."

The girls found their friends fighting Firex and a second Featheren. Aldyn was wielding a rusty sword that she'd found somewhere. She and Nathan were out on the balcony and were slowly getting edged back.

"STOP!" Firex yelled, her voice had a hint of desperation under her anger. She had spent years working to get her position and losing them would damage that.

Nathan turned to Aldyn; he knew they wouldn't both be able to escape. "Run Aldyn!" He yelled.

Her eyes widened, realizing what he planned. "No, I won't leave you. I promised your mother."

"You don't have a choice." He whispered as he pushed her over the balcony.

Aldyn fell through the air, somehow keeping her grip on the rusty sword. She looked absolutely furious as she fell out of sight.

"Nathan!" Everen yelled surging forward, Erica grabbed her arm and yanked him back. "We have to save him!" She yelled.

"No, we have to get away, this is our chance! They won't kill him." Erica argued, pulling Everen's arm. Firex and the other Featherens surrounded him, Nathan was a good fighter, but he didn't have any weapons to even try and hold his own against them.

Erica pulled Everen's arm, which was frozen to the spot. Nathan glanced at them and nodded. Everen's heart sank as she let Erica drag her away, leaving Nathan behind.

Chapter Nine: The Blood Of Sisters.

They found Aldyn with the horses, looking bruised and battered from her fall. Her nose was bleeding, and her lip was split. She walked stiffly and winced as she climbed onto her horse, before grabbing the reigns of Nathan's as well.

Erica and Everen silently climbed onto their horses, the three girls were all in too much shock to speak. Everen passed Aldyn her sword, who nodded her thanks solemnly.

The three girls stirred the horses into a gallop and rode towards the tree line, away from the Featherens and away from Nathan. Everen heard shouts from behind them and glanced back, but at that point, they were already too far away to make out the details of the outpost.

It took a while, but the girls eventually got deep enough in the forest that Aldyn was willing to slow their pace.

"We have a few hours before they send a legion after us. Let's let the horses rest." She said. Erica and Everen nodded and the three dismounted.

Aldyn fell against a mossy tree trunk and slid to the ground. She leaned her head against it and closed her eyes. Erica also rested, lying on her back on the grass.

"What about Nathan?" Everen asked, crossing her arms, and refusing to rest.

"They'll interrogate him, find out he's not a threat, then lock him up and throw away the key." Aldyn sighed.

"Aldyn was the only one they were going to put on trial or kill. They wouldn't have even gone after you, Mistry." Erica explained. Everen winced and the girl scowled. Erica was irritated they hadn't trusted her with the secret, but she recognized that Everen had made her choice.

Everen didn't take that answer, "But we're just going to leave him there?"

Erica sighed. "He sacrificed himself and we have to be out of Ralaji before they come after us."

Aldyn stood up. "No, we're going after him. We'll go to Agatha and ask for her help."

"What about your mission?" Erica snapped, sitting up and crossing her arms.

"I don't care about the dragons; I care about my friend!" Aldyn yelled.

"Then why did you go on this mission in the first place?" Erica yelled back.

"Because Agatha asked me!" Aldyn shouted.

"She asked the one girl who hates dragons the most, to try and save them?" Erica's voice was incredulous. "I doubt that. I bet you volunteered. You wanted to get close enough so you could join the Hunters!"

"Don't test me!" Aldyn snarled, lifting her sword from the ground and stumbling to her feet.

"Or what?" Erica hissed. "You kill me like you killed Angela?"

Aldyn went stiff. "I didn't kill Angela. She gave her life defending us. How dare you forget her sacrifice!"

"Forget her sacrifice? It's your fault we even took that mission! It was risky and foolish. You had no right to make us go along with your thirst for revenge!" Erica screamed.

"I didn't make you do anything! You came with me, and then you left. Don't dare blame me for your choices!"

"You wanted revenge, we came with you, you wanted to kill the dragon, we tried, we failed, and Angela died saving us. And then you wanted to go find her body, instead of escaping with our lives!"

Aldyn's knuckles turned white on her sword's grip. "We owed her a burial. It's the least we should've done. We were her friends."

"We made oaths to be sisters! We'd already lost her; I couldn't lose you too. Going after her would've gotten us both killed!" Erica screamed and her voice cracked with emotion.

"If you cared so much, why did you leave? When I went after her, you left me to find her body alone. You broke your oath!" Aldyn's voice rang across the forest. If she was right, and Erica had broken her oath, under Eldenvine law Erica should've been killed.

Erica drew a long knife from the folds of her blood-colored cloak, "I. Did. Not." She snarled.

Aldyn raised her blade and slid into a stance, leaning on her toes, bending her knees, and tensing her arms. The sword she held had been with her for years. She'd found it in the ashes of Cedar, in the smithery of the city's renowned blade forger. She'd been looking for signs of life, what she'd found was a tool of death.

"I hate you," Aldyn whispered, before charging to meet Erica's blade. "You don't care about Angela; you care about me. You hate my choices. But you're selfish, vain, cruel, and cowardly!" She yelled as the blades crashed.

"You can only depend on yourself! You shouldn't have tried to take care of all of us. My family taught me that!" Erica broke away and swung at Aldyn's exposed side.

"My family taught me differently. They believed in loyalty and honor!" Everen backed away from the furious girls, mentally scrambling for a way to intervene. This was new to her. The physical fighting, the danger, the death, she didn't know how to deal with any of it.

"Your family is dead! You can't change that! No matter who you kill, or what ancient relic you find, they are never coming back! Revenge is worthless!" Erica screamed, "Whatever they believed in died with them!"

"You never cared about anyone except yourself!" Aldyn cut a scarlet slash across Erica's high cheekbone. The blood flowed freely down Erica's face and dripped off her chin.

Erica stepped back, "I cared about you and Angela! You got her killed!"

Aldyn surged forward with anger, "She made her choices. You have no right to discount that."

"You wanted revenge, not justice! Don't defend yourself!" Erica screamed.

"You're right! I did want revenge!" Aldyn swung her blade so strongly that she knocked Erica's knife from her hand.

"Aldyn!" Everen yelled, trying to stop them, but Aldyn snapped and was deaf to her screams.

Erica let out a short scream as Aldyn's blade nicked her arm.

Aldyn kept moving forward and attacking. "I *know* I went too far. I *know* revenge blinded me." Erica barely blocked the sword and continued stumbling backward. "You don't have to tell me." Aldyn brought her sword down to Erica's trembling throat. "But I will not apologize for someone else's actions. Do not hate me, when Angela is the one you are angry with."

"Yield!" She ordered and Erica glared defiantly at her. "I said, yield!" Aldyn repeated, this time touching the cold metal to Erica's skin.

With barely checked fury, Erica bowed her head. "I yield." She whispered.

Aldyn was silent as she backed away and sheathed her sword. Erica stayed there on the ground, glaring up at her, with an unusual mix of guilt and anger.

Erica calmly got to her feet, holding her head high with dignity, she wasn't going to apologize.

Aldyn turned to Everen, "Going back to Agatha will take days, I don't want Nathan to be stuck here any longer than necessary."

"What are you saying?" Everen asked, unsettled by how quickly the tone had changed.

"I'm choosing to go back. If the Featherens catch me, they will kill me. But I owe it to him. You can either follow me or go back to Agatha. She will be able to get you home."

Everen hesitated, all she wanted was to return to her father. But she didn't want to abandon her friends. Especially when leaving would probably make Aldyn go in alone and get killed. "I'm coming." She promised.

Aldyn nodded, then turned to Erica. Erica held her gaze for a long moment, before sighing softly. "I do regret that I left you to find her body alone. I am sorry I blamed you for her choices. You're right, I'm angry at her, not you. I'll help you rescue Nathan, afterward, I'll leave, and you never have to see me again."

Aldyn set her hand on Erica's shoulder, "No. Stay with us. Help us defeat the Dragon Hunters. Make someone pay for everything that has happened to us. Don't leave again."

To Everen's absolute shock, both girls immediately wrapped each other in a tight hug. Both of their shoulders shook with silent sobs, and they held each other tightly, like long-lost friends. "Why did we let them break us?" Erica whispered and a tear leaked from her eye.

Aldyn stayed silent, choosing to hold onto her best friend, the one who represented the brief period of stability in her childhood. The two had been bitter for almost four years, but now their anger was forgotten.

Chapter Ten: Freedom Is Its Own Reward.

"We get in, grab Nathan, and get out as quickly as possible." Aldyn summarized. The three girls were camping just behind the tree line waiting for the right moment to go after their friend. Erica had special binoculars and was watching the Featherens.

"I count four Featherens around the outpost. There are probably another four inside, they must have gotten more guards." Erica reported.

"We are not going to be able to get close without cover, it's a field of barren ash between us. I can use magic to make us invisible." Everen said.

"Do it." Aldyn said, "Can you also cover our scent? Featherens can smell us."

Everen shrugged, "I can try."

Ten minutes later the three girls were at the wall of the outpost, it was built rather close to the tree line, so it wasn't a long walk. Once they reached it, Aldyn knocked out the Featheren guard by the door and the three snuck inside.

They dodged guards easily and quickly reached the prison. Everen dropped the enchantment that was covering them and breathed deeply in relief, she had stretched herself to hold the magic for so long.

They searched the entire prison twice and couldn't find him. "Where is he?" Aldyn hissed.

"I don't know, where else could he be?" Everen replied in a whisper.

Erica opened her mouth to argue when the sound of footsteps stopped her. A Featheren walked around the corner.

"Scales and bones," Aldyn muttered. The Featheren looked shocked to see the girls and then he frowned.

Everen smiled when she recognized the reddish-brown wings and hair.

"Hello, Robin. You wouldn't know where our friend is do you?" She asked. Aldyn whirled around to stare at her, and Erica tried to conceal her snort of laughter.

"You shouldn't have come back for him, Firex is counting on it." He said quietly. Aldyn frowned.

"That doesn't matter, do you know where he is?" Aldyn asked.

"Yes, they moved your friend to the cells under the palace, they didn't want to risk losing him," Robin replied.

"Thank you, now we have to go." Aldyn turned back to Everen and Erica.

"You will not get a step inside the palace without my help," Robin commented with crossed arms. Aldyn glared at him and crossed hers as well.

"Are you offering it then?" She asked.

Robin smiled. "As long as Firex and Phinx never find out that I helped you. The royal family is legendary for their punishments."

Aldyn smiled slightly, "You have my word we will not betray you."

"Follow me."

With the combined abilities of Robin's Featheren knowledge and Everen's magic, the group of four was able to easily get to the Featheren capital, Featherwind.

Featherwind was beautiful. The pale stone buildings were tall and covered in elaborate artwork. There were many balconies and tall open windows. Some bridges connected the buildings and massive feathers and tapestries hung underneath them. The main colors were gold, red, and orange, but there were also violets, yellows, and turquoise. Featherens flew throughout the city. Almost all were in armor, but some wore dresses and togas in a variety of bright colors.

"This city is over five thousand years old, even older than Lady Mistic and the War of Magic," Robin informed them. "We used to have other great cities like it. Now only Featherwind is left."

Everen frowned lightly, "I thought the Pearlings burned this place to the ground."

Robin nodded solemnly, "If you look closely, we still are rebuilding. Featherwind was our pride and the heart of Ralaji, so when she fell, it destroyed the spirit of our people. Now, we defend her with our claws and the spilled blood of our enemies." His grin turned threatening.

"I have heard similar words uttered by a Pearling," Erica commented and Robin turned to her with a raised eyebrow.

"Unlike the sea-bloods, we have a sense of honor, and we are loyal to one another." Robin said, "Anyway, we need to move on if we are going to rescue your friend."

Robin led them through the city and down an alleyway. A door was on the side and led to a staircase underground.

The path was lit with torches that illuminated the bare stone. "They took your friend to the secure prisons, we have to be quiet, or the guards will hear us," Robin whispered. The girls nodded and followed him through the rest of the tunnel.

Finally, they reached a more decorated area. Robin explained they'd crossed into the actual palace. It was even more stunning than the capital. The pale stone walls were adorned with brightly colored tapestries and embedded with gold designs. Candles hung on the walls and there were large hearths placed periodically with flickering fires and glowing embers.

They were in the underground part of the palace, which was built into the mountains, so there were no windows or balconies. Featherens hated being away from the skies and sunlight, so the lower levels of the palace would be mostly empty.

Robin led them through several more halls until they reached the prisons. The prisons were deep in the center of the lower floors and were surprisingly not well guarded. Robin explained they had very few prisoners because they were hiding in exile and the population was small.

In the center of the prisons was a large circular room made of marble. A star constructed of golden feathers was ingrained on the floor and Everen ran her fingertips on it. She wondered how the Featherens had so much gold and why the Pearlings hadn't taken it.

Everen stood back up beside Aldyn and Erica. The room was poorly lit by lanterns and her neck prickled. Everen glanced at the columns that supported the ceiling and checked for hidden figures on the balcony that encircled the room.

As their eyes adjusted, Everen noticed a large iron cage concealed in shadows at the back of the room.

Inside it, was a familiar Elven boy. "Sharp-ears, you're alive!" Aldyn called, running to him and grabbing onto the bars.

"Nathan!" Everen echoed and ran after Aldyn. He grinned when he saw them, but his grin faded swiftly and was replaced with misery.

"The Featherens thought you might come after me, they're already here." He warned them.

Robin's senses alerted him to the threat, and he immediately paled with terror. "If I get out of this alive, I'm never helping a prisoner again." He muttered under his breath.

Suddenly a tall Featheren warrior leaped down from behind a column on the upper balcony and landed between Nathan and the girls.

Across her face was a trademarked smirk that dripped with arrogance and confidence. She had gorgeous massive brown wings and dark red hair. Her skin was darkly tanned with warm undertones, and she had thick dark brown eyelashes. In her ears were golden earrings and she had a gold chain around her neck. She wore a simple silver and leather armor set with gold cursive writing on the neck and her claws were unsheathed to fight.

Robin paled at the sight of the girl and breathed a single word "Phinx."

Everen turned around to glance at the exit a second Featheren dropped into a low fighting stance in front of it.

This Featheren had wavy light red hair and elegant silver-grey wings. Her bright storm-colored eyes shined with wisdom and intelligence. She had a paler complexion than her sister and her skin was creamier in color. The second Featheren had diamond earrings and her armor was engraved with wind patterns. She had a genuine smile on her face and also had unsheathed claws.

Everen noticed that this Featheren seemed slightly weaker than the other Featherens they had encountered. Her limbs were lean, and she was probably only Everen's height. She was small and her face was sharp, rare for a Featheren.

"Welcome to Featherwind." Phinx smirked, "You will never leave."

"Phinx, be reasonable," Robin said coldly and glared at her.

She bared her teeth at him. "I am Princess Phinx Fireena Feathercrown, daughter of Queen Athala and King Feathron, I am being very reasonable, traitor." She spat.

Robin flinched. "They shouldn't even be here, and we shouldn't keep them trapped here."

"And who are you to decide that?" Phinx replied, "We must protect Ralaji and our people. The war with the Pearlings almost destroyed us, if they learn that we are alive they will not hesitate to come and finish the job." She said.

"Robin, you know the law just as we do." The second Featheren said softly, with unusual gentleness.

"Auks, I know the laws." He snapped. "I also know what's right. It's not right to hold someone prisoner when they committed no crime." Phinx crossed her arms and Auks' smile vanished.

"Our mother ordered us to contain the threat. Nothing you say can change that." Auks told him stiffly.

"Even we are subject to her rules," Phinx added. Her eyes studied the three girls and she suddenly scowled with fury.

"Aldyn." She growled, "What are you doing here? Where's Angela?" She demanded. Aldyn flinched and didn't reply, not knowing how to answer.

Erica stepped forward. "She died with the bravery and ferocity of the best Featheren warriors. She was killed by a dragon, saving our lives." Phinx's threatening stance collapsed and her eyes widened with horror.

"No. No, no, no." She stumbled backward and her voice shook. Auks was pale and reached out to her sister, who turned away. "Not Angela. She promised she would come back to us, she promised me." Phinx's voice broke. She recovered her decorum and turned back to them with a cold anger. "I should kill you all where you stand." She hesitated. "But I won't. Angela wouldn't want me to. Just give me a good reason to not throw you into our deepest, darkest cells under the mountains." She snarled furiously.

"Because we are not a threat to Ralaji. No one will ever know that the Featherens are still alive. We will leave and never come back." Aldyn promised and her voice was void of any emotion.

"Can you promise that?" Phinx asked. "Angela is dead, a broken promise. So why should I risk my people's safety by trusting you?"

Aldyn didn't even hesitate. "I know I've made more than my share of mistakes. My past is covered in scars. I swore on the shell of Eldenvine to keep your survival secret, and I did. Now I'm swearing on the shell of Eldenvine that you can trust me."

Phinx was quiet for a long moment, before asking, "How did she die?"

Both Erica and Aldyn tensed and looked at each other. "A dragon was threatening to burn down a village and demanded tribute as protection. We wanted to help, and I was blinded by the idea of revenge for my family, they were killed in the burning of Cedar. We tried to fight it, but we underestimated the beast's power. I was injured and Angela was killed after pushing me away." Aldyn explained.

"Why are you back now, if Angela is dead," Phinx asked.

"We are following the Dragon Hunters," Nathan repeated, annoyed at not being listened to.

"Who are they?" Auks' voice had a soft tone of genuine curiosity.

"A group of terrorists who are killing dragons across Mytharica. They are targeting mothers with eggs and are taking the eggs; we don't know why." Aldyn answered.

Auks' eyes flashed with anger, "What?" She gasped; it was a horrific act to separate a child of any species from their mother. Phinx didn't react as strongly, but her gaze darkened.

The sisters were quiet for a long moment staring at each other in silent communication. Auks finally asked, "Phinx, what are your orders?"

Phinx turned to her. "Stand down." Phinx sheathed her claws and Auks did as well. Robin sighed in relief and Auks sent him a smile.

"What about Mom, she's going to demand an explanation for this," Auks warned her sister.

"We will tell her the truth," Phinx replied curtly. She turned to the others. "We will bring you to meet her, and you can share your story. She will decide what to do with you. I cannot change her final decision."

"Is it really smart to go to the Queen, you just tried to kill us." Everen reminded her.

Phinx grinned, "Queen Athala is the deadliest and most dangerous woman alive, even more than me. Of course, it's not smart to confront her."

Auks rolled her eyes and muttered under her breath, "Yet you're somehow more arrogant."

Phinx's ear twitched, but she ignored her younger sister. "Don't worry about it. Auks and I will speak on your behalf. Follow me, I'll lead you to her."

Phinx spun on her heel and opened a hidden door built into the stone walls. It opened into a large corridor with flame designs painted on the walls in orange and gold.

Everen noticed that Aldyn's fingertips traced the fire as they passed. She remembered how Cedar had burned and Everen wondered how close Aldyn had been to it. The fifteen-year-old girl was the only survivor of the several thousand that lived there.

The end of the corridor exited into a large, tall hallway filled with Featherens. Phinx led them through the palace and up several floors. The Featherens they passed stared in shock at the prisoners and respect for the princesses.

A Featheren in elegant white armor passed Auks to approach Phinx. "Your Highness, what are you doing?" She asked.

"I am bringing these infiltrators to speak to my mother." She answered, "Athala will decide their fate." The woman nodded and stepped aside for a second Featheren, this one a teenage boy, to talk to Phinx.

He had golden brown wings and dirty blond wavy hair. "Phinx, need any help?" He asked.

"Eagle, do you know me?" Phinx laughed, "I can handle it." He nodded and walked away. Phinx smiled after him and Auks shoved her, not very effectively. Auks was too small to off-balance Phinx.

She led them to the center of the palace on one of the highest levels. It was the most secure position in all of Ralaji and ten Featherens were guarding two tall golden doors.

The Featherens moved out of their way and Phinx confidently shoved the doors open. Inside them was a massive room with a tall arching ceiling. Several narrow windows hid on the walls and let in natural light. Tapestries hung beneath the windows that depicted scenes of past rulers and famous moments in Featheren history. Orange orbs hung from the high ceiling and glowed with faint fire.

A raised dais was in the center of the room. On it was a large golden throne covered in golden feathers and rubies where a beautiful woman lounged. On her head was an intricate crown made of golden feathers, rubies, and garnets. Her dark red hair was braided and hung down onto her gold breastplate. She had golden feathers on her wings and her skin was warm and tan. Her eyes were bright orange. She also had golden shin guards and arm guards. All of her armor was engraved with immense detail. She had a thin pale gold cape loosely on her neck, secured with a golden feather at her shoulder.

She radiated power and confidence, like her elder daughter, as she watched the group walk in.

"Phinx, what is this?" She demanded calmly. Any Featheren would flinch under the harsh look of the Queen, but Phinx only grinned.

"Love you too Mom. Auks and I recovered the escaped prisoners, and we brought them to you to plead their case. It is more convincing than I originally thought." Phinx explained, taking the lead like usual.

Athala thought for a moment, "Let them explain themselves, I'll judge what we will do next." Phinx nodded and stepped to the side.

Aldyn stepped forward and some Featherens growled, smelling her unusual ancestry. "I am Aldyn, these are my friends Nathan Willowsar, Everen Thatcher, and Erica Wolf." Each nodded their heads in greeting when Aldyn said their name. "We came to Ralaji to follow the Dragon Hunters, not to interfere with the Featherens. Erica and I were already aware of your existence, and we kept our promise to keep it secret. We were not intending to go anywhere near Featherwind, so we would not have threatened you. If you let us go on and continue our mission, we will respect your wishes and keep everything secret."

"I respect your blunt honesty and appreciate your promise to keep our secret. However, this is unnecessary. I see this as the perfect opportunity for the Featherens to return to Eldenvine from our exile." Athala announced.

"You can't be serious." A teenage Featheren boy interrupted, who was standing near the throne. He was probably part of the extended royal family. He had brown spiked hair with natural highlights and dark brown wings. He wore basic silver armor and dark brown eyes.

"Hawk." Athala scolded, "I have thought of this for a long time, I know the risks and dangers better than anyone. But I also see the benefits of reopening alliances. If the rest of Eldenvine learns that the Featherens of Ralaji are alive, the Pearlings will not be able to quietly extinguish us. If they dare to start a war, the rest of Eldenvine will react in sympathy. We can open trade routes and bring wealth and prosperity back to our weakened lands."

"We have been in hiding for over two hundred years, why are we breaking that now?" He asked.

Athala smiled at him, proud that he was thinking critically. "Because there is a new threat in Eldenvine. It is a group of terrorists slaughtering dragons, our prisoners followed them here. If we help our prisoners, by association helping the rest of Eldenvine, that will show us the best way for our return. Also, we are unable to hide forever, so we should take advantage of this good opportunity." She explained and Hawk nodded, respecting his queen and her wisdom.

Athala turned back to Aldyn. "Now, I do want to let you go. However, I am not a fool. Your plan to sabotage the Dragon Hunters is weak and destined to fail. My investment will not pay off as of right now. But, if I send you with several Featheren warriors, your mission is guaranteed a higher chance of success."

Aldyn hesitated for a moment, before answering "I accept your offer."

"I am glad." The Queen said. "Phinx, Auks, are you willing to accompany them?" She asked suddenly, looking at her daughters. Everen noticed that Athala's gaze lingered on Auks, and she realized that the Queen was probably very protective of her daughter.

Phinx looked stunned and Auks was excited. "Are you serious?" Auks asked.

Athala laughed at her younger daughter. "Yes." Auks' face broke into a wide grin while Phinx crossed her arms.

"Who will protect Ralaji while we are gone?" Phinx asked and Athala sighed.

"You are not the only capable warrior Phinx, there are many other Featherens who can adequately protect Ralaji." Phinx scowled, but then the corner of her mouth twitched.

"I always wanted to go on an adventure." She said, Athala smiled.

"I am glad we have agreed." She faced Aldyn. "Phinx and Auks will join you." Aldyn frowned faintly but she didn't fight with the Queen, it was more important to get their freedom.

Thinking ahead, Aldyn asked, "Do you know where the Dragon Hunters are now?"

Athala's face darkened, "They camped on the edges of our southern territory and left for Klondor less than two days ago. They hit several nests on the coast, with no survivors. That is part of the reason Firex captured you, she thought you might have been a part of their organization." Nathan looked offended at the idea.

"We would never!" He exclaimed and Erica rolled her eyes.

"We know." She snapped. He glared at her.

"What should I call you four? You are a team, and you need a name." Athala said, smiling.

Aldyn hesitated, they hadn't collectively created a group name yet, and she didn't have any ideas.

Nathan grinned and stepped past her. "Call us the Elden Order." He said. Aldyn raised her brow and Everen smiled. Erica sighed.

"Alright, Elden Order, for the rest of today and tonight you can stay in the palace. Tomorrow my daughters will accompany you to Klondor." Athala nodded to Phinx after she finished, and the elder princess guided the newly christened Elden Order out of the throne room.

Phinx took the lead and walked up the floors to the towers. Everen found herself walking next to Auks.

"Hello." Auks greeted Everen, "I know we haven't formally met, I'm Auks. I'm sorry about the whole prisoner situation, I hope that doesn't mean we can't be friends."

Everen laughed kindly. "The first time I met Aldyn, she threatened to kill me. You are already doing better than her."

Auks laughed, "What land are you from?" She asked.

"Actually, I am from Earth," Everen replied, making Auks' jaw drop.

"You have to tell me that story!" Auks begged. Everen grinned and spent the rest of the walk telling Auks about her journey so far with Aldyn, Nathan, and Erica.

Phinx led them up to the top of one of the tallest towers of the palace. Half of the room was open to the mountain air and the golden roof was supported by tall stone pillars. The room was beautiful and old with gold wing designs engraved on the walls. It fit in well with the rest of the artistic style of Ralaji and Everen's eyes widened as she saw it.

Around the room were a dozen wooden and leather contraptions that resembled wings. "What are these?" Everen asked as her fingertip traced the carved feathers of the wood.

"It's a Soarer, they are ancient Featheren inventions made of skywood. They were created to allow non-Featherens of Ralaji to fly, you can use it as well." Phinx answered.

"I can fly with it?" Everen clarified.

Phinx smirked, "Yes. It's the closest you can come to actually flying as a non-Featheren." Auks rolled her eyes at her sister.

"Don't worry, flying is amazing. I can't imagine life without wings." Auks encouraged them.

Auks helped Everen get the soarer on and the two joined the others at the edge of the balcony to jump.

"This is how you fly," Phinx shouted over the howling wind and jumped backward off the balcony.

Phinx free-fell for several seconds before she flipped herself and dove. She spread her wings right before she crashed and glided upwards at a steep angle. When Phinx reached the same level as the tower, she paused in the air and gently beat her powerful wings to keep afloat. "Come on! Just jump!" She yelled.

Nathan was the first to join Phinx. He leaped off the edge, trusting the contraption to keep him alive. He yelled as he fell towards the ground but managed to catch himself.

Everen had a wide grin as she followed him. She twisted as she fell and then spiraled upwards. It was easy to fly with the wooden wings and absolutely amazing.

Aldyn stared at the stone edge of the balcony and took a deep breath. She took several steps back and narrowed her gaze. She broke into a run and spread her wings in the open air.

Erica went last, she was probably the least daring of the four and the least likely to trust an unknown device to keep her alive. But she still jumped and joined the others in the sky.

Auks was right. Flying felt like freedom. The force of the wind flew Everen's hair back and made her eyes water. Everen laughed when she saw it was the same for the others. Nathan flipped in the air and Everen followed his lead. Aldyn flew like a natural and was shockingly able to keep up with the Featherens.

Phinx was a dangerous daredevil in the sky. She would free fall and catch herself at the last second and dive tightly through branches of trees. She was incredibly fast and easily able to outpace the rest of them.

As they flew, Auks' light red hair glinted in the evening sun. She flew beside Robin, yelling teasing insults as he attempted to catch her. The seven teenagers had the time of their lives as they flew, but eventually, they had to return to the palace.

They ate dinner with the royal family. King Feathron and Queen Athala sat at the head of the table. Feathron had dark grey wings and brown hair so dark it was almost black. Ransha was Athala's sister and was next to her. She had light brown wings flecked with gold, dark brown skin, and black braided hair. Her husband Flaredor was on her other side. Next to Feathron was his identical twin brother Ro and his wife Laylia. Laylia had white wings and pale blond hair with sky-blue eyes. The siblings, Hawk and Firex were next to their father Flaredor at the end and Skyri and Skyron were next to their mother Laylia. Skyri and Skyron were twins, she had rare pale purple wings and pure black hair while he had navy wings.

The meal was pheasant marinated in a sweet spicy sauce with a side of tangy orange fruits.

"Not bad," Aldyn commented.

Firex grinned, "Much better than anything in Islaria. They can't handle even a bit of spice." Firex turned to her cousin, "Phinx." She said slyly. "I think we should take our guests out to the woods after dinner."

Phinx's face broke into a wicked grin.

"What's out there?" Aldyn asked.

"We dug out a large pit in the woods that's perfect for Pit Brawl" Phinx answered.

"Has Pit Brawl changed since the last time I was here?" Phinx shook her head.

"What is it?" Nathan asked.

Phinx turned to him, "It's a casual fighting game. Free for all, but no claws or weapons. There's always at least a few Featherens out there, you should come with." She offered. Aldyn grinned.

"I'm in." She said. Phinx turned to the others.

"Heck no," Erica replied. "I'd like all of my limbs to be functioning tomorrow." Nathan laughed.

"Suit yourselves." Phinx and Firex stood up and left with Aldyn beside them. Hawk leaped to his feet and followed his sister.

"Say hi to Kasia for me!" Robin yelled after him.

"Will do!' He saluted before running after the girls.

"While they are gone, how about I show you my favorite place in all of Ralaji?" Auks offered.

The Featheren princess led them to a mountain peak about half an hour's flight from the palace. They landed on a large ledge cut into the stone. A waterfall cascaded down from the cliff into a pool on the ledge.

It was sunset at that point and the setting rays hit the falling water which turned the white water golden.

"This is Fire Falls, the most beautiful place in Ralaji," Auks whispered reverently.

"I see why," Nathan replied, his voice echoing softly across the mountain.

"Thank you for showing it to us." Everen breathed, Erica nodding. Auks replied with a smile, still gazing at the gleaming falls.

"Beauty deserves to be shared."

Part Two – Surviving A World Such As This

Chapter Eleven: Flight Of The Featheren.

The next day the Elden Order and the royal sisters stood in the tower room with the Queen and Robin. King Feathron had a council with the Sky Giants, so he said his goodbyes the night prior. Athala hugged her daughters tightly.

Athala let them go and set her hand on Phinx's shoulder, "Phinx, you have reached an age where everything is a test. After you return from the mission, we will discuss handing over some royal duties." Athala smiled at her eldest daughter. Everen didn't miss the expression of disappointment that flashed across Auks' face.

"I will not fail," Phinx promised, before hugging her mother again.

"Valas," Athala whispered the Featheren word for strength and honor, it was the customary farewell to warriors before they went off to war. It was also the word for goodbye.

Auks nodded at her mother and went to speak to Robin. "It will be so lonely without you. Tell me everything when you get back!" Robin set one hand on Auks' shoulder, he was several inches taller than her, and Everen could tell he was trying to hide how worried he was.

"Have fun putting up with Firex while I am gone!" Auks teased, "I will miss you too." She added softly.

"See you in a month or two?" He asked.

"Probably." Auks hesitated before adding, "Valas, Robin." Auks suddenly wrapped him into a tight hug and kissed his cheek. Robin blushed as he hugged her back and closed his eyes, trying to hold on to the moment forever.

"Valas, Auks." He whispered in her ear, he added something else, but Everen couldn't hear what he said.

Everen turned her attention away from the two best friends back to the Queen, who was speaking with her eldest daughter.

"Phinx, hear me. Watch out for Auks, take care of her." Athala's hand firmly gripped Phinx's shoulder, hard enough for her to flinch.

"I promise." Phinx nodded her head with conviction, however, Athala still looked worried.

"You know she isn't as strong as you, she's weaker than everyone your age." She sighed, "It's my fault she's like this."

Phinx reached out and gently held Athala's hand. "Don't blame yourself. You were poisoned with Fire Bane."

Athala shook her head, "I shouldn't have flown a mission while pregnant." She trailed off and looked away, "Just take care of her."

"I will," Phinx vowed.

"Thank you," Athala whispered.

The flight to Klondor was easy and smooth with Phinx and Auks in the lead. It would have been many days on foot or horseback but in the air, it was only eight hours before they were on Islaria's eastern shore. They took a break on the beach before flying out into the ocean, the ocean was beautiful. Everen observed with awe, the soft teal waves that sparkled in the evening sun.

Phinx and Aldyn spent the majority of the flight avoiding one another. Phinx blatantly despised the pirate-like girl. Aldyn didn't care, the feeling was mutual. Every time Phinx looked at Aldyn she remembered her friend Angela, who had been so excited to see the world, and who died beside Phinx and Auks flew together, like the sisters had done their entire lives and discussed their friends and family back in Ralaji. Everen turned her head and saw Erica flying behind Phinx and Auks, she was silently observing the water pass beneath them.

While they flew, Everen stayed in the back and talked with Nathan and Aldyn, the three had become close since meeting in Wryrom.

Everen shifted the weight of the bag hanging at her chest. Before they left Ralaji, Robin had picked up all their gear and released their horses, Aldyn's and Everen's were rented from Jack, and they would return to him. Nathan's would run ahead to Elvara and Erica's would stay in Ralaji.

Soon, a tall island with cliffs came into view. It rose out of the water like a massive white collum from ancient Rome. On the flat top, it was covered in small green hills and thick underbrush. The waves of the ocean crashed into the white cliffs and the sound of their churning could be heard up in the sky.

"We will camp on the island for the night. To land the Soarers, lightly angle downwards so you will be as level to your landing point as possible, don't do it too much or you will speed up into an uncontrollable dive, and none of you are Featherens." Auks explained. Featherens were born with innate physical abilities which helped them fly. They were light, durable, and strong. Also, they had incredible reflexes, and eyesight, and were able to adapt to pressure changes quickly. Historically, non-Featherens were terrible flyers and many had been injured by overestimating their skills on the Soarers.

Phinx rolled her eyes at her logical sister. "Race you to the shore!" She challenged and dove out of the sky at an alarming speed. Aldyn scowled and chased after her. Aldyn would rarely refuse a challenge, and Phinx knew it.

"Don't! You are going to crash!" Auks yelled, holding her hand out. "Follow them, carefully!" She yelled to Everen, Nathan, and Erica. Auks dove out of the sky, trying to catch Aldyn before she killed herself.

Everen dove as fast as she dared to follow Auks. She quickly reached the ground and Aldyn, who was dangerously close to the cliff face.

"TILT UP, YOU ARE GOING TO CRASH!" Auks screamed. Aldyn tried to bring up her Soarer, but she was going too fast. Phinx raced to Aldyn, but she fell through the air too quickly for Phinx to catch her. Phinx cursed very loudly and creatively in the Featheren language.

"If we don't stop her, she will crash into the cliffs. At her speed, she'll die!" Auks yelled. Nathan's eyes widened. He sped up his soarer and dove after Aldyn. He hit her Soarer in the side and both of them crashed on the cliff's edge.

Auks swiftly dove down to them and Everen and Erica followed. Nathan and Aldyn's soarers were pulling them off the edge with their heavy weight so the three forward and grabbed them. Everen felt like she was using all her strength as she helped the Featheren pull Nathan and Aldyn back. Finally, they were no longer in danger.

Everen fell back into the grass and breathed deeply, relieved, and exhausted.

Meanwhile, Auks stormed across the cliffs over to Phinx, who'd just landed. "PHINX!" She roared in her sister's face.

"Fayra's feathers," Phinx muttered, backing away.

"Do you remember what mom said? She's trusting us to make sure this mission is a success. How could you risk that? If Aldyn died it would've been on your head." She snarled.

Auks probably would've been able to calm down if Phinx hadn't rolled her eyes. "You don't deserve the crown!" Auks yelled suddenly. Phinx's jaw dropped, as though she had been slapped. "You would be a terrible queen! You are reckless, overconfident, and arrogant! I should be queen!" Phinx's eyes darkened, and she glared at her sister.

"Since when do you want the throne?" Phinx demanded.

"Since I realized how terrible of a queen you would be!" Auks yelled.

"I would be a better queen than you, at least I'm a real Featheren." Phinx snapped.

Auks' eyes widened at the jab, "And what's that supposed to mean?"

"You're weak!" Phinx snapped, "You spend all day hiding in the palace and you never train."

"I train! You just don't see it!" Auks argued.

Phinx raised her brow, "Last week you lost a match to River!" Auks flinched, and she spread her wings.

"Fine." She beat them down and climbed into the air.

"Phinx!" Everen snapped as Auks flew away.

"Shut up." Phinx growled, "Don't get involved." She turned around and leaped into the air, flying in the opposite direction from her sister. Everen couldn't help but notice how easily Phinx flew, compared to Auks.

Everen stomped over to Erica who was gently pulling Nathan further away from the cliff edge onto the grass. Everen saw the blood on Nathan's face and immediately forgot about the Featheren sisters.

"Scales and bones, please be alive," Everen whispered as she knelt beside him.

"He's alive, but that was a heck of a crash," Erica replied as she gently took off the broken soarer and tossed it aside. Everen opened her pack and pulled out the spell book that she'd stolen from Eldersa.

She flipped through the pages until she reached the healing section. "Sanar." Everen sang softly and waved her hand over his chest. Gold magic knit his cut lip back together and his bruises faded. The blood evaporated into stardust, and he breathed deeply.

"Oh, thank Eldenvine." Everen breathed and leaned back.

Nathan began to move, his eyelids twitched, and he shifted. "What in Mytharica happened?" Nathan asked, opening his eyes, and raising his head.

Everen began to laugh, slightly hysterical. "Nothing much." She replied, attacking him with a tight hug. "Don't do that again." She ordered.

"Don't worry, I don't plan on intentionally crashing anytime soon," Nathan answered cheekily. Everen rolled her eyes and climbed off him. She grabbed his hand and helped him stand.

Erica hugged Nathan once he stood up. "You almost had me worried there." She said before letting go. Nathan smiled at Erica.

"Where's Aldyn?" He asked. Everen glanced over to Aldyn and hurried to her friend's side.

Aldyn looked surprisingly less beat up than Nathan. Erica frowned when she saw her. "She should be injured worse." Everen shrugged, Nathan had probably taken the worst of the fall in the crash.

Everen kneeled beside Aldyn, but Erica stood back with crossed arms. Although the girls had made up, it was still tense between them.

Everen repeated the spell and Aldyn groaned before jumping to her feet. "When I get my hands on that Featheren I will shred her wings and throw her corpse off the Featheren Palace!" She yelled furiously. Aldyn turned to the others, "Where's Phinx." She demanded.

"Whoa, there will be no killing, torture, or murder of any kind," Nathan said stepping up to Aldyn. The two were nearly the same height, but he was taller by enough to irritate the one-eyed girl.

"Fine. Where are the Featherens?" Aldyn asked, her voice still carrying an edge of a threat, but Phinx was probably safe.

"They got in a fight and flew off. Phinx is furious and Auks snapped after something she said." Everen explained.

"So Phinx is normal, and Auks' secret dark side is revealed," Aldyn repeated and Erica snorted.

"That's one way of describing it." Erica retorted. The corners of Nathan's mouth twitched and Everen laughed.

"While we wait for the Featherens to come back, we can set up camp," Aldyn said, that Aldyn was a natural leader and effortlessly took charge of the situation. Under her direction, Erica and Nathan worked with Everen to set up the tents and start a small fire. Aldyn gathered a bag of wild berries and nuts. Aldyn also borrowed Nathan's spare bow and killed three large hares.

Aldyn passed the food she had gathered to Nathan who started to cook it in a small iron pot. Aldyn was rarely put in charge of cooking because she liked things too spicy for the others to handle.

Everen sat next to Nathan as he cooked the meal. Erica joined them and the three talked causally. A bit beside them, Aldyn rested on a stump, carving into a small stick with a knife she'd gotten from her belt.

"Where did you get that knife?" Everen asked Aldyn, making the girl glance up. The firelight glinted over her black eyepatch, and it made her look intense.

"I don't recognize it; you must have gotten it after we separated," Erica commented.

"I did," Aldyn replied. She twisted the blade in her hand. "Someone very close to me gave me this knife, I saved his life, and he gave me this knife in gratitude."

"How did you save his life?" Erica asked.

Aldyn's face broke into a soft smile as she remembered, "The idiot got pickpocketed and lost all our gold, so he tried to bargain with a Klondor merchant, except his northern Klondon is *terrible*." Everen and Nathan joined in with her laughter. "He threatened the merchant, accidentally he swore, by I doubt it. The merchant's crew, who were actually pirates in disguise, attacked us. I had to save him, and we fought pirates all the way out of Klondor!" Even Erica was laughing at Aldyn's animated tale.

"You never told me that story." Nathan pretended to be hurt, and she shrugged.

"It's not my best, we lost a lot of money, and my shoulder didn't turn all the way for a week," Aldyn replied. Everen's eyebrows shot up.

"What did you do?" She asked.

"Yeah, I kind of had to jump from the crow's nest." Nathan choked. "I caught the netting with one arm, it yanked my shoulder out of the socket." Aldyn rolled her shoulder at the memory.

"You never change," Erica said, shaking her head. Aldyn grinned, showing her white teeth and Nathan laughed.

"She wouldn't be Aldyn if she did." He commented. The group of four laughed.

Auks and Phinx showed up shortly after. Phinx had a bruise on her jaw and Auks looked ashamed. They raised their eyebrows at the sight before them.

"What happened?" Phinx asked, voicing the question for both of them.

"Aldyn's telling us about her knife," Nathan answered, easily breaking the ice.

"May I see it?" Phinx asked with interest. Aldyn passed the knife to Phinx, who turned it over in her hand and looked at it from different angles. The blade was a blueish metal with small groves. The handle was white and smooth.

"Sea-steel with heart-pearl, worn but still in excellent condition, forged at least twenty years ago. I don't recognize this symbol; it is probably a family symbol or blacksmith's trademark, possibly even a pirate's insignia. This is a fine blade, where did you get it?" Phinx asked as she reverently handed it back to Aldyn, who set it back on her belt.

"From a friend," Aldyn replied.

"How did you know all that about the knife?" Nathan asked.

"My sister only bothers with her education when she's interested in it. For example, she loves weaponry. Our cousin Firex is the same. Both of them know more about war history, weapons, and battle strategy than anyone in our wing." Auks cut in and took a seat beside Everen and Erica.

"It's true. But now Firex has been studying more so that she can become Peakatroir." Phinx said.

"What's that?" Aldyn asked.

"The head of the entire Ralaji military, only the best of the best can even try for the position. Firex wants to be Peakatroir by her twentieth birthday, and she might even make it. The Peakatroir is second only to the King and Queen of Ralaji." Phinx explained.

"That's impressive," Everen commented. The group continued to talk and get to know each other better. Aldyn repeated her story about receiving the knife and Nathan shared several of his adventures.

"So, then my idiot brothers had managed to set the roof on fire. They'd used some strange chemical mix they'd bought off a Klondor merchant and it made the fires purple and almost impossible to put out. Finally, we had to get the local enchanter to put it out. Mom grounded them for a month." Nathan said.

The others rolled on the ground in laughter. "I hope I can meet them," Everen said when she was finally about to talk through her laughter.

"I hope so too. Lance and Leo are the best. Once the mission is over, I'll take you to Elvara." Nathan promised.

"Could I come too? Otherwise, I'm just going back to running from the Wolfmoon royal guard." Erica asked.

Nathan grinned, "Sure. You're all welcome."

"So, Aldyn," Phinx asked, turning to the girl. "Any idea why you smell like a sea-blood?"

Aldyn's laughter evaporated and her expression became guarded. "I told you already I don't know. I might have Pearling ancestry."

"Must be recent." Phinx pushed, "Like maybe a Pearling mother or father?"

Aldyn stood up, "I don't know. My parents dumped me in a river; I know nothing about them."

"People are rarely loyal when it matters, my family taught me that." Erica's voice was bitter as she interjected.

Everen flinched, thinking about her own mother's abandonment. "But maybe," Phinx began.

Suddenly, Aldyn's head snapped to the side. It was like someone had whistled and only she had heard it. "Quiet." She ordered.

"What's wrong, Aldyn?" Nathan asked.

She ignored him, instead looking out at the ocean. "Someone's calling me." She said.

"Aldyn, there's nothing," Everen said.

The girl shook her head and began walking towards the cliff. Everen stood up and followed her. "Aldyn stop!" Everen yelled, realizing what she was about to do. Everen grabbed Aldyn's wrist and she twisted out of it, not looking away from the dark water.

Aldyn reached the edge of the cliff. She breathed deeply and dove.

Chapter Twelve: Daughter Of The Ocean.

"ALDYN!" Everen yelled as Aldyn fell to the water. She slowly moved her hands in front of her like an arrow point. Her brown hair flew back in the wind. Aldyn struck the water between the black slick rocks and didn't resurface.

Nathan and Erica ran to Everen's side, with the Featherens right behind them. Nathan started to pull off his green cloak and stepped back as though he was going to dive in after her.

Everen grabbed his strong arm and yelled at him, "The rocks could kill you! Don't be stupid!"

"We have to save her!" Nathan yelled angrily.

"I know!" Everen yelled back. She found her spell book and leafed through it desperately. Erica smacked the book shut.

"We don't have time for you to find something, Aldyn could be dead!" Erica snapped.

Before Everen could do anything, or Nathan could jump after her, Aldyn rocketed out of the water into the sky. Her body was weightless for a moment before she landed on the cliff on one knee with her head bent.

Aldyn whipped her head back, knocking most of the water out. Her hair and clothes dripped as she stood.

The other five were silent in shock. "How?" Erica demanded.

Aldyn's strange expression vanished, and she looked confused. "I don't know why I did that." She murmured and looked out at the sea again.

"You *are* a Pearling. That's how you survived Cedar!" Erica realized.

"I, yes." Aldyn stumbled and Nathan caught her. He helped her sit down on a fallen log and she rested her head in her hands.

"You were right," Aldyn said finally, looking at Phinx. "One of my parents was a Pearling. It doesn't matter anymore. I already revealed myself."

"Why did you keep it hidden?" Everen asked.

Aldyn looked at her, "About fifteen years ago the Pirate King Graves had a grudge against the people of Islaria. He slaughtered them by the hundreds. He was especially against half-Pearlings. If his surviving supporters found out that a Pearling and an Elve had a daughter together, they would hunt me down."

Erica nodded and glanced at Everen, "He's dead, but his old men still keep his ideals."

"We wouldn't have told anyone," Nathan said, sounding hurt.

Aldyn shook her head. "It doesn't matter, the second you tell a secret, people start to find out. I was protecting myself. Like it matters anymore." She muttered.

Nathan set his hand on her shoulder. "We'll protect you." He promised and Everen and Erica nodded.

Everen turned to the Featheren sisters, who were exchanging solemn glances. "You know our people are sworn enemies," Phinx said.

Auks sent Phinx a look, "We promised to accomplish this mission. Once this is over, we won't turn you in, but there's not much more we can do." Auks said, her grey gaze filled with pity.

"Thank you," Aldyn said, getting back to her feet. "That's far more than I would've expected." Auks nodded.

"Do you have gills or something?" Everen asked suddenly.

Aldyn stared at her for a moment before breaking into laughter, "No. The water I breathe filters out through special skin on my neck. I can also see underwater, and when I'm in water my physical abilities are enhanced." Aldyn explained. "I'm nowhere near as powerful as a full-blooded Pearling, but I can hold my own."

"I can't believe my first mission outside of Ralaji is with a sea-blood," Phinx whispered.

"What did you hear?" Auks asked. "When you freaked out and dove off the cliff." She clarified.

Aldyn gazed out at the water, "Something about the disappearing islands, I think we should go there."

"Of all the places in Klondor!" Erica groaned.

"What's so bad about the disappearing islands?" Everen asked.

"The islands are ghost islands, everyone who goes there disappears. It's near Islaria, and even pirates stay away from the place." Aldyn answered.

"So of course, we have to go there," Everen said sarcastically.

Aldyn smirked, "It will be an adventure." Aldyn turned away from the ocean. "We will head out tomorrow morning. Get some sleep."

Everen wrapped herself in her blanket after they figured out the night's watch. The second her head hit her pillow; she was out.

Everen was running through the Dark Woods of Wryrom, at night with four of the seven moons new and the others barely illuminating the shadowed forest. She dared to look over her shoulder as she panted for breath, her heart pounded in her ears. She saw a blur of a shadow and red eyes. She pushed forward, knowing that the creature was at her heels. The forest thinned. It faded to a rocky barren mountainside, like the majority of Ralaji. Everen screamed in fear as she ran. Then her luck ran out. The mountainside ended in a cliff face overlooking a dark ocean of pure black water. She barely managed to stop herself from diving off the edge. Everen turned around to face the creature that hunted her. It melted into the shadows, obscuring a full picture, but what she did see were red eyes and pure white fangs dripping with silver blood that gleamed. Everen tried to step back, to escape the horrid beast. She got her wish. She tripped over the edge and plummeted towards the black waters below.

Everen woke up gasping and covered in sweat. The cold night air swept into her bones her blanket fell on the ground and she sat up.

Nathan rushed over to her, "Are you okay?"

Everen nodded and wrapped her blanket back around herself. "I'm fine. Just a nightmare." She told him.

"Do you want some tea?" He asked.

"We have tea?" Everen replied with a raised eyebrow.

"I keep a secret stash." Nathan grinned. He opened a pouch on his belt and the fragrant smell released into the air.

"Thanks," Everen replied when Nathan handed her a wooden cup filled with tea.

"You're welcome." He winked at her, and she laughed quietly.

The two didn't talk much. Everen just sipped her tea and tried not to think about her dream. Eventually, she finished it and handed the empty cup over to Nathan. "Goodnight." She said, barely hearing his reply before falling back asleep.

The next morning Everen awoke to the smell of burning meat. "What is going on?" She asked as she stood up.

"It's Phinx's turn to cook," Nathan replied, coming over to her. "You okay?" He asked.

"Yeah, thank you," Everen answered.

"No problem, I'm always here." He promised. The two walked over to the fire. The Featheren had caught four rabbits and set them in an iron pan to cook.

"Is it edible?" Erica asked sarcastically when she joined them.

Auks snorted, "My sister's talents may be on the battlefield, but she knows what she's doing." Erica was unconvinced, but she accepted the plate of rabbit meat and wild onions.

Everen finished hers quickly. "Not bad." She nodded to Phinx.

Aldyn walked into the camp as they finished eating. Nathan held a plate to her.

"I ate out in the ocean." She waved the food away. "I was scouting. Let's pack and get going."

"How are we going to travel, two of the soarers are broken." Erica reminded them.

"I can swim. Everen, do you know repair magic yet?" Aldyn asked.

"A little." Everen shrugged.

"Work with Auks on it, Nathan also can help," Aldyn replied. Everen and Auks looked at each other and nodded.

The camp was packed up within half an hour, but it took twice as long for Auks and Everen to figure out how to repair the Soarer. In the end, Everen was able to use her magic to make it fly again.

They were flying over the ocean before lunch. The ocean was beautiful. Gold glints of sunlight sparkled atop the turquoise waves. The pleasant wind blew Everen's hair out of her face which was warmed by the sunlight. Everen felt more daring and did a flip with the Soarer. She laughed and twirled through the air.

She heard the sound of laughter and saw Nathan flying above her. He waved at her, and she waved back.

Aldyn led them to an island after a few hours of flight, which Everen loved. Phinx and Auks could've done it in half the time if they were alone.

The island was in the center of the disappearing islands, they had seen some of the phantom islands, but Aldyn warned them away, so they stayed on track. As they flew, Nathan told them the legend about the islands. They were cursed by a group of Pearling sisters to drive seafarers mad after their youngest sister's heart was broken by a sailor.

The group of six flew over the island. It was beautiful and mysterious. Lush, tall tropical trees covered the island with light green grass sloping over the hills. Streams flowed across the vibrant land and the clear blue water bubbled.

The island's hills sloped up to a light grey mountain in the center of the island. A river flowed beside it and down a waterfall.

Everen and Nathan landed on the dusty golden sand of the beach. They both stretched as they removed the wooden flight contraptions. Everen watched as Aldyn swam out of the water and heaved herself onto the shore. She collapsed in the sand on her back. Everen heard a shout and looked up, just in time to see Phinx dive out of the sky into the water, splashing water all over Aldyn.

Aldyn yelled and splashed Phinx when the Featheren princess surfaced for air. Auks laughed and joined them.

"We might as well get in on the fun," Nathan suggested. Everen laughed and the two joined the others.

"We have to search the island," Erica argued, but the others ignored her as they drenched each other in water.

"Come on Erica, it's fun!" Nathan teased. Erica rolled her eyes and removed her signature red cloak. Then she kicked off her soft leather boots and ran towards them kicking up sand.

Phinx and Aldyn were splashing each other, and Aldyn was insane in the water. Her Pearling ancestry made her strong, fast, and practically unbeatable. Her reflexes were on high speed, and she brutally splashed the Featheren.

Aldyn didn't normally physically look Pearling, but when she was in the water, her skin became more vibrant and had a faint iridescent shimmer and some strands of her hair looked like gold. Her eyes turned a clear blue and the dark circles vanished from under her eyes. Her bruises and scratches faded, and she looked more alive.

Auks dive-bombed the water beside Phinx, at the last second, she spread her wings to increase the splash. Phinx yelled and tackled her sister and the two rolled and laughed. The two Featherens rolled in the water laughing.

Phinx was laughing as she dunked her sister under the water. Aldyn moved behind her and knocked Phinx's face into the water. Phinx shot into the air and pinned Aldyn under the water.

Everen and Nathan ran into the water and joined the fight. Everen yelled as she shoved Aldyn under the surface. Aldyn pulled her down and Everen jumped up sputtering.

Nathan challenged Auks and the two chased each other around. Erica cackled, but when Phinx dunked her, she furiously chased the Featheren down.

Everen saw Nathan and she ran to knock him over. She accidentally overbalanced and the two fell into the water laughing.

"Alliance?" Nathan whispered when they got to the surface. Everen splashed him one more time.

"Fine." She agreed and got to her feet.

Several hours of fun later, the group staggered onto the beach with drenched clothes and dripping hair. They collapsed onto the sand and continued laughing.

"We needed that," Aldyn said after a little while.

"Yeah." Auks agreed. With a mischievous smirk, Phinx pushed Aldyn into the sand. The two started wrestling again. Everen laughed and accidentally fell backward on Nathan, who shoved her off, also laughing.

They spent the night on the beach. In the morning, Erica woke Everen up and the group of six followed Aldyn into the jungle.

It was beautiful. The tall trees filtered out the excessively bright light and the shade kept them from being overheated. Everen picked several hibiscus and wove a small crown, she'd learned how to do it a few summers ago from a friend at a camp.

"I hate this stupid jungle! It's not made for warriors!" Phinx grumbled when her wings kept bumping into vines and trees. The others tried to conceal their laughter, unsuccessfully. "What?" The Featheren asked.

"When do you graduate?" Erica asked.

"End of next year, my wing will join Gold Legion," Phinx answered. "The most elite division of the army."

"If the Featheren army is so powerful, how did the Pearlings almost wipe you out?" Everen asked, making the Featherens scowl.

Auks sighed before explaining, "Most of our strength and physical abilities come from our years of training. Our senses can be fooled, and our claws are not unbreakable." Auks rubbed her wrist remembering when she'd broken her claws, "Pearlings also have increased abilities in the water, even half-Pearlings like Aldyn are incredibly powerful."

"Why do you hate each other so much? What was the point of all the bloodshed?" Everen asked.

"The War of Magic, also called the Ancient War, was between Mistic and Elderic. It is the reason Mistic magic is outlawed and why Mistic and Alder are dead. The war dragged all of Eldenvine into the conflict and Featherens and Pearlings fought on opposite sides. Although that war ended, it left a deep hatred between the species. Shortly after, the Queen of Ralaji was Stella. Her husband died on Pearling soil by pirates, and the Pearlings watched as he died. She was devastated but it was not enough for her to declare war. Then one night, years later, she was murdered. Her son

Hawkthorn ascended to the throne, determined to avenge his mother. Shortly after he came to power, his sister, Stormowl, disappeared. He followed her with his best friend, Jaycall, who was deeply in love with her. They found her with a Pearling pearl seeker named Seaspray. The two had secretly wed. Jaycall and Seaspray fought to the death. The Pearling cheated and killed Jaycall. Hawkthorn in his rage murdered the Pearling. Stormowl fled and disappeared from history. The Pearlings declared war. This war became known as the Sea and Sky War." Auks explained.

"Don't forget that the Pearling Massacre happened during that war." Nathan interrupted. Both Auks and Phinx flinched.

"Yes, the Featherens massacred the Pearlings in a particular battle and they swore vengeance. The Pearlings found a plant named the Blood of the Sea and derived a terrible poison from it, called Fire Bane. They used the Fire Bane to cut through Featheren forces. We retaliated by executing all prisoners of war. The Sea-Sky war ended with an uneasy truce." Auks explained.

"What happened to start the Great War, the one that burned Ralaji down?" Everen asked.

This time, Phinx explained. "Three hundred years ago, a battle broke out on the coast of Pearling Bay. It was two small groups of border guards; it shouldn't have started anything larger. But we'd had centuries to feed our fury and grow our armies. Both sides had been waiting for the chance to attack. As time passed, both sides became desperate and cruel. While the army was fighting, the sea-bloods sent a strike force north into Ralaji. They sent the land aflame and slaughtered the Featherens sheltering in Featherwind. The victims were all injured soldiers, the elderly, mothers, and young children. At that point, almost all the Featherens across Eldenvine were hiding out there. So, in a single night, the Night of a Thousand Tears, the Featheren population was almost eradicated. The only survivors were the army. The Queen at the time, Deathwing, led the survivors into the tundra of the north, practically into Vlarcia. She is our great-grandmother."

The group was silent after Phinx's explanation, and Everen felt sick to her stomach. How could people be so absolutely ruthless and heartless? She didn't ask any more questions and simply followed Auks deeper into the island.

After an hour of intense, quiet hiking, they found a tall tower hidden in the jungle. It was beautiful. It was carved from a dark green stone which shifted to dark blue and black around the foundation.

They walked up to the door, and it opened automatically. Aldyn was the first one to step into the tower, she was followed by Nathan and Everen. Erica, Auks, and Phinx came after.

They slowly made their way down the stone hall which was illuminated by pale blue light. The walls were now a deep blue, and the floor was covered with a thin layer of sand. Woven tapestries depicting ocean scenes hung on the walls.

At the end of the corridor were two tall, silver doors framed with massive sapphires. At the center of the door was an emerald turtle with a tree designed on its shell. Everen traced one of the engraved roots of the tree and suddenly the door glowed and opened.

The room was white stone with a high domed roof. Six white stone pillars stood on the sides of the circular wall. In the center of the room was a dark green stone platform, which was almost level with the river of water that ran around it. An arched silver bridge connected the doorway to the platform. The clear blue river was the clearest blue water Everen had ever seen. Directly across the stone platform from the doors was a beautiful white waterfall that ran into the water.

Aldyn led them to the center of the green stone platform. "Hello?" She called out, "Who are you?"

"One who wishes to help." A melodic voice answered which seemed to come from all around them.

"How?" Aldyn demanded, drawing her blade.

"I know where your enemies are."

"The Dragon Hunters?" Everen asked.

"Yes. From here I cannot see the extent of their power or the plan they have. But I see enough to know they are dangerous and must be stopped, or Eldenvine will burn."

"How?" Nathan asked, "I don't know about the rest of you, but I don't really want the world to burn."

Aldyn ignored him, instead focusing on the strange voice, "Why are you helping us?"

"My purpose in existence is to preserve the balance of magic in Eldenvine and protect her inhabitants. These Dragon Hunters are upsetting that."

"Who are you?" Aldyn repeated. Erica sucked in a breath sharply, realizing it before them.

"I am Oceana."

Chapter Thirteen: Return Of The Alpharics.

Nathan, Phinx, and Auks gasped. Erica was frozen and Aldyn was in shock. "How? Oceana disappeared almost two centuries ago, after the Great War!" She shouted.

"I chose to step back from the active world. In my exile, I have remained in peace." She replied.

"You are one of Eldenvine's seven daughters." Everen realized.

"Yes. I am Oceana, the Alpharic of Oceanic. I am entrusting you to keep this secret. Now, I will speak to you individually, the others may wait in another room." A door opened out of the walls. "First I will speak to Aldyn."

Aldyn tensed. "I will be fine, go." She ordered the others, they looked like they wanted to argue, but with her glare, they kept silent. Everen watched Aldyn with worry, as Erica led her out of the room.

The doors closed behind them with an ominous thud, trapping them in the waiting room. It had light blue walls and soft white couches. But no one could relax. Nathan paced the floor and Everen nervously tapped her fingers on a driftwood table. Erica sat stiffly on a couch and stared off into space. Phinx leaned against the wall and crossed her arms and Auks sharpened her claws with a thin dagger.

Twenty minutes passed, but it felt longer before Aldyn opened the door and came in. Her cheeks were pale, and her expression was grim.

"What did she say to you?" Nathan asked, pausing his pacing.

Aldyn didn't answer his question, "She wants to talk to you next." She said instead. She shrugged him off and collapsed on the couch beside Erica. Everen turned to Nathan with worry, if Aldyn had been so upset, he probably would too. Nathan sent Everen a reassuring smile before going to meet Oceana.

Each second that passed made Everen more nervous. Aldyn hadn't said a word since speaking with Oceana, and it only worsened Everen's worry. She kept glancing at the closed doors like she was hoping Nathan would walk through them.

Nathan returned after about fifteen minutes and looked a lot better than Aldyn had. His smile was off, but overall, he seemed fine. "Your turn." He said tapping Erica's shoulder and taking her seat next to Aldyn.

They waited in patient silence until Erica returned, "Everen." Erica announced and pushed Nathan onto the ground so she could reclaim her seat.

Everen blanched, "You sure?" She asked.

Erica rolled her eyes, "Pretty sure." Everen swallowed and stood up. She glanced once more at her friends, before going out to meet Oceana.

Everen slowly stepped out onto the stone island and waited for the Alpharic to speak. "Everen, descendent of Mistic."

"How do you know that?" Everen asked.

Ocean made a soft sound like laughter, "I knew Mistic very well. Your magic sings like hers. But your magic doesn't make you special."

"What are you talking about?"

"Anyone born from Mistic's line has equal potential. But you are unique. You were raised on Earth, without magic. You weren't raised in rigid training where you would've leashed your power. But this unlimited power comes with a heavy cost, it makes your control weak and unstable." Oceana warned her.

"What if I don't want power?" Everen spoke up.

A spire of water formed in front of her and solidified into a beautiful woman. She had floor-length blue hair, green eyes, and pale pink skin. Oceana laughed, "You can't get rid of your power, you can't even ignore it. The best you can do is learn to control it. Someday, you must return to me, and I will help you. But that day is not here yet. When you return, I will give you all the answers you seek."

"What answers? Do you know anything about my mom?" Everen demanded.

"Yes, but that answer is not free. If I tell you about her, you must swear on the shell of Eldenvine that someday, when I need your help, you will give all that you can." Ocean said. Everen remembered Agatha's warning about promises and magic.

"On Eldenvine, some promises are infused with magic. Do not make deals lightly, do not bargain with powerful beings, or I swear on the shell of Eldenvine, you will regret it." Everen shivered at the memory of Agatha's words. But she was too desperate to heed them.

Everen faced Oceana. "Fine. I swear on the shell of Eldenvine that one day when you need me, I will do whatever in my power to help you." Everen agreed before she could change her mind.

"Good. Your mother's real name is Inaria. Ara was an assumed name she used to hide her identity for her safety and yours." Oceana explained, making Everen frown.

"Is there anything else?" She asked, crossing her arms.

Oceana sighed, "You will find out the rest soon. If people always tell you everything, how can you learn?" Everen seethed with irritation, she shouldn't have made the deal.

Everen spun on her heels and stormed out. She exited the main room and then slumped against the door and set her head in her hands. She couldn't believe what she had done. She hadn't learned anything valuable, just another name. Everen forced herself to stand and wiped away the tears that were beginning to form.

Everen found the others deeper in the tower, they were in a large room with bowls of fruit. When she came in, Nathan jumped up and ran over to her. "How did it go?" He asked.

Everen shook her head, not wanting to talk about it. She took her seat beside Aldyn and took a slice of mango to eat.

Nathan sat on the arm of the chair beside her. "One of Oceana's attendants brought us here. She told me that the Dragon Hunters are called

Blackshard, and they are going to use the baby dragons to conquer Eldenvine."

"What about you, Erica?" Everen asked.

"My family." Erica spat with cold fury. Everen grimaced, Erica's relationship with her family was terrible at best, and she knew that Erica would be in a horrid mood for the rest of the day.

Everen glanced at Phinx, "Don't look at us, she's the Oceanic Alpharic, she doesn't talk to Featherens. We're lucky she didn't kill us for stepping on her territory." Phinx said.

"We wouldn't be caught dead associating with her either, the only reason we are here is the mission," Auks explained.

"What about you Aldyn?" Nathan asked.

Aldyn looked up from her spot on the couch. "She told me where we're going next. Blackshard is camping in southern Elvara." Everen got the feeling that Aldyn wasn't being fully honest, but she knew better than to push it at the moment. "We will head out tomorrow, she promised me that we can rest and recover tonight."

"Because we're stuck here for a bit, we should figure out how we're going to handle Blackshard," Auks said.

"We could probably just burn their base to the ground." Erica muttered, "With them inside."

Nathan shot her a stern look, "Our mission isn't to kill them all, it's to stop them." He snapped.

Auks unsheathed her claws, "Actually, to finish the job, we probably do have to kill them."

"No," Everen said, standing. "We're not killing anyone. We'll destroy their base and drag their leader to justice."

"Actually, I agree with Erica and Auks," Aldyn said. Everen stared at her with wide eyes. "We aren't assassins, but we do have a mission. If we don't take them out they will come back, and the problem will continue."

Everen felt slightly nauseous, but she understood what Aldyn was saying. They didn't want to become killers, but stopping Blackshard was more important. She knew that to win the war, sometimes they had to lose the battle. In this case, the battle was mercy, and the war was victory.

A woman came into the room. She had dark skin, indigo eyes, and waist-length black braided hair. A loose pale green dress, which resembled a toga, hung from her shoulders and touched the floor.

"Hello, I am Okcria, a Pearling apprentice of Oceana." She dipped her head. Phinx and Auks stiffened but thankfully didn't say anything.

At an early age, Pearlings learn how to shift back and forth between a humanoid form and their tail. The humanoid form allowed them to walk on land while their tail let them swim. In both forms, Pearlings could breathe underwater, see in the dark, and handle extreme cold.

Okcria waved her hands and a long table made of pale driftwood appeared in the center of their room. It was covered with plates of seafood and more fruits. "Enjoy your meal. I will return in a few hours to take you to your rooms." She informed them.

The meal was mostly silent. Everyone was thinking about the mission, or what Oceana had talked to them about. Everen was stressed about her mother, the stupid deal she'd made with Oceana, and the situation with Blackshard. She stabbed her silver knife into an orange slice and brought it to her mouth seething.

Okcria led her to a large room that was high in the complex. The tower was only the main exterior entrance to Ocean's fortress. It also continued underground and up into the mountain. Everen's room had a large open window that looked over the forest and sea and the pales were painted pale blue.

She made her way to the bed and fell asleep the second her head hit the white silk of the pillows.

She awoke to the faint sound of singing. Everen sat up and stretched, she was more rested than she'd been the entire time in Eldenvine. Everen glanced around her room and noticed that it was beautifully decorated. Colored glass vases stood on shelves and were filled with shells and scraps of driftwood.

Over the window hung a large white semi-transparent curtain, Everen pushed it to the side and looked out the window, searching for the source of the singing.

Phinx was flying through the sky in the early morning sun. She was twirling and laughing as she sang an old Featheric song. Everen smiled, she hadn't seen this side of Phinx before.

"I'm soaring high,

through the northern sky.

I am flying.

I am dreaming.

My fears all fade like mist on dawn.

This is the land where I belong.

My home is up high, here in the sky,

Here where the sun touches,

the clouds drift, and wind roars.

Oh sky, let my wings soar." Phinx sang and the last note of the song faded. Everen turned from her window to get herself cleaned up. She washed her face and arms with a steamed towel and made her way down the halls to the room where they'd eaten yesterday.

Nathan, Erica, and Auks were already on the white couches enjoying the breakfast Oceana had supplied them. Everen filled a small silver plate with sweet rolls and berries and joined them. After a little while Phinx came into the room, grabbed a whole fish, and sat beside Erica. She held the red spice-coated fish in her bare hands and bit into it. Erica wrinkled her nose and scotched to the side.

"You're a princess, get a plate." She grumbled. Auks rolled her eyes and threw Phinx a plate.

After Phinx had silverware Everen asked her, "What song were you singing?"

"How did you hear?" Phinx looked both surprised and embarrassed.

Auks laughed, "The entire kingdom hears you every morning."

"Why did no one say anything?" Phinx demanded.

"Because everyone remembers what you did to Raven when she commented on your ripped dress at the Sun Ball five years ago." Auks reminded her.

Phinx crossed her arms, "That's completely different, she made Mom notice it and got me caught for sneaking out to play Pit Brawl with Eagle, Hawk, and Firex."

"You challenged her to a duel of single combat! If Mom hadn't interfered, you probably would've killed each other." Auks shouted.

Phinx scowled, "It's still different." She went to get more food and Auks sighed in exasperation.

"I swear my sister." She grumbled as Aldyn came into the room.

Aldyn's hair was dripping water and she smelled like salt and seaweed. "Where were you?" Nathan called.

Aldyn chucked a small fruit at his head. He caught it with incredible reflexes and popped it in his mouth. "Scouting around the island. I also got us packed with extra supplies from Okcria. We need to leave in an hour."

"An hour? Why?" Everen asked.

Aldyn rolled her eyes, "Because Earthborn, we have to get to Blackshard. If we leave soon, we'll get to land early enough to make our way to southern Islaria."

"Islaria's next to Elvara, right?" Everen whispered to Nathan, who nodded.

"We won't stop there though, if my mom sees me, she'll force us to stay for a couple of days." He added.

Everen nodded, hiding her nervousness. She didn't want to confront her mother, but she wanted answers. She didn't want to face the woman who'd abandoned her, but she wanted Ara to know how angry she was.

After they finished eating, Aldyn led them to the beach. It was a beautiful spring day, and the water was warm. Phinx would lead them by air because Aldyn was swimming. Erica, Everen, and Nathan got on their soarers, Auks would have to help them up.

Aldyn nodded at the others before diving into the water, she rocketed off leaving a streak of white bubbles in the teal water. Phinx beat her wings and leaped into the air, and Auks helped pull Nathan up. Then she pulled Erica up.

"Are you coming Everen?" Auks yelled.

"Just a moment!" She called back, adjusting the straps of the wooden wings.

"Come on Everen!" Nathan yelled. Everen took a deep breath and pushed her palms toward the sand. A burst of wind pushed her up and she panicked.

Auks dove towards her, and she reached out desperately. Everen was terrified as she spiraled towards the waves, but somehow, right before she hit them, she caught herself with magic. Everen took a few deep breaths as she stabilized her flight. Her heart pounded in her chest, and she flew towards her friends.

"You good?" Erica asked.

Everen nodded as she caught her breath, "At least I know that worked." She muttered.

Nathan snorted, "You might need to practice." She grinned at him.

After several long hours of flight, they returned to Mytharica. They landed in the trees by the shore of Pearling Bay, Islaria. Everen removed her wooden wings and stretched. She was exhausted and hungry.

"I'm going hunting, who wants to come?" Aldyn announced.

Phinx, who was irritated after the long flight, replied, "I'll go alone, I'm not hunting with a Pearling." She took to the skies with one beat of her powerful wings.

Aldyn scowled and turned to Auks, "What was that about?" She demanded.

Auks sighed, "Phinx is tired. I'll talk to her." She took to the skies after her sister. Erica joined Aldyn in hunting and Everen and Nathan were left to set up the camp. "Did Oceana talk to you about anything else?" Nathan asked as they built the fire.

Everen stiffened, she did not want to tell him about it, "Nothing. She just said stuff we already knew."

Nathan frowned, "She talked to me about my family a bit. She said my parents are worried."

"Don't they know that you went with Aldyn?" Everen asked.

"Yes, but when I told them I played down how dangerous it was. I also thought I'd be home sooner. The whole situation with Erica and the Featherens slowed us down." He explained.

"Don't worry. We're almost to Elvara, you'll see them again in a week or two." Everen reassured him.

He grinned, "Do you want to check out the bay? I know we looked at the ocean all morning, but it might be interesting."

"Sure." Everen followed Nathan through the trees to a white sand beach. Nathan was right, it was amazing. The water of the bay was a lot smoother than out in the ocean and it was greener and more transparent. She found small shells in the sand and anemones hiding in the water.

Everen looked around and noticed a woman sitting on a large rock several yards away from the shore. She was beautiful with long ebony hair braided in tiny cornrows and dark brown skin. The tips of her hair were dyed pale pink which matched her shining metallic pink eyes. Instead of legs, she had a long tail with transparent coral fins that were covered in rose-gold diamond-shaped scales starting at her waist.

Chapter Fourteen: A Man Named Cat's Eye.

Everen's jaw dropped when she saw the Pearling. The Pearling was stunning, and the sea breeze blew her pink-tipped hair back as she splashed her tail.

"Hello." Everen greeted, Nathan was too surprised to speak. The Pearling turned and looked at her in surprise.

"Oh, hello. My name is Shellea, who are you?" Shellea asked.

"I'm Everen, and this is Nathan."

"What are you doing in Islaria this close to Cat's Eye?" Shellea asked.

"We are searching for something," Everen replied vaguely. Shellea frowned.

"What are you looking for?" She asked, in an unsettling tone. Everen stepped back nervously.

Suddenly, a scream of Aldyn's rage thundered in the forest nearby. Everen turned from the mysterious Pearling and bolted after her friend with Nathan beside her. She soon broke through the trees where Aldyn and Erica were fighting a tall man. He wore ripped jeans and a loose cream cotton shirt, and his shoulder-length ginger hair was pulled back in a messy ponytail. He also had frigid blue eyes and his nose and cheeks were covered in freckles.

Aldyn's custom broadsword clashed with the cutlass. She had to duck as he swung his blade, and a second pirate leaped out from behind. They were fighting too close for Erica to use her bow, so she fought with her knives. Erica slashed and dodged, but the two pirates had caught them off guard and had them cornered.

Everen didn't have a sword, but she pulled out a knife and focused her magic. Beside her, Nathan drew his bow and an arrow in a smooth motion, "Leave her alone!" he yelled, releasing it. The sharp and heavy arrowhead struck one of the pirates in the forearm. He shrieked in pain and dropped his sword. In that second the other pirate got behind Aldyn and held his sword to her throat.

"One more step and she dies." The other pirate hissed. Aldyn's eyes were filled with so much rage, that Everen was surprised the pirate didn't drop dead there. "You are coming after Cat's Eye's treasure again, aren't you?" Nathan stood still and Phinx and Auks landed behind him.

Phinx unsheathed her claws and prepared to charge, but Auks raised her wing to hold her back. Phinx's eyes flashed with fury, she hated being held back from a fight.

The pirate holding Aldyn continued, "This time you won't catch us unprepared. We patrol the forests regularly. Now, come with us and Cat's Eye will decide your fate. If you value your friend's life, you will not fight further."

Everen's hand twitched and a blast of air smacked into the pirate's face. Nathan shook his head at her, and she scowled. She wanted to wipe the smirk off the pirate's face by flinging him back into a tree, but Nathan was right. They couldn't risk Aldyn.

Erica dropped her knives to her side and Nathan lowered his bow. Phinx and Auks stood straight and sheathed their claws. "We surrender," Nathan said.

The two pirates led them towards the bay, and they reached the cove where Cat's Eye's ship was berthed. The large vessel had spiderwebs of nets, tall imposing sails, and an elegant dark chestnut hull. While they walked, the pirates kept their weapons drawn and ready to fight. Everen's fists were clenched, and she desperately wanted to do something.

A gangplank was dropped to the sand, and it wobbled as they marched up it. On the deck, there were about twenty pirates. They were sparring with swords, playing with cards, and shooting pistols at marked barrels.

Many of the men and women stared at the Featheren princesses. Phinx held her head high and glowered at them while Auks tensed and scowled. After all, most of Eldenvine believed that the Featherens were extinct.

As they were marched down towards the prison, Everen caught sight of a boy. He looked to be just a bit older than Aldyn. He had sun-belched blond hair, turquoise eyes, was tall and well-built. His eyes widened when he saw them, and he stared at Aldyn like she was a ghost. Aldyn glanced at him and immediately paled, but before she could say anything, they were thrown into an iron cell at the belly of the boat.

The cell was cramped, dark, and miserable. The pirates had taken their weapons, including Erica's hidden daggers. Every thirty minutes a pirate would check on them, apparently someone had escaped in the past, so they were extra cautious. Erica leaned against the wall and crossed her arms while Nathan and Aldyn sat on the floor. The Featherens leaned on the opposite wall and Everen paced.

"Who was that?" She finally demanded, pausing Nathan's pacing, and staring at Aldyn.

"No one." Aldyn snapped defensively. Her voice shook slightly and Everen's suspicion turned to concern.

"Aldyn, what's wrong?" Nathan asked gently. Aldyn turned sharply towards him.

"I don't demand that you share all your secrets, why should I be different?" She snapped.

"In case you haven't noticed, we are trapped on a pirate ship, and we need to hurry. Anything you know could help us get out of here." Erica interjected.

"Fine. I didn't survive on my own after Erica left. I met a boy who saved my life. He taught me how to survive and gave me my knife. He was…" Aldyn hesitated. "He got captured by pirates and told me to run, I didn't even know he was still alive." Aldyn's mind flashed back to waiting for weeks on a small island, where they'd promised to meet, desperately hoping he'd somehow survived. Eventually, she was forced to conclude that he was dead.

Erica raised an eyebrow at Aldyn's brief explanation but didn't ask any more questions. She liked the appearance of being all-knowing and only asked when she wasn't able to figure things out herself.

"We must figure out how to get out of here. We need to finish the mission." Phinx reminded them.

"And I have to get home, Dad might be losing hope by now," Everen added, her voice turning quiet.

"You both at least have family, mine threw me to the wolves." Erica snapped bitterly. Phinx looked like she wanted to make a joke about the wolf reference, but she wisely held her tongue.

"And Oceana told us we have to hurry." Nathan reminded them all. Usually, Aldyn took charge in these situations, but the half-Pearling was quiet and lost in thought.

"I think I have an idea," Everen said. Magic was quickly becoming her main defense and ability in Eldenvine. Aldyn's talent was fighting and leading, and Phinx's was brute strength. Auks' was her ability to reason.

Nathan and Erica were great archers, among other assorted skills, but Nathan was incredibly loyal, while Erica was probably smarter than all of them combined.

The others looked at her, "I can use my magic to break the bars, like back in Ralaji. But when I do that, we will alert the guards and we don't have weapons to fight them."

"Speak for yourself," Phinx said, showing her white claws.

Nathan grinned, "But we should attract the guards over here, so we can take them out at once. Aldyn and Erica, because you two are so good at arguing, could you start something?" He asked.

Aldyn looked up at that, "Phinx should help, even after two hundred years the pirates will know that a Featheren in a fight will probably end with someone dead. They won't want to risk that."

Phinx nodded, solemn for once. "We will have to put up a good show, I promise to be careful though."

Aldyn nodded, she knew that getting in a fight, even a fake one, with a Featheren warrior was incredibly dangerous. She was incredibly brave for choosing to do so. "After everything with Oceana, we are all exhausted. Let's stay here for tonight and escape in the morning."

Several hours passed before the pirates brought in an evening meal. While they waited, Everen taught the others how to play games she'd learned on Earth to pass the time. After a bit, Erica was practically unbeatable in chopsticks, concentration, and coconut. Phinx and Auks arm wrestled a few times, Phinx threw a few of the matches so that Auks won, if she'd been using her full strength she could have broken Auks' arm. Nathan told stories and Aldyn broke out her hidden deck of cards.

"I've been captured a lot." She explained at Everen's questioning look. They played several rounds of poker, and Aldyn managed to destroy Erica. Once they escaped, the half-Pearling would get a small fortune off of her victory.

Nathan also taught them how to play Honesty, a game where someone says a word, and everyone must go around saying their best story related to it. The six of them were practically rolling with laughter as Phinx detailed some of the chaotic pranks she'd pulled in Featherwind.

Finally, dinner came. It was simple, fish and potatoes. Everen finished the bland dish quickly and used her cloak as a pillow. The others followed her lead and they adjusted to make themselves comfortable for the night.

Somehow, Everen found herself using Erica as an extra pillow. The Featherens were curled beside each other, and Nathan slept in a seated position against the wall. It wasn't comfortable, but they were all able to rest. In the middle of the night, Aldyn carefully got up from beside Everen and Erica. She wasn't a light sleeper and she'd heard her name being called.

"Aldyn, wake up. It's me." The voice repeated.

"Jayden?" She asked quietly, stepping over Everen's legs to get to the bars of the cell.

"Hey, Princess." He whispered. He stood on the other side, and the moonbeams that fell through the cracks of the deck partially illuminated his face. His blond hair had grown out past his ears and his turquoise eyes seemed a bit darker. The last time she'd seen him he'd been scrawny and the same height as her, but now he had filled out and was a head taller.

He grinned when he saw her, and she smiled back. It was good to see him. "You cut your hair." He commented bittersweetly.

"It was getting long." She replied, her hair used to hang to her hips in a long braid, now it was at her shoulders and cut unevenly, she'd done it herself the day she thought he was dead. "I thought you died."

Jayden glanced away. "I'm sorry. But I couldn't come back."

"Why not?" You promised." Aldyn's tone turned hard.

"Because I was keeping Cat's Eye from hunting you down. He was furious that you'd tried to take his treasure, staying protected you."

"You didn't get to make that choice!" Aldyn snapped, "I thought my best friend was dead, and it was my fault!"

"Cat's Eye would've killed you!" Jayden protested.

"He can't hurt me. What hurt was you dying, and thinking it was my fault!" Aldyn's voice raised in volume, and she had to lower it to not wake her friends.

Jayden stepped back, looking hurt. "I would have died for you a hundred times."

Aldyn blinked and turned away, crossing her arms. "Too many people have died for me."

He leaned closer to the bars, "They knew what they were doing, they knew you deserved to live."

"What did they possibly see in me that made them believe I was worth their sacrifices?" Aldyn's tone was bitter and harsh.

"They saw what I see," Jayden replied quietly. "You're still my best friend Aldyn, I promise to get you out of here."

Aldyn's face was still turned away. "We're both escaping this time. I'm not leaving you behind."

Jayden didn't answer, instead, he looked at her one last time before disappearing into the shadows. Aldyn noticed that he didn't promise to come with her.

Aldyn kept her gaze turned away and felt a shard of her heartbreak. It was a long time before she went back to sleep.

The next morning the group silently ate a small breakfast of bread and bacon. Everen loved bacon but the bacon the pirates gave them was too salty and burned to be enjoyable. She missed her father's cooking. He would make bacon and cook it with a little bit of maple syrup, so it was amazing.

A little while after they ate, Aldyn and Erica started to argue. "Your stupid ego brought us against the dragon." Erica snapped, but her tone didn't have much heat in it. She no longer blamed Aldyn for Angela's death.

"The dragon was threatening to burn down an innocent village unless they paid him ridiculous taxes, we were helping them," Aldyn argued, even louder. At this point, the pirates who were guarding the prison came over. There were three of them and they all looked very annoyed.

"We were eleven years old; Angela was twelve. We were too young for dragon slaying!" Erica yelled, jumping to her feet, and glaring at Aldyn. Aldyn also got to her feet and the girls tensed. Everen stared in surprise, if she didn't know better, she would've tried to intervene and stop it.

"Cedar burned when I was six. In this world, age doesn't matter." Aldyn growled.

"Maybe age doesn't matter, but you got her killed!" A flinch of hurt flashed across Aldyn's face and Erica cringed.

"You didn't seem to care back then. Why do you care now? We can't avenge her now, but you could've helped me bury her!" Aldyn shot back, more vicious than necessary.

"We would've died before reaching her body!" Erica slammed her fist towards Aldyn's jaw to escalate things.

Aldyn stumbled back, she had bitten her lip when struck and it started to bleed.

"Alright break it up. Cat's Eye doesn't like dead prisoners." One of the pirates said, banging on the bars. Suddenly, the bars blackened and turned to ash. The Featheren sisters flew out and knocked the pirates to the deck unconscious in seconds.

"We aren't out yet," Aldyn warned them. "Erica, Phinx, find our gear. The rest of us will distract them." The group nodded and split up. Erica and Phinx towards the cargo bay of the ship, while the others ran to the ship's deck.

When they reached the deck, several dozen pirates whirled to face them. They unsheathed their swords in sync and glared. "Prisoner escape! Someone, alert the captain!" One yelled. Aldyn gritted her teeth.

"Tell Cat's Eye I have a message for him." She whispered coldly, before charging into the pirates, she had stolen a sword on their way out of the prison and used it with extreme skill. Auks unsheathed her claws and somersaulted in the air landing in the mist of Cat's Eye's crew. She laughed as she fought, and her strawberry blond hair flew behind her like a flickering flame.

Everen used her magic to create tiny bursts of golden stardust that pushed the pirates back. Nathan had also grabbed a sword and was fending off the pirates, however, he wasn't as talented with blades as Aldyn and had several near misses.

Aldyn slashed viciously with her sword, she saw red and didn't flinch when she hurt the pirates. She plowed through them and before long, most chose to pick on the others, who were easier targets. Her fighting was a perfect dance, a deadly twirl of blades and blood.

Everen was shoved back, and she yelped in surprise. Everything was happening too quickly, and she was overwhelmed. The tip of a sword slashed across her cheek, and she cried out. Nathan stumbled over fallen barrels and ropes as he backed away from the bloodthirsty pirates. A massive net fell over Auks, and she panicked, trying to cut through it while defending herself. They were losing.

Then, Phinx and Erica appeared with their weapons. Phinx tossed Aldyn her sword, Aldyn smirked and caught the blade, replacing the one she had been using. Erica threw Nathan his bow and drew her own before leaping into the battle.

Nathan climbed the ropes into the crow's nest where he used his bow to take out pirates. Phinx fought brutally and cut the net imprisoning her sister. Everen joined Nathan up at the crow's nest and used her magic to help.

"This reminds me of a video game I used to play with my dad!" Everen called.

"You'll have to show me someday!" Nathan replied, shooting a pirate in the arm. Everen grinned at him and threw another magic blast.

As the two camped in the crow's nest, the others fought on the deck. Aldyn was laughing as she cut through the pirates. She was careful not to kill anyone, magic could only heal so much, but she was bitter and angry, and not afraid to inflict damage.

For a moment, it looked like the six of them were going to make it, but then the pirates pushed back brutally. Nathan and Erica ran out of arrows. Everen was exhausted from overuse of magic, and Aldyn was knocked to the ground with the lucky strike of a sword.

The Featheren sisters were the only ones standing, but even they couldn't take fifty pirates at once.

"Aldyn!" Nathan called, as a pirate reached down to grab Aldyn's neck. The woman wore a red bandanna and she looked incredibly strong. She picked Aldyn up by the neck and Aldyn gasped for air. She held her blade at Aldyn's chest.

"Stop this madness!" An intimidating voice yelled before the woman could stab Aldyn through. "I do not allow foolish fighting on my ship. Stand down." The person ordered. The pirates immediately lowered their weapons and stood straight. Nathan and Erica lowered their bows and Phinx and Auks sheathed their claws. Everen lowered her glowing hands. The woman dropped Aldyn, who fell to the ground and coughed. The man who had stopped the fight had shoulder-length brown hair with a neatly trimmed beard. He was strong and handsome. He wore a long navy and gold coat and a white shirt with elegant black pants. He had a healthy tan and sharp pointed ears. His eyes were bright blue with flecks of neon green like a jeweled ocean.

"Cat's Eye." The pirates murmured. Aldyn carefully got to her feet and her grip tightened around the hilt of her sword.

"I hope you are not stupid enough to get yourselves killed in a weak escape attempt. I will not extend such mercy a second time." The pirates moved around the Elden Order and grabbed their wrists. "Keep the Featherens separate." Cat's Eye ordered his crew, before turning around and marching back to the captain's quarters.

They were placed in a different cell with stronger thicker iron bars. Everen groaned and slumped to the floor. "I can't believe we failed."

Nathan crossed his arms and leaned by the cell bars. Erica was seething and silently brooding in the corner.

Suddenly, Aldyn slammed her fist into the hull of the ship. Aldyn was usually very controlled, so it was surprising to see her lose it.

She screamed in anger and frustration. "How can he always win?" No one knew what she was talking about.

"We have to get out of here." Everen groaned.

"It's pointless, we will never be free," Aldyn growled.

"Why did he even capture us in the first place? We never showed aggression." Nathan wondered.

"Because of something *I* did years ago." Aldyn snapped.

"What?" Nathan asked quietly.

"A bit over two years ago, I stole Cat's Eye's most valued treasure. I didn't realize the trouble it would unleash. I escaped with the treasure, unlike everyone who had tried before, but Cat's Eye caught me and recovered it. I underestimated how important the treasure was to him, he personally tracked me down, taking his treasure, and my best friend as compensation. I escaped with my life." Her voice died. "After that, Cat's Eye has guarded his treasure against every threat, many have tried to steal it, he must have assumed that we were after it as well." Aldyn was quiet after her explanation as if she accepted the anger and judgment her friends felt. Finally, Erica's irritation boiled over.

"And why in Eldenvine's name, would you do that?"

"Because I hoped I could see my parents again," Aldyn explained. Everen and Nathan frowned at each other, they knew Aldyn's family was dead. "There were stories about Cat's Eye's treasure. It was believed he had a set of pearls that would allow you to speak with dead loved ones. I was desperate and young. I wanted to tell them-" She cleared her throat. "It doesn't matter why I stole them, all that matters is escaping now." Erica opened her mouth, but Everen beat her to it.

"Aldyn's right." Everen came to her defense. "We should stop arguing so we can actually get out of here, we have a mission to complete."

They spent a while trying to come up with ideas, but no one had anything. "We will figure it out tomorrow. Get some sleep." Aldyn finally sighed, defeatedly. Everen and Nathan nodded and lay down. Erica also leaned against the wood walls.

In the middle of the night, Jayden returned, he'd been able to slip past the barracks' guards by drugging their drinks with sleeping powder. "Why didn't you tell me you were going to try to break out?" He asked.

"Because you would've tried to stop me." She countered, she was awake, and she'd expected him to show up. "If it had worked, I'd expected you to run after us. And it doesn't matter, we failed worse than that time in Klondor."

"Which time? I remember a lot of bad fights." He replied, and a smile twitched on her lips.

"We have to get away, Jayden, this is important. I have a mission, and I intend to see it through." Aldyn's voice turned serious with a hint of desperation.

"Let me guess, Agatha?" Aldyn nodded. "What is it?" He asked.

"You've heard of the Dragon Hunters?" He nodded, the terrorists were well known across Eldenvine, even if no one had met them. The trail of carnage they'd left traveled like wildfire in gossip. "We're following them so that we can sabotage the organization."

"I thought you hated dragons, after everything that had happened." He commented.

"A lot has changed in two years," Aldyn replied vaguely.

Jayden glanced at Nathan, "I can see." His tone took on a hint of coldness.

Aldyn stared at him in surprise, "You can't think," She broke off. "No. You are my best friend, Pirate-Boy; besides, he likes another girl."

Jayden's tone warmed considerably, "What happened after we split up?" He asked.

Aldyn shrugged. "I was on my own for a while, then ran into Nathan. We became friends, and I brought him along for Agatha's mission. Then we met Everen and the others. What about you?"

"Cat's Eye let me join his crew, it was better than being a permanent prisoner. He doesn't trust me, he knows I just want to leave. But if I did leave," Jayden trailed off and Aldyn shuddered. Pirate Kings were known for their ruthlessness, especially towards treasure thieves; he had already shown mercy to them once, and he wouldn't grant it again. "I just wish we could finally stop running. The playful game ended long ago."

"Yeah," Aldyn answered softly. "But we don't know anything else."

Jayden's grip on the bars tightened. "I will get you out of here Aldyn, then we will be free." His eyes traced her face which had changed so much but was somehow exactly the same. "I promise."

Chapter Fifteen: A Man Named James.

Elvara – Fifteen Years Ago.

James reached the border between Elvara and Islaria in just a few hours. He slowed his ride as he reached his destination. The small cottage was crafted of driftwood in a secluded cove of Pearling Bay. Pale blue curtains hung at the windows and thick grass from the surf thatched the roof. A rock and seashell path led up to the threshold and dried lavender bouquets stood in glass jars on the windowsills. James smiled softly; he'd built every piece of the cottage with her beside him.

As he got closer to the house, he realized not even a single candle or lantern was burning. He frowned and quietly drew his sword before opening the door.

"Pearl?" He called out, with no response. "Pearl!" He yelled again. "Oceana." He breathed, seeing the shattered glass and smear of blood on the wooden floor, beside her favorite sword.

James ran outside, still yelling her name, and frantically searching for a sign of his wife. "Oceana." He whispered desperately, hoping the ancient being of the sea heard his plea.

James ran across the familiar white sand and reached the dark water. He scanned the churning waves and his throat caught as he spotted a black shape, nearly invisible in the darkness. James dove into the shallow water and began to swim towards the ship, praying to all the Alpharics that the worst hadn't happened.

Graves was the King of Klondor, and the most powerful pirate lord in over a century. He was infamous for hunting Pearlings and slaughtering them with his cursed blade. So far, he'd personally killed a hundred and sixty Pearlings. He was the most dangerous man currently alive, even more than Sonoson. James had begged Pearl to go to Mythea, but she'd refused to leave Islaria.

James' heart clenched with terror. He was going to lose his Pearl, he knew it. Graves was ruthless, even her incredible luck couldn't save her. He remembered meeting her at Pearl Rocks and then being married there by a Priestess of Oceana. He'd promised to never leave her or let her come to harm. He'd broken his vows.

James trod water and yelled as loud as he could. "PEARL!" The black ship was now only a hundred meters away. The sails were a ghostly grey and the flag was designed with a malevolent black skull with blood dripping from its jaws.

James swam harder and he gripped the chain of the anchor tightly. His hand split open on the spikes, but even the pain couldn't push through the fog of terror in his mind. He reached with his other hand to grip a second spike and used it to pull himself up the hull of the ship.

James gritted his teeth and pulled himself over the rail. He landed on his feet and sharply inhaled.

In the center of the deck was a beautiful Pearling, around twenty years old. She sat awkwardly on her tail on the deck and was surrounded by darkly clothed pirates. The one directly behind her kicked her back, making her fall onto her elbows. She glared with anger, but James saw the mirroring terror in her eyes. She had long wavy mahogany brown hair with amber highlights that gleamed in the orange lantern light. She wore a loose light blue top with shells woven into it and her waist melted into a long tail covered in pink and white scales. The scales were diamond-shaped with an iridescent shimmer. She had striking amber eyes that once had stolen his heart.

The pirate who'd kicked her forward drew his blade and held it to the middle of her spine and faced James. James' chest burned with rage, and he shoved through the pirates to defend her.

James reached the front of the crowd, and the evil man noticed him. He began to laugh wickedly, filling James' veins with ice. The man was taller than the other pirates and a captain's hat rested on his head. His clothes were dark and layered, and his face was shrouded in inky blackness, except for two orange glowing embers in place of his eyes.

"*Graves*," James snarled the man's name. "Let her go." He demanded.

"James, you have to know-" Pearl interrupted, her voice desperate and panicked. He saw the streaks of tears on her face and his heart broke. He'd only seen her cry once when her mother had been killed by a Featheren survivor.

"That's enough speaking, *Pearling*," The Pirate King spat venomously. James lunged but froze when Pearl gasped.

"Go," she mouthed, even though she knew he would never be able to leave her. They had taken vows; James refused to break them again. He raised his sword to Graves' throat.

"I said, Let. Her. Go." James repeated.

"She will be freed, of life." Graves grabbed Pearl's neck and lifted her off the ground; she gasped for air and clawed at his grip, thrashing with rage. She was determined to die fighting, as it was the most honorable death. James yelled and stepped forward holding his sword, trying to find a way to stab the pirate without hurting his wife. Graves continued laughing as he stabbed her in the stomach. She let out a scream of pain, her eyes wide, her head snapped back, then her cry cut off. Graves released her, and she collapsed to the floor, gasping for air.

"Pearl!" James lowered his sword and rushed to her side. He kneeled and ripped the end of his shirt to try and stop the bleeding, but he knew it was too late. "Why? Why!" James screamed at Graves as she coughed up blood.

"I will give you the answer which many have begged for." The pirate leaned right before James, and he saw the outline of what was once a face, but now it was a black bone and soulless. "I kill them because they deserve to die, Featherens and Pearlings destroyed this world with war. Featherens got their punishment, the Pearlings didn't."

James gently laid the barely breathing Pearling on the deck and stood back up. He picked up his sword and slid into the defensive stance his father taught him years ago. "Even if the war killed many innocents, their descendants don't deserve your rage." James' quiet voice carried across the eerie ship, and he lunged at Graves, who didn't even try to dodge. His sword caught deep in the man's ribs, a lethal strike on anyone else, even Featherens. However, Graves still stood, and James removed his sword and stepped back. The inky shadows knitted together and closed the wound.

"What are you?" James asked.

"More powerful than you, or your Pearling bride." The pirate lunged forward like a blur of shadows. James deflected the blow with his sword and ducked. As a prince, he was trained by the best swordsmen in the kingdom. They clashed blades several more times, and James realized that the pirate was much better than him. Graves swung his sword, cutting across James' shoulder. His skin felt as though it was on fire and his blood became acid flowing through his veins. He screamed in pain and collapsed to the ground. He glanced at the injury; the skin around the cut was quickly turning dark and thick black blood dripped down his arm. James remembered the horror stories of Graves' cursed blade that inflicted terrible deaths.

The infamous King of Klondor stood over the fallen prince and laughed. James looked beside himself to see Pearl, who was barely breathing. He stretched out his hand and touched her fingertips, still warm in the frigid air. A tear fell down his cheek and he longed to fix the mess that this had dissolved into.

Now, he had a choice. He could die fighting or accept his fate and die beside his wife. He knew that she would want him to fight. James kept his eyes on Pearl as he gritted his teeth and pushed himself onto his knees. He dragged himself to his feet and covered his stomach with his bleeding arm. James raised his sword and felt sweat sting his eyes. Graves laughed coldly as James stumbled towards him.

"Foolish boy, still fighting me when you're already dying. Although, few are brave enough to do so." Graves' cruel laugh faded. "I respect your strength. In another world, I would've chosen you as the next Pirate King." James was so surprised at the man's words that he almost forgot his mission.

After a second, James shook his head. "I never wanted a throne; all it symbolizes is the powerful crushing the weak." Inaria had been the one who wanted power, he'd never really had the opportunity.

"A harsh truth for a prince," Graves replied. "But my offer stands. I will make you my right hand if you drop your sword and bow before me."

James hesitated longer than he was proud of. "Never," he spat. "I will die wielding this sword and I will never bow to you."

"A pity to see such bravery and talent wasted. I wish I didn't have to kill you." Graves raised his cursed sword.

"I'm not afraid of death." In a last act of desperation, James dove forward and stabbed his blade, covered with his blood, directly through the pirate's heart.

James knew the king would live, the man was said to be immortal, so he was shocked when the Pirate King gasped in pain and stumbled back. Graves clutched his chest, bleeding a dark red liquid, the only human part of him. He stumbled away from the prince.

The shadows around his face faded, revealing a grey-bearded face that once had been handsome. His grey eyes resembled the storm over the ocean and his features were weathered from age and the harsh life on the sea. Those eyes filled with shock, and even a trace of fear, as though he believed death would never overcome his strength. Graves reached out and grabbed the rail of the deck to remain standing.

"It's not possible." The man choked out. James remained silent. The King of Klondor's grip failed on the rail. He fell back on the edge of the ship.

Time slowed and the pirate was caught between life and death. James could have pulled him back and saved him. James' blue eyes darkened and the mercy in his heart died. The wounded prince lunged at the pirate with an animalistic roar and slashed his chest with his sword, knocking him over the edge into the black waters below.

The dreaded pirate that claimed the lives of so many never resurfaced. The remaining pirates screamed as they dissipated into shadows, they were cursed beside their leader and would die with him.

James gasped as the venom in his wound faded and his blood returned to a more normal color. He lowered his sword and ran to his still-breathing wife.

He collapsed beside her and held her dying body in his blood-soaked arms. "Oh James," she whispered. She held her hand up and touched his wound. He flinched and she dropped her hand.

"I will live. What about you, what do you need? The Elven healers might be able to" She interrupted him.

"No, you are never going back there, even if they could heal me. We both know I will not survive; I don't have a miracle way out of this one." She lifted her hand to his cheek.

"No, you always escape. Death can't claim you now, not when we finally won!" He cried.

"This is my last fight, but it isn't yours. Live your life, just remember me." She insisted.

"I have no life without you!" He yelled.

"I refuse to argue with you in the last minutes we have together. I must tell you-" She gasped in pain.

"Just breathe, I will be here." James comforted her. She gave a sad smile and her bright amber eyes looked into his green-flecked blue ones. She once said that he had eyes like a cat's, intelligent and mysterious.

James remembered Pearl's laugh, her smile, and the way she held a sword with casual confidence. He remembered the day they first met. They hadn't had enough time.

"James, I love you so much. I wish we could have had our family. James, while you were gone-" She gasped in pain again. James felt her strength fading and her pulse lowering.

"I love you, Pearl." His voice cracked and he wished he could trade his life for hers.

"The rocks James, go to Pearl Rocks. James, I must tell you, your-" She struggled as she gasped in agony. "James." Her voice faded and her last words died on her lips. James let out a soft cry as her body went limp. Her hand fell back on his arm and her bright, mischievous eyes glazed over.

"Pearl don't leave me. Pearlise. Please, my Pearl." He cried. He rocked her in his arms and tears streamed from his eyes. He leaned down to her lips and kissed her gently. "Pearl." His voice broke and he sobbed.

A while later he kissed her forehead softly. "Goodbye Pearl." He whispered.

A man with striking blue eyes stood on the beach in the first lights of dawn. He watched the black ship become consumed in fire and sink forever into the seas. "Goodbye," he whispered again to silence. His heart shattered into a thousand pieces.

Present Day.

Everen awoke to Aldyn shaking her. "Come on, we have to hurry!" Everen groaned in annoyance.

"What is it, Aldyn?" She asked.

"I'm getting us out of here." She replied. That jolted Everen awake. Nathan and Erica were stretching.

"How are we going to get out of here? My magic is drained after yesterday's mess." Everen asked. "Not to mention the fifty pirates on this ship ready to fight."

"We have help," Aldyn said. Suddenly, the door of their prison was unlocked and swung open. A handsome boy, who looked slightly older than

Aldyn, stood on the threshold. He had sun-bleached blond hair, a healthy tan, and turquoise eyes. Aldyn hesitated a second, but she ignored how angry she was with him and ran to embrace him.

"Do me a favor and don't get captured again." Aldyn broke the hug and hesitated just a moment before stepping away from him.

"Then how will we pull off half of our crazy plans?" He grinned. She laughed as well before hugging him again.

Erica rolled her eyes and interrupted, "Don't we have something to do? Like escaping this blasted ship?" Aldyn and Jayden broke apart and Aldyn crossed her arms.

"Maybe someday you'll understand Erica." Aldyn snapped, and Erica glared at her.

"We don't have much time, follow me," Jayden warned them. Aldyn walked beside them and the two started to catch up.

They soon reached a thick iron cell on the other side of the ship. The black metal bars made their prison seem weak in comparison. Phinx's claws were unsheathed, and she slashed at the metal, but it didn't even scratch. She hit it as hard as she could and grimaced in pain when her claws bent back on her hand. She sheathed her claws and rubbed her hands. Auks, like usual, kept up a calm exterior as she brainstormed plans. When she saw the others, Auks smiled. "I was about to break out," Phinx informed them.

Auks rolled her eyes. "This is titan iron; you can't break it with your claws." She explained, her tone sounded bored. Phinx growled in annoyance.

Aldyn rolled her eyes at the sisters and unlocked the cell. Phinx leaped out and smiled. "I will hang the pirates' corpses from the north cliffs of Ralaji!"

"You know, Phinx, there are other ways to kill people that are shockingly less bloody and difficult," Auks informed her.

Phinx laughed, "Where's the fun in that?" She elbowed her sister teasingly. At that moment Everen realized something about the sisters, they weren't too different. Phinx was a fighter, and Auks was a strategist, but they were both loyal, strong, and goodhearted, although a bit bloodthirsty.

"The reason your earlier escape attempt failed was because you tried to fight your way out. Instead, we are going to sneak out and swim to shore. Were berthed close enough that even terrible swimmers can make it." Jayden explained. Everen was suddenly grateful her father had forced her to take swimming lessons when she was little.

All the pirates were sleeping, passed out beside mugs, throwing knives, small piles of gold, and scattered cards. The group of seven kids slowly crept across the deck towards the railing which faced the shore. They were almost there, and the Featherens leaped into the air.

Then Erica cried out, she had tripped over one of the sleeping pirate's arms which he had moved while sleeping. The pirate opened his eyes, he quickly became alert, "Oi! Prisoners are escaping!" He yelled, awakening the other pirates.

Aldyn cursed worse than Everen had ever heard, even worse than Phinx's expansive vocabulary. The pirates climbed to their feet. "Into the water, now!" Aldyn yelled. She turned, but they were surrounded by the newly awakened pirates.

Then, Cat's Eye pushed his way through them and faced Aldyn. "You almost got away; I'm impressed." He looked over the group and frowned at the sight of Jayden. "A traitor. You know the punishment for treason, yet you still made your choice."

"We are pirates, betrayal is in our blood." Jayden scoffed.

"Many would say the same of loyalty." Cat's Eye countered.

"My only loyalty is to my friends; it was never you. I remained with you to protect her." Jayden shifted his body so that he stood between Aldyn and Cat's Eye.

"You held him prisoner, he owes you nothing," Aldyn interjected angrily.

"Ah, you were that girl, Aldyn, if I remember." He raised his eyebrow. Aldyn froze. "You never even knew what you stole."

"Aldyn may have stolen your treasure years ago, let the past rest. Let us go." Everen demanded.

Cat's Eye turned his gaze to Everen, and his blue and green eyes flickered with something like recognition. "Come with me." He ordered them. Jayden stepped forward. "Except you. Take the traitor to the cells." Cat's Eye ordered. Four pirates grabbed Jayden. He tensed and tried to pull away.

"Don't touch him!" Aldyn yelled, she slashed her sword and left a bleeding gash on the arm of one of the pirates holding Jayden. She refused to lose him again.

"I'll be back Princess. I promise." Jayden turned and went willingly with the pirates, while Aldyn watched in worry.

Cat's Eye led them to the captain's quarters, which were beautifully furnished. Two magenta couches surrounded a circular wooden table that had gold accents. A massive map of Eldenvine covered one wall and it was covered in intricate details. A large window covering the back wall revealed a scenic view of the sea. Cat's Eye took a seat at the desk in front of the window and leaned back.

"Please take a seat." He instructed, gesturing to the couches. Phinx and Auks sat down on one couch, their wingspan reaching entirely across it. Everen, Erica, and Nathan took the other couch while Aldyn remained standing.

"What do you want." She asked Cat's Eye.

"First, I would like to know the names of the prisoners who almost escaped twice." Cat's Eye replied.

Aldyn rolled her eyes, "Aldyn Ryre, of Cedar." The king of the pirate's relaxed pose vanished, and his eyes widened in surprise.

"Cedar was turned to cinders by an insane dragon. How did you survive?" He asked.

She glared at him, refusing to answer. Nathan sensed the tension and spoke up. "Nathan Willowsar, fourteen years old, Elvara." He introduced himself.

"Phinx Fireena Feathercrown," Phinx announced afterward, enjoying the pale expression on the Pirate King's face. Feathercrown was the classic name of Ralaji royalty, and it was considered an act of war to hold a royal heir captive.

"Auks Aysia Feathercrown," Auks said after her sister.

"Erica Wolf." Erica's arms were crossed as she answered in a bored tone. She had deliberately left off the last half of her name, choosing to abandon her legacy.

Everen was last. "Everen Lily Thatcher, I'm thirteen."

"You are a unique group. How did you come together?" Cat's Eye asked. "Especially considering that at least three of you are supposed to be dead." He glanced at Aldyn, Phinx, and Auks.

"That's a long story." Aldyn snorted. "Basically, we are on a mission to track down the Dragon Hunters and stop them."

"So, you are not after the treasure?" Cat's Eye asked slowly.

"No, we were passing through Islaria from Klondor, I had no intention of even coming close to your territory," Aldyn said bitterly.

"Then I apologize for your capture, however, you had stolen my treasure before, I couldn't risk it." Cat's Eye explained. "I doubt you even understand what you stole."

He pulled a silver chain out from underneath his shirt. On its end hung two rings, a dark, thick silver band and a thin one holding a small sapphire. Aldyn sucked in a breath sharply. She remembered holding those rings and feeling disappointed, and how much she had lost due to her search for the treasure. "This is my last connection to my wife." He said quietly, holding the wedding bands so they could better see them.

"Who was she?" Aldyn asked, her voice was low, and she felt a familiar sting of guilt.

"Pearlise, I called her Pearl. I loved her more than all the realms combined. We married secretly; my family would've killed her if they'd known." He bowed his head.

"Why would your family kill her?" Aldyn asked.

"She was a Pearling, and I was the prince of Elvara." He replied.

"*You,* are the lost prince of Elvara?" Nathan gasped, "King Sonoson supposedly killed him in revenge after he abandoned the throne, but it was never confirmed!"

"Yes, I never wanted the title, or to be my uncle's puppet. I met Pearl and I realized I didn't have to accept my fate, she freed me." Cat's Eye replied.

"If you are the prince, then who is currently on the throne?" Everen asked.

"My sister, Inaria." Cat's Eye answered. Everen's heart froze, and she made the connection to what Oceana had told her.

"Inaria?" Everen repeated, her voice raising several octaves, Nathan looked at her with worry.

"Yes, my sister is Queen Inaria. I called her Ara." Cat's Eye explained, causing Everen to pale and step back.

"I will tell you my story, but first tell me yours." Cat's Eye said.

"Fine." Aldyn sighed. "A few years ago, dragon loners were mysteriously disappearing, the evidence has become stronger in recent months, so Agatha sent me and Nathan to find out more. We encountered Everen, she had come through a portal from Earth. Shortly after we met her." Everen coughed loudly.

"I think you mean *threatened* me," Everen argued. Aldyn rolled her eyes.

"Fine. Shortly after, we discovered a dead dragon and learned that the Dragon Hunters were targeting mothers with eggs and were taking the eggs for an unknown purpose. We found a hidden hatchling and took her to Agatha. There, Agatha taught Everen the basics of magic. We left Pine and ran into Erica in the forest by Wolfmoon. We agreed to travel together to Ralaji, where the Dragon Hunters had been most recently. In Ralaji, we were captured by the Featherens, who were alive and in hiding. Queen Athala sent Phinx and Auks with us on our mission, directing us towards Klondor. In Klondor we met Oceana, and she finally gave us answers, she told us where the Dragon Hunters' base is, and we were going there before you captured us." Aldyn finished her story; she left out a lot of the details, but it was an accurate summary.

"You all are young for the mission you have." The Pirate King said.

"But if we don't do it, who will?" Nathan countered. "We are all qualified for this, Phinx and Auks have trained their entire lives, Everen has magic, Erica's lived on her own for years, and I am training for the Queen's Bow. Aldyn is one of the best swordswomen in Eldenvine and she is half-Pearling."

"Half-Pearling, and half-Elve, it appears. You said you were raised in Cedar, which was a city in Mythea." Cat's Eye commented.

Aldyn shrugged. "My mother left me in a river. My adoptive parents found me; I was raised as their daughter, Aldyn Ryre. The only connection I have to my birth mother is this necklace." Aldyn pulled her shell necklace out from underneath her shirt. It was a large cream-colored clam shell with both sides intact. It was simple but beautiful.

"I recognize that necklace." Cat's Eye breathed in sharply. "Open it." He ordered. Aldyn gave him a look; she hadn't even thought she could open the necklace, and she hated taking orders.

Aldyn tightly gripped both edges of the shell and yanked them apart. They snapped open revealing a folded scroll that had deep blue writing on it. Aldyn lifted the paper out of the shell to read it.

"Read it." Cat's Eye's tone left no room to argue.

Aldyn scowled at him but obliged. "My dearest daughter Aldyn, I doubt I will ever see you again. Care for your brother Maximus, I do not know where he will drift to. I sent you both into the water to keep you safe. Graves is approaching as I write this, and I am trying to save your lives. Find your father James and wait for him at Pearl Rocks where we met. I love you forever and always, Pearl." Aldyn was an expert at covering her pain and emotions, even from those who would help her. But something about reading her mother's letter broke the control that she had built up over almost a decade. Her hands trembled as she read, and her emotions spiraled.

Beside her, Cat's Eye whispered, "Pearl Rocks, I understand."

Aldyn's eyes widened. Her hand which held her mother's letter dropped to her side. She whipped her head to Cat's Eye. "You." She said.

"Yes, I am your father."

Chapter Sixteen: The Pain of a Father.

Aldyn's little control left snapped. Her voice cracked, "How?" She asked.

Aldyn didn't care that he was the King of Klondor, whom she hated and had been running from for years, or that he was the lost prince of the Elves. She had once wanted to search for her biological family, but that dream had died long ago. Now, she had a father for the first time in almost nine years.

Cat's Eye awkwardly set his hand on her shoulder. "I'm sorry." He whispered. "I didn't know I had children. I didn't know it was my own daughter I was hunting down."

"How did you not know?" Erica asked incredulously.

"I fell in love with Pearl shortly before my sister disappeared. I thought she was dead and ran away from the palace; after leaving I married Pearl. Months later, I received a message from her, saying she was alive and begging me to help take down our uncle. I was a fool to follow her and leave Pearl, she must have been pregnant then, but we didn't know it. I fell into my uncle's trap and remained imprisoned in the palace for over a year. With help from two of my closest friends, I escaped the palace and returned to Pearl. While I was gone, she must have had Aldyn and Maximus, and when I found her, she died before being able to tell me." Cat's Eye explained.

"How did she die?" Aldyn asked.

"Graves." Cat's Eye spat. His rage was evident even years after her death. At the name of the previous Pirate King, Nathan, Adyn, and Erica all paled.

"Who was he?" Auks asked, the Featherens had been separated from Eldenvine society for over two centuries and did not know him.

Cat's Eye looked slightly surprised at her question but still answered it. "He was the cruelest pirate in history, and the King of Klondor before me. He was obsessed with killing Pearlings. He found Pearl in our home by the bay, mere hours before I arrived. She didn't expect him to be nearby and thought she was safe. He took her to his ship and waited for me. I ran to the rocks to look for her and saw the pirate ship, I realized what must have happened and made my way on board. Graves killed her in front of me. I avenged her by killing him, unintentionally taking the pirate throne. Over the next few years, I hunted down every last one of Graves' supporters, until I was certain no one else would suffer Pearl's fate. At the end of my conquest, I remained as Pirate King to prevent anyone else from becoming another Graves." Cat's Eye, or rather, James finished.

"Here." Aldyn yanked her shell necklace off her neck, and with a shaking hand, she dropped it into Cat's Eye's. "She was your wife. This should be yours."

Cat's Eye's fingers closed over the shell. "Thank you." He said softly.

Aldyn nodded, not knowing what else to say. Suddenly, the sound of shouts came from the door and Jayden burst through holding a bloodied sword. His shoulder was bleeding, and he had a developing bruise on his jaw, but he saw Aldyn and looked relieved.

He turned to the Pirate King and his face darkened. He held his sword threateningly. "Let them go." He growled.

"Consider them free." Cat's Eye replied. Jayden's sword lowered in surprise. Aldyn laughed at his expression. His surprised look faded into a joyful smile. He sheathed his sword and wrapped her in his arms.

"I told you we'd be free someday, Pirate-Boy." She whispered into his shoulder.

"You were right, Princess." He replied softly.

The two embraced long enough to make Cat's Eye cough. "I recommend releasing my daughter."

Jayden released Aldyn with a pale expression and turned to look at her sharply, "Cat's Eye is your father?" His voice was low and dangerous.

"Yes, neither one of us knew, we figured it out shortly before you arrived," Aldyn explained, and he scowled.

"Even after everything-" He started but was cut off by a warning glare from Aldyn. "Explain." He demanded Cat's Eye.

Cat's Eye raised his brow at Jayden's outburst, but he explained the story without argument. Afterward, Everen turned to the King of Klondor, "Tell us about your sister." She asked.

"I would recommend sitting down, that story is long." He replied. Nathan joined the Featheren sisters on the couch while Aldyn and Jayden joined Everen and Erica.

"I will tell you what I know, but I do not know everything." He warned them, "My parents, Elkon and Niara, ruled Elvara before my uncle. Shortly before my ninth birthday, my sister would have been eleven, our parents vanished. Our father's brother, Sonoson, took the throne and announced that my parents had been assassinated by insurgents. My sister and I couldn't do anything. When we were older, Inaria started a rebellion against our uncle, he was a cruel king and refused to give her the throne. She disappeared right before her massive strike, and I believe Sonoson had her killed. I ran away where I met Pearl and we married. Sonoson used a message that I thought came from Inaria to trick me into coming back to the palace. I was trapped there for over a year before I escaped. That is when everything with Graves happened. After a few years, Inaria suddenly returned. She challenged Sonoson for the throne and killed him in the conflict. He'd been behind our parents' deaths, so he was a traitor and had no claim to the throne. She was a good ruler and asked me to return. But I can never go back there. Now, we live in two different worlds, she is the Queen of Elvara, and I am the King of the Seas."

"Did Inaria tell you about her time away?" Everen's voice was hard and angry, unusual for the usually kind girl.

"Yes, actually." Cat's Eye said, giving Everen an odd look, "She said Sonoson found a way to banish her to Earth using ancient magic. There she met and married a human and had a daughter. One day, the enchantress that sent her to Earth in the first place, arrived on her doorstep and begged her to save Elvara. The enchantress took her back to Eldenvine where she took the throne. She never knew why the old enchantress helped her."

"What about the daughter?" Everen demanded, "Why did she leave her behind?"

"I don't know, but my sister always had her reasons." He shrugged.

"What reason could anyone have for leaving her child?" Everen's tone was low and dangerous.

"Everen," Erica started before her eyes widened in horrified realization.

"Oceana told me, Cat's Eye just confirmed the story," Everen explained. Nathan looked pale and he leaned back on the couch, he admired and respected Queen Inaria and didn't like how Everen's experience changed his view of her.

The Pirate King looked shocked and sympathetic, "I don't know why she left, you'd have to ask them yourself." Everen scowled and crossed her arms, furious.

Aldyn turned to her, with a developing grin on her face. "We are cousins." Aldyn's realization vanished the tension. Everen smiled slightly as Aldyn hugged her for the first time. "I always knew you were cool. Now we only have to find my brother, I wonder if he is looking for me."

"I doubt it." Cat's Eye interjected. "I only gave Pearl one necklace, and it is around your neck. You will have to find him yourself." Aldyn frowned.

"I can help you find him." Everen offered. "After all, he's my family too."

"Thank you." She whispered.

"Don't we have a mission to finish? You know, before we got captured." Erica reminded them, in her classic sassy tone.

"Erica, it's so obvious you want to stay here." Everen retorted, making the others laugh.

"As much as I hate to agree with our depressing pessimist, she does have a point. We are on a mission; we can save the less time-sensitive side missions for later." Auks reasoned.

Aldyn turned to her father. "I hate to leave so soon; I don't even know you."

Cat's Eye set one hand on her shoulder, "Now that we have found each other, I promise we will meet again. Know that I am prouder of you than anything else in my life, I will always be here for you." Then he surprised them all by gently hugging her. Aldyn was stiff, but she accepted the embrace.

Auks set a hand on Aldyn's shoulder, "We have to go, we want to stop Blackshard before they murder any more innocent dragons." Aldyn nodded and let go of her father.

The Pirate King led them out of his office to the deck. His crew looked surprised, but they didn't say anything. No one questioned Cat's Eye. He sent three pirates to retrieve the soarers and the rest of the confiscated gear. They returned several minutes later with their arms laden.

"We will land in northern Elvara. The Queen's bow has an old camp there where we can stay the night." Nathan decided as Auks helped Erica fasten a soarer onto her back.

"We only have three remaining soarers, Aldyn's got destroyed when she crashed." Erica reminded them. Cat's Eye raised an eyebrow at that comment. "Aldyn can swim, but we don't have anything for Jayden, and these soarers are not designed for two."

"I may be able to help with that," Cat's Eye interrupted, "I have an old glider stored in the ship. It works the same as a soarer, it is just less maneuverable."

"That should work." Auks nodded as she thought it through.

"I'm worried about Aldyn, that's a long way to swim alone," Nathan interjected.

"I will be fine. I am half-Pearling remember?" She laughed and gently elbowed Nathan.

"That's over a hundred miles of straight swimming, and you will have to be fast to keep up with the soarers."

Aldyn rolled her eyes. "I've swum farther. Stop worrying, I know where the camp is. We should leave now if we want to reach it before sundown." Auks helped them get on the soarers and the glider on Jayden. Before long, everyone was ready to leave.

"I promise we will meet again, and we can talk about everything," Aldyn told Cat's Eye. He looked at her for a moment and removed his hat.

The Pirate King's hat was black with gold trim. Small diamonds and pearls were woven in with the gold. He placed it on Aldyn's head. It slipped down, his head was bigger than hers. "I will see you later, Aldyn." His voice was low and gruff to cover up his emotions, but some still leaked through. He stepped back and Aldyn walked to the edge of the ship. She climbed onto the railing and jumped off. She cut into the sea like an arrow and shot through the water. Her Pearling blood gave her underwater speed that was unable to be rivaled.

Erica leaped into the air and flew up while Auks and Phinx lifted Jayden into the sky. They let go and Jayden glided after Aldyn. The four quickly caught up with Aldyn. Only Everen and Nathan remained. She took a deep breath as she observed the early morning sun.

"I know that look," Nathan said knowingly. She turned to him guiltily.

"After we finish the mission, what next?" She asked, "Do I go after my mother? She left me. But if I don't go, I'll never know why."

"You don't have to worry about it right now. When you do, it's your choice." He suggested.

"I'm so angry at her. How could she just leave with no explanation and not try and contact me? I'm not like Aldyn. I'm not going to forget everything she did."

Nathan shook his head, "Trust me, Aldyn hasn't forgotten what happened between her and Cat's Eye. You don't have to either; I just ask that you talk to her. I know Queen Inaria, she'd not be a bad person."

Nathan leaped into the sky, and she followed, using her magic to lift them high up. The wind flew her hair behind her, and sunlight warmed her face. A smile broke onto her face as she looked down at the turquoise waves which glinted gold. She loved this world.

Chapter Seventeen: The Line That Shouldn't Be Crossed.

It took several hours of flight from the *Pearl Sword,* Cat's Eye's ship, to reach Elvara. The border was the edge of the trees, which went right up to the strip of golden sand before the water. The massive forest extended all the way to the southern shore of Mytharica and was one of the larger territories. Nathan led them several miles into the forest, and they gradually reduced altitude.

They landed in a clearing near the beach and took off the soarers. Nathan led them to the camp from there. The camp was surrounded by tall maples and was carpeted with soft moss. Tall trees shaded the camp so no one would be able to see them from above.

Aldyn arrived at the camp after them, holding seven large fish on a chain in one hand. Her hair dripped seawater, so she twisted it and shook her head, but it was still damp. Cat's Eye's hat was still on her head, it was waterproof and enchanted to be resistant to damage.

"It's perfect on you, Aldyn." Everen complimented sincerely.

"Thanks, Everen." Aldyn smiled and the two cousins walked over to the camp. Erica was building a fire and Nathan was setting up several tents.

"How are you not freezing?" Erica asked with a raised eyebrow, it was nearly sundown and cold enough to need a cloak, Aldyn's clothes were soaked.

"Pearlings' bodies naturally contain and conserve heat, we can survive in extreme cold," Aldyn replied.

"But you're only half-Pearling," Erica said. Aldyn shrugged.

"I don't know about genetics, but it doesn't bother me much. Anyway, I caught dinner!" Aldyn handed the chain of fish to Erica who rolled her eyes.

Everen looked around the camp. Nathan had finished setting up the tents. The smallest was Erica's, who hated sharing a tent. Nathan and Jayden would share one and Everen and Aldyn would share. Phinx and Auks had the biggest tent, due to their wings. A wide stump was in the center of the ring of tents with the soarers stacked beside it and Auks and Phinx were sparring with their claws unsheathed. Aldyn went over to Jayden and said something to him. He nodded and drew his sword, before following her a bit farther away to duel.

Phinx and Auks' claws rang when they clashed. The sisters laughed as they narrowly dodged blows. Auks lunged and Phinx leaned back, before surging forward to slash Auks' breastplate. Auks growled in annoyance as she stood up from her fighting stance and sheathed her claws.

"You always win." She grumbled and Phinx set an arm over her shoulder.

"You're getting better, if you actually trained more, you might beat me." She teased and Auks scowled.

"Even if I did train more," Auks trailed off and the two joined Erica at the fire where she was cooking.

"Dinner is ready!" Erica yelled, Aldyn and Jayden lowered their swords and came over. The group crowded around Erica, and everyone grabbed a fish and a tin plate. Nathan had a bottle of a creamy drink he'd heated over the fire. He poured everyone a mug of the drink. It tasted like cinnamon, cream, and coffee.

Erica ate next to Everen who was beside Nathan. On Nathan's other side were Aldyn and Jayden, with the Featherens across from them. They formed a loose closed circle as they enjoyed their meal. After she finished, Aldyn told a dramatic story that made the others laugh. Jayden rolled his eyes, but he also smiled. When she finished, Nathan told jokes until Phinx eventually called a game of Dare.

"What's that?" Everen asked. She had been the quietest during the meal.

"It's a game we play in Ralaji. Everyone gets in a circle, and someone starts. They start by creating a dare for the person beside them. That person can either do the dare or pass. If they pass, they are out of the game and the dare passes on to the next person, or the person daring can change it. If you accept the dare, you must do it and then you create a dare for the next person. Whoever lasts the longest wins." Phinx explained.

"Oh no." Nathan groaned. "This will not end well."

"Have you played it before?" Everen asked.

He nodded, "It's very popular at Emerald Elite, my school. My brothers are absolutely ruthless."

Aldyn laughed and elbowed him. "Count me in, Phinx!" The group tightened the loose circle and Phinx rustled her wings.

"I called the game, so I start. After me is Auks, then Erica, Nathan, Everen, Jayden, and Aldyn." She turned to her sister, "Auks, I dare you to join me and Firex for training when we get home." Auks groaned.

"First, that is totally breaking the rules, I can't do that right now. Second, you both are the best fighters under the age of twenty." Auks complained.

"I could've dared you to spar Eagle, he broke Falcon's jaw last time they sparred." Phinx pointed out. Auks scowled at her.

"Was that the match where you and Firex won all the gold?" Auks asked.

Phinx nodded with a grin, "I knew to put my money on my boyfriend." Auks sighed.

"Fine."

The group kept playing and eventually, it was Erica's turn. "Alright. Nathan, I dare you to ask Everen to the Emerald Ball." She announced.

"What's that?" Everen asked.

"The Emerald Ball is an annual Elvara event on the last night of summer. It's a big deal." Nathan explained. "I'm already going with someone; I have to pass." Nathan sounded slightly relieved and Everen was strangely disappointed.

"The girl with the curly blond hair?" Aldyn asked and raised her eyebrow. Nathan nodded.

"She asked me right before I joined you for the mission." He explained and Aldyn started laughing.

"Do you brothers know?" She asked and Nathan paled. "Ha!" Aldyn laughed. "I'll have to talk to them when we go to Elvara."

"Nathan's out and I get to dare Everen." Erica reminded them. "Everen, I dare you to steal Aldyn's eyepatch."

"I hate you," Aldyn said as Everen made a weak attempt for it. Aldyn smacked her hand and Everen laughed.

"I pass." Everen shrugged and the group played a few more rounds.

"Auks, I dare you to tell who your secret boyfriend is, Firex and I have a bet." Phinx grinned and Auks' scowl could freeze the ocean solid.

"Pass." Auks crossed her arms and Phinx groaned.

"Please?" She asked and Auks smirked.

"Like Fayra I'd tell you."

Finally, only Phinx, Aldyn, and Jayden were left. Phinx had gotten more vicious in her dares, her competitive nature shining through. But Aldyn and Jayden were equally stubborn.

"Jayden, I dare you to kiss Aldyn." Phinx declared with a grin.

Jayden's eyes flickered to Aldyn, whose arms were crossed. "I pass." He decided and turned away.

Phinx grinned and turned to Aldyn, "I dare you to let someone cut your hair."

Aldyn raised her eyebrow, "Easily. Here," She passed her knife to Jayden and turned her back to him so he could trim the uneven edges.

"It's just like old times." Jayden teased and her scowl faded. He didn't spend long on it, but afterward, her waves hung just past her shoulders. Erica nodded her approval and passed one of her many silver daggers to Aldyn, who used it as a mirror to check his work.

After, she turned to Phinx with a wicked gleam in her eye, "I dare you to ground yourself for the next month."

Phinx's eyes widened in horror and her victorious smile vanished, "You can't be serious, flying, that's a part of *life*."

Aldyn just raised her brow, "Anything's legal." She quoted and Phinx grimaced.

"Fine, you win."

Aldyn grinned and high-fived Jayden. Auks laughed at Phinx and Erica, the latter who was twirling an arrow over her fingers.

"Anyway," Nathan said after a little while, "It's getting late, and we need to rest for tomorrow, we'll be confronting Blackshard."

The others nodded, "I'll take the first watch." Jayden volunteered and Aldyn nodded gratefully at him, she usually took the first and stayed up later than necessary.

After a quick clean-up of the camp, the teenagers climbed into the tents and curled up in blankets. As she fell asleep, Everen wished she could see her father. This whole trip reminded her of camping with him.

She remembered the previous summer, how the two of them went backpacking with Grams across part of the Pacific Northwest. She had many good memories from that week, fishing with Dad, and smores with Grams, a tear slipped down her cheek.

No matter how happy she was here, it wasn't home. She missed her family. Once she helped the others take down Blackshard, she was going back to Agatha's, the Mistry would contact Grams so that she'd be able to go home.

Everen turned onto her side and saw Aldyn's sleeping form. The girl took off her black vest, boots, and belt to sleep, but otherwise wore her normal clothing. As she slept, the edge of her cream blouse slid down her back slightly. Underneath, Everen caught sight of the tell-tale splotches of burns.

The scars probably covered her entire back, Aldyn hadn't escaped the burning of Cedar, she'd just been the only one to survive.

When Everen awoke, Aldyn had adjusted her shirt, and the burn was no longer visible. "You good?" Everen asked and her cousin glanced at her oddly.

"Yeah, I'm fine." It didn't take them long to pack up the camp. They were able to take off at dawn, flying south across the edges of Elvara.

The seven of them were lucky to catch a breeze that sped them across the land, before midday, they were able to see the southern beaches of Elvara. As they flew, Phinx and Auks carried Aldyn, so that the half-Pearling wouldn't have to swim around the entire peninsula of Elvara.

The sight of the aqua ocean sparkling under the yellow sun took Everen's breath away. "Looks like we're here!" She called and beside her, Nathan laughed.

"Head for the beach, we'll plan there!" He yelled back, over the wind and she nodded, angling the wooden wings downward toward the ocean.

She was careful not to spiral into an uncontrolled dive, but she enjoyed the wind rushing into her face as the Soarer sped up.

She touched down on the white grains and stumbled under the weight of the artificial wings.

Behind her, Nathan and Erica landed. After a bit Jayden joined them, the glider was a lot slower than Soarers, so he'd fallen a bit behind.

Aldyn yelled as Phinx dumped her in the sand. "Scales and bones." She cursed and Phinx cackled, Auks sighed as she dropped to the ground beside them.

"Any clue where Blackshard is?" Erica asked before Aldyn could yell at Phinx, "Oceana only told us vaguely where to go."

Everen noticed a thin trail of smoke in the trees coming from a small mountain within walking distance from where they landed, west of where they were. "Maybe Oceana helped us more than we thought." She pointed towards the smoke. The others turned and Erica scowled.

"It's worth a shot." Aldyn decided, coming up beside Everen. The young woman led the way through the forest towards the smoke. They'd left the Soarers with their gear on the beach, the forest was too thick to carry it with them. Jayden had complained about leaving it unguarded where it could be stolen, but Nathan argued that this particular region of Elvara was nearly uninhabited.

As they traveled through the forest, the team brainstormed ideas on how to deal with Blackshard. "A frontal attack would be idiotic," Aldyn shot down Phinx's plan, "we're going against an army, we need to use strategy."

"What about an ambush?" Jayden suggested and Aldyn hesitated.

"It's less dangerous but more risky. If we aren't careful, we could get cornered."

"We could do a two-front ambush," Nathan added.

"We'll figure it out once we find the base." Aldyn shrugged, "And look, we're here." Everen's eyes widened as the source of the smoke was revealed.

She'd been right. Oceana had helped them more than they'd expected. The smoke came from a cave, carved into a massive bare mountain. The cave was sealed off with two enormous, reinforced iron doors. Two guards in silver armor and dark clothes stood at either side and they held spears in their hands and daggers at their waists. Everen briefly wondered why neither of them was armed with more modern weaponry, but remembered that most Eldenvine fighting styles revolved around melee weapons and martial arts.

"If we take the guards out, we can sneak inside, that'll delay a confrontation," Nathan whispered.

"Wait." Auks stopped him. "If we go in, we might not be able to get out. Who knows what's in there, we could get killed." She reasoned.

"Our mission is to stop them, if we get closer, we can do that," Everen argued. "We must at least check it out. If we encounter any trouble, I can protect us with my magic."

"We can't just rely on your magic, it's not foolproof," Auks argued back.

Phinx snorted, "Nothing's perfect." Auks gave her sister a dirty look rival to one of Queen Athala's.

"How are we even going to get in? We don't want the guards to alert the others we are here." Jayden spoke up.

"Leave that to me." Phinx stood up.

"Are you crazy?" Erica hissed at Phinx who walked towards the guards.

"She's a Featheren what do you expect?" Aldyn retorted. Auks unsheathed her claws and glared at her. Before Auks did anything, Phinx stepped in front of the guards who saw her wings and raised their spears at her. Even two hundred years after their extinction, people still were terrified at the sight of an angry Featheren.

"I recommend running into the forest before I decide I don't care if I get my claws dirty." Phinx unsheathed her claws and Everen could see how sharp they were. The guards dropped their spears and bolted away, leaving Phinx grinning.

Auks looked furious as she walked over to her sister. "You are going to compromise the mission. Now all of Blackshard will know we are here!"

Phinx rolled her eyes. "We can deal with them later."

"Loose ends lose lives." Erica quoted coldly.

"And there are dragons who might have died if we had been held back by the guards." Phinx crossed her arms.

"Just because you're the eldest, perfect daughter doesn't mean you get to do whatever you want!" Auks yelled.

"We are supposed to be a *team*," Nathan said. "We aren't supposed to be arguing, we are supposed to be saving dragons."

"No, we are stopping terrorists, I don't care about the beasts." Aldyn snapped.

"We're not a team, we all have our reasons for being here." Jayden interrupted.

"Who's forcing you to do anything? You're just here for Aldyn." Everen snapped, and Aldyn whirled to face her, furious.

"Why are you here? You could've stayed with Agatha, she'd do a better job of getting you back to Earth!" Aldyn spat back.

Betrayal flashed across Everen's face, and the words stung like a slap. Aldyn was right of course, if Everen had stayed with Agatha she'd be closer to home by now.

To her surprise, Auks stepped to her defense, "We don't have time for this." The Featheren declared, ending the argument. Aldyn and Jayden scowled, and Nathan cringed.

"Fine. Let's go, the sooner we get this done, the sooner I can go home and never see you idiots again." Everen spun on her heel and used her magic to open the massive iron doors.

"Everen," Aldyn tried, but Everen refused to listen. The girl from Earth led the way into the cave. Aldyn exchanged a glance with Nathan before following.

The seven were silent as they traveled through the cave. The tension was thick enough to cut with a sword. Everen chose to focus on their surroundings and noticed that the walls of the tunnel had torches bolted into stone and the roof was slanting downward, making it feel claustrophobic.

"There should be claw marks or any sign of the dragons," Erica commented softly as they neared the middle of the cave.

"The hunters took eggs, not fully grown dragons. The eggs would hatch in captivity, going insane." Auks explained and Everen shivered. In her short time in their world, she'd realized how dangerous some things could be, and she did not want to add another thing to her growing list.

Finally, they reached the end. The cave was cut off with a wall of iron bars. It was dark and difficult to see inside the cell, but Everen saw the faint outlines of shattered eggshells and dark blood covering the floors.

Everen raised her hand and made it glow a low gold. The light illuminated the cavern and her eyes widened with shock and horror.

The room was smaller than Everen had thought it was in the darkness. It was filled with over a hundred thin dragonettes. Dark metal armor covered the dragons' frail bodies and chains hung from their ankles. Their eyes were bloodshot, and they glared at the uninvited visitors. They hissed, revealing unusually sharp blood-stained teeth.

One of the dragons charged the bars, clawing hopelessly at the metal. The dragon collapsed backward, and another dragon leaped at the fallen dragon, ripping open the dragon's chest and killing it.

"Fayra's blood." Phinx whispered, "They are making an army."

"What?" The others whirled to look at her.

"It makes sense. Blackshard is hatching the dragon eggs and training the dragonettes. They are going to use the dragons to conquer Eldenvine." Phinx explained, and they stared at her in surprise. Her comment was incredibly insightful, something Everen hadn't seen from the Featheren.

"She's right." Erica realized with horror. "Infant dragons are vulnerable and can be turned into powerful weapons when trained, remember Black Scale from six centuries ago." Nathan turned pale and Aldyn looked confused, she hadn't taken a history course in years and hadn't learned about the man. Erica glanced at Aldyn and Everen and elaborated, "He kidnapped eggs while the dragons were away at war and turned them into his insane army. The dragon tribes united to kill him. I can't believe Blackshard would be foolish enough to even attempt his plan."

"We can't free these dragons," Aldyn said quietly. "If we do, they will burn Eldenvine to the ground. *Tens of thousands* will die."

"There has to be a way to save them." Everen insisted desperately.

"They were born here, there is no way to reverse the damage Blackshard caused. These dragons will *never* recover." Erica whispered.

Everen felt her eyes water and her cheeks flush with anger. It broke her heart to see the devastated innocence of the dragonettes. They should've been raised by their mothers; they didn't deserve torture and insanity. Dragaria shouldn't have been so torn by war that their eggs were hidden across Mytharica to escape the bloodshed.

Nathan set one hand on Everen's shoulder. She wiped her eyes with her palms.

"What do we do now?" Everen asked quietly.

"The only thing we can do, stop Blackshard at any cost." Erica surprised them with her determination.

"How? With these dragons," Auks' eyes lit up. "Of course!" She exclaimed.

"What?" Aldyn asked.

"We don't have much time before Blackshard returns, thanks to Phinx. When they do come, we can trap them with the dragons." Auks explained.

"Aren't they vicious and insane?" Jayden asked worriedly.

"Exactly," Erica explained. "The dragons will fight Blackshard and keep them busy."

"Giving us enough time to trap them all in the mountain." Auks finished.

"Which will save Eldenvine." Nathan finished. Auks nodded at him.

"Blackshard has already done so much damage, they need to be stopped." Everen said, "We will all have to work together to pull this off. We can't be fighting each other, we are a team, we should act like it." Auks and Phinx exchanged guilty glances, out of all of them, the sisters argued the most.

"We will," Aldyn said finally. The others nodded and agreed with her.

"By now, Blackshard knows we are here, and they are going to try to corner us. We have to get around them and shut the doors on them. Once the doors are shut, we can release the dragons." Everen decided.

"I can stay back and cut the bars." Phinx proposed. Auks gently squeezed her sister's shoulder.

"I will stay with her."

"Jayden and I can shut the gates; we just need a way to get to them." Aldyn grabbed his hand and they looked at each other.

"I will stay with Phinx and Auks. I will use my magic to get us out after we free the dragons." Everen said, trying to hide her nervousness. She hadn't yet used a portal with other people, it was a risk.

"Nathan and I will go with Aldyn and Jayden; we can fight if there are any Blackshard members who don't get trapped," Erica added.

Suddenly they heard the sound of voices and the clang of metal. "Go." Everen opened a crackling gold portal, relieved that it worked. "It will take you right behind the trees." Aldyn nodded to Everen in respect before walking through. Jayden, Nathan, and Erica followed her.

Everen let out a sigh of relief she had not realized she was holding. She closed the portal and immediately felt a surge of exhaustion. She hoped she would have enough energy to last through the fight ahead. The three girls backed against the bars and waited for the fight.

Suddenly forty warriors passed from the turn in the cave tunnel. Everen unconsciously stepped back, her back hitting the bars.

"Wait," Auks whispered. Everen lifted her fists loosely in front of her chest, she wouldn't go down without a fight.

The Blackshard members stepped closer. "NOW!" Auks yelled, slashing her Featheren claws through the iron bars with Phinx. The soldiers panicked.

"They will kill us all!" One Blackshard warrior screamed.

"No, only you." Everen retorted and created a second golden portal. Auks and Phinx dove through it as the dragons lunged through the now-broken iron bars. Everen closed her eyes and leaped through the golden portal, ignoring the screams.

The portal closed behind her, and she opened her eyes. She was standing behind the Featheren princesses in front of the closed gates of the cave.

Next to them were Aldyn, Jayden, Nathan, and Erica, each with their weapons drawn. The assorted weapons were directed at a woman surrounded by ten remaining warriors.

"You children have cost me greatly. Years of work were put into this army." She growled. Her hair was short and bleached white with black roots. Her irises were grey with streaks of white that looked like electricity. She wore ripped black jeans, a silvery-grey shirt, black boots, and a knee-length black coat. She looked like she was in her late thirties, younger than Everen's father, who was forty-three.

The boots and coat, Everen noticed with disgust, were made of dragon-hide. "Who are you?" Aldyn demanded.

"You can call me Shard, Blackshard is my organization." She replied.

"Why did you take all those dragonettes? Why were you building an army?" Everen demanded.

Shard laughed. "You ask why I wish to rule Eldenvine?" Her voice hardened. "This world had wronged me. I was left starving and scavenging for scraps on the streets. I finally built a home away from all the pain, and it was burned to the ground by the armies of Dragaria." She hissed, before taking a second to compose herself. "I was powerless once, and I will never be again."

Phinx lunged at her with the full might of a Featheren warrior, her claws unsheathed and held out before her. Shard stumbled back and a young Blackshard warrior stood to defend her, holding twin swords.

"You can't stop me. I will rebuild my army and I will rule Eldenvine." Shard announced bitterly.

"We will stop you." Everen shot back.

"You will not have the chance." Shard snarled. The Blackshard warriors started to circle them, holding their spears. "You, like many others, dared to cross me. Say hello to my daughter for me." She grinned widely and wickedly.

Everen screamed a spell Agatha taught her to use in an emergency. She, Erica, Aldyn, Jayden, and Nathan, instantly grew white sparkling wings. They leaped into the air, used to flying thanks to the Soarers, and the spears fell beneath their feet.

The Blackshard warriors drew bows and shot arrows at the escaping teenagers after their spears failed. Aldyn dodged most of the arrows, but two hit her arm and leg. The girl somehow managed not to cry out in pain, but Jayden dove towards her anyway. Erica fluidly dodged the arrows like a fish in water.

Everen gasped as an arrowhead nicked her upper arm, but she was lucky. Most of the arrows were concentrated on the Featheren sisters. Everen heard Phinx grunt out in pain as an arrow caught her in the thigh. The Featheren then yanked out the bolt and flew higher.

Auks was more careful in dodging the attack, but even she wouldn't be taken down by just a couple of arrows. Featherens were strong. Most injuries inflicted by the arrows would heal before they could die of blood loss, granted it didn't strike anywhere vital.

Beneath them, Shard shrieked in rage and grabbed the bow of the warrior next to her. She pulled a vial filled with black liquid out of her dragon-hide coat and dipped the arrowhead in the liquid before setting it on the bow and pulling back the bowstring. Shard lined up her sight with the arrow and lifted the bow as she breathed out, she released the string.

"PHINX!" Everen heard herself scream as the arrow streaked towards the Featheren.

Phinx heard the warning and she tried to move, but she was too late. The arrow was going to hit her. Suddenly a blur of grey feathers slammed into Phinx.

A loud shriek cut through the night, followed by Phinx screaming a horrifying string of curse words. Auks' wings failed and she fell out of the sky with an arrow embedded in her breastplate, right at her heart.

The Featheren's eyes glazed as she fell through the clouds. Everen's heart stopped, and her mind froze.

"AUKS!" Phinx screamed and dove after her sister. Aldyn, Jayden, Erica, Nathan, and Everen dove after the two Featherens.

Chapter Eighteen: The Cost of Love.

Auks crashed in the forest below. Her wings lay on the ground, never to fly again. Her hand fell and her light red hair spread out. Everen watched as a last tear slipped down the Featheren's cheek. Phinx landed first, sobbing uncontrollably, as she collapsed to her knees by her sister.

"Auks, *Auks!*" Phinx screamed. "Wake up! *Please!*" Phinx cradled her sister's limp form in her arms as her wings shook with emotion. "No. No, no, no, no! Auks! Answer me, please!" She cried.

The magic wings faded into stardust. Everen walked over to the Featherens but stopped when she saw Phinx sobbing. Erica covered her mouth with her hand when she saw Auks and tears slid down her cheeks. Aldyn clenched her fists and leaned into Jayden, who wrapped his arms around her. Nathan stood beside Everen, his hands were clenched so tight his nails dug painfully into his palm.

Everen was destroyed. Auks had become her friend, and if she had just listened to her, she wouldn't be dead. Auks knew that it was dangerous to go inside the cave, Auks had warned them that everything could go wrong.

When Auks' pulse faded out, Phinx let out a shrill scream louder than the roar of the thunder. Her cry came from her shattered heart, and it shifted into blood-thirsty rage, stronger than the heat at the center of a forest fire.

A bolt of lightning flashed. Phinx dropped Auks' body and spread her wings as she stood. Her rage echoed across the forest like a surge of energy. Her head snapped back, and her tears blended with rain. Her eyes glowed orange like they were on fire.

Fire started on Phinx's chest and spread to cover her whole body in orange flames. Her wings were made of golden feathers and her claws looked like molten gold. Her dark red hair brightened to a scarlet. Phinx cried out like a bird of prey before the kill. Golden fire spread from her and encircled Auks. The others leaped away so they wouldn't be burned. The fire guarded Auks' body and left the Featheren untouched. Phinx leaped into the air with one beat of her powerful wings, before soaring after the sky to kill the one who'd killed her sister.

Everen didn't even hesitate before she followed Phinx. Nathan, Aldyn, Jayden, and Erica ran after her.

They ran through the forest after Phinx. No one spoke. Everen felt her heart break with every step she took. Once the adventure had made the danger seem laughable. Now they had been struck down. The fight was no game. People had died. Dragons had died. *Auks* had died.

They broke through the trees where Phinx was confronting Shard. Everen tried to step closer to Phinx, and Nathan yanked her back before the flames could burn her. A wave of fire spread from the furious Featheren, knocking the surviving Blackshard warriors to the ground. Phinx threw a blast at Shard's face, and the woman blocked it with her arms. When the fire faded, Everen could see the scorched Dragon scales and Shard was flinching like she had been burned, but she somehow kept her ground.

"YOU KILLED MY SISTER! I WILL SEND YOU TO THE PIT OF BONES, YOU SICK HEIR OF BLOOD!" Phinx roared at Shard, who was stepping backward. Around them, trees were covered in fire, and Everen smelled smoke. The howling rain of the storm barely held back Phinx's vicious fire.

Shard snarled. "This world is crumbling into chaos; she would've died eventually. Ask your friend Aldyn, a dragon decimated Cedar; she is the only one to survive. There was no one left to bury the charred bones that remained."

"How do you know that?" Aldyn demanded with fury rival to Phinx's.

"You could join me." Shard proposed, ignoring her question. "You could help me stop the chaos that orphans children. You can take vengeance on the dragon that murdered your family. You could save other villages from the fate of yours." Aldyn hesitated, and Everen could see the conflict flashing across the girl's face.

Finally, Adyn shook her head, "Dragons are not the problem." She answered and Everen felt a surge of pride for her cousin. Before, Everen wouldn't have been surprised if Aldyn accepted the offer.

"That Fire Flight, who killed thousands in a single day, seemed like a problem to me." Shard snarled.

Aldyn narrowed her eyes. "How did you know it was a Fire Flight, I was the only survivor who could confirm the dragon responsible, and I never told anyone."

"You never connected the dots, did you? She was guarding a nest. We were after the eggs, a pity a whole village had to die as well."

Aldyn froze. Her fists trembled with rage. "You killed them. It's your fault the village burned!"

"A small price to pay," Shard replied.

Aldyn lunged forward, her hand on the hilt of her blade. Jayden grabbed her arm and held her back. "Let me kill her!" Aldyn yelled, "She killed them, she killed them all!" She broke out of his hold and drew her sword.

Aldyn joined Phinx before the woman. As the three faced off, each had a slightly different light. Phinx's claws glowed with her orange fire, Aldyn's sword glowed blue in the absence of sunlight, and Shard's coat emitted faint purple smoke.

"You have made your choice," The woman whispered coldly. She pulled out a blue book from inside her dragon-hide coat. Its pages were yellowed with age and golden lines spelled words on the cover.

Everen couldn't make out the title, but she was able to see the shape of strange spirals and circles. Her veins turned to ice as Shard turned the pages of the magic book.

"Nighteria Terrorana." Shard yelled, holding out her hand as Aldyn charged.

A dark blue mist suddenly shrouded them, blocking their vision and making Everen feel oddly dizzy. "What's going on?" Nathan asked as he stumbled to the ground. Shard started laughing.

"One of the most powerful spell books in all Eldenvine lost for centuries, and I used it against children." She shook her head. "Appreciate the power that will destroy you."

Everen's vision swam, and she collapsed to the ground, somehow, she stayed conscious. Her magic felt so much stronger than it should be. She looked across the ground, where Aldyn lay, her hand inches away from the hilt of her sword. Tears had slipped down her face, Everen had never seen Aldyn cry. Everen stretched out her hand, her arm felt like heavy lead, and it took all of her willpower to inch her fingertips forward and reach her cousin.

With one last burst of energy, Everen's fingertip touched Aldyn's bare arm. With a flash of white light, Everen stepped inside Aldyn's cursed nightmare.

Aldyn was eleven. Her hair was chest-length and was a lighter shade of brown. Both of her blue eyes were intact, and she held the same sword she still had. She wore soft leather pants and a white shirt with rolled-up sleeves. Beside her, stood two girls. One was Erica and the other was a young Featheren with pale blue eyes, very dark brown hair, a dark tan, and white wings.

In front of the three girls was a massive dragon with sharp silver scales. Chains of gold and jewels hung from the dragon's neck. The dragon had been demanding treasure from the nearby village and threatened to burn it if the people refused to pay the tribute. Aldyn drew her sword and stood defensively, but she was just a girl. Erica drew her bow. The Featheren unsheathed two of her claws; they were pure white and very sharp.

The dragon roared in stubborn rage and slashed her claws at the girls. They jumped back and Erica let the arrow fly, right into the beast's left eye. The dragon roared again but this time in pain and lashed out with her talons.

The Featheren shoved Aldyn away and flew into the air. She drove towards the dragon, but she was not fast enough. The dragon's deadly claws sliced across her chest. The Featheren shrieked in agony and blood soaked through her shirt.

"ANGELA!" Aldyn screamed after the Featheren. Angela fell out of sight into the forest.

The dragon turned towards Aldyn and slashed her while she was distracted across the face. Aldyn shrieked and collapsed to the ground. The mark from the dragon's claws had slashed directly through her eye and blood spilled over the girl's face. Erica screamed and tried to run towards her. The dragon turned to her, and Erica stopped.

Everen dove under the dragon's scaly belly after Aldyn. She wrapped her arms around her cousin and held her unconscious, bloody body tightly. She closed her eyes.

Everen tried to calm down. She regulated her breathing and focused on needing to save Aldyn.

A gold glow surrounded the girls. Everen opened her eyes.

She remembered Shard and the spell. Everen climbed to her feet, Aldyn right after her. On the ground around them lay the bodies of their friends trapped in their worst nightmares and memories.

"How," Shard asked.

Everen smiled. "We are the Elden Order." Everen knelt beside Erica and touched her forehead while Aldyn drew her sword to defend them.

Everen opened her eyes and saw a young girl, barely seven years old, hiding next to a wooden door in a castle corridor. The girl had dark curls, brilliant green eyes, high cheekbones, and porcelain skin. The side of her head was pressed against the door and her brow was furrowed in confusion.

Everen stood beside the girl and was able to overhear the conversation.

"We will announce Erica's betrothal to Prince Thorne at the Lunar Ball. Hopefully, this will create the alliance we need to build our wealth and avoid war."

"This plan will go against tradition! Erica is the heir, Aronna is available." A second voice protested.

"Tradition would have Wolfmoon in ruins. Erica is too stubborn to rule Wolfmoon the way we need. Aronna is easier to control. Aronna must be queen, and after several years all Wolfmoon will forget about Erica's claim to the throne." The first voice insisted.

"I will send our proposition to Crowthorne." A third voice decided.

Erica gasped and stumbled back from the door with tears gathering in her eyes. "Mother?" She whispered. The door opened and the Queen walked out. On the Queen's head was a silver crown of spikes and moons. She paled when she saw her daughter.

Erica turned and ran. "Get her!" The Queen roared to the men beside her and Everen bolted after the girl.

She found her hiding in an adjoining hallway, on the ground sobbing. Everen knelt beside the girl and wrapped her arms around her. "You are safe," Everen whispered as the golden stardust carried them away.

She opened her eyes to Aldyn who was fiercely dueling Shard. Shard had a long silver sword she swung overhead against Aldyn. Aldyn blocked with her own blade and gritted her teeth.

"Hurry up Everen," Aldyn growled. Everen nodded and reached towards Jayden as Erica shakily brought herself to her feet.

"Keep her busy," Everen said to Erica, nodding at Shard. Erica weakly nodded and drew one of her daggers. She charged after Aldyn and joined the fight against Shard.

"Just like old times." Aldyn sent the girl a grin.

Erica smirked, "I'm still better than you." The two fought Shard and the tide of the fight changed. Erica and Aldyn fought incredibly well together and could probably defeat Phinx if they wanted to.

Everen smiled at the two and turned back to Jayden. She grabbed his fallen hand and closed her eyes.

Jayden was fighting a group of vicious pirates. Aldyn stood beside him with a drawn sword. In Jayden's mind, Aldyn seemed to glow like an ethereal being. Her hair fell in waves, not the jagged layers she had currently. The Aldyn beside him was lighter than the girl Everen knew. She was laughing in the danger and smiled brightly.

Everen knew the real Aldyn would have been the girl he pictured if her life hadn't been so cruel.

Jayden turned to Aldyn. "Aldyn, I-" she turned to him with an angelic smile. Then she froze as a sword stabbed through her chest.

"Aldyn!" He yelled. She gasped and her eye glazed over. She fell to the deck. Jayden sliced through the pirates and caught her. He yelled her name again, but he was helpless as she bled out in her arms. He'd failed her.

The pirates closed around the grieving boy. "I'll kill you all!" Jayden screamed at the pirates, gently setting Aldyn's body down. He raised his sword, and his eyes were dark and without mercy.

The kindness and laughter that Everen knew was gone from him. Aldyn was everything to him, her death broke him, even if it wasn't real. Jayden raised his sword, prepared to slaughter the pirates. Everen rushed towards him, she didn't want him trapped in the mental prison any longer. She wrapped her arms around his chest and closed her eyes tightly.

Everen opened her eyes in reality holding Jayden's hand. He opened his eyes and met hers. "Thank you." He said softly, sitting up. Everen nodded. He looked around for Aldyn, who was pushing Shard back with aggressive powerful swings of her sword. His face faded into relief when he saw she was alive and already free.

Everen turned to her last two friends, painfully remembering Auks. She touched Phinx's forehead.

Everen opened her eyes in Phinx's mind. The shattered Featheren held Auk's dead body. Phinx shook with hysterical sobs. The world around the sisters was fractured like a broken mirror. The fractures shifted and changed constantly, and Everen worried about what that meant for Phinx's mind.

"That arrow should've hit me," Phinx cried. "Sisters stick together. Why Auks? Why did you have to save me? How can I go home without you and say that I failed?"

"Phinx," Everen whispered to the Featheren warrior, not wanting to prolong the Featheren's agony any longer. "Wake up." She whispered touching the Featheren's shaking shoulder.

Everen started to panic when nothing happened, they didn't wake up. Everen tried again, "Phinx!" She yelled, "Wake up, this isn't real!"

"My fault. My mind. My death. My time." The Featheren shouted as she stood, Auks' body turning to ash and grey feathers. The Featheren faced her and Everen's heart stopped. "My fault. My mind. My death. My time!" She repeated over and over again.

Phinx's eyes were solid white, and her hair floated and flickered like fire. Aldyn, Erica, and Jayden hadn't seen her when she'd pulled them out, but for some reason Phinx did. "Do not tell me what is real when you saw me hold her body!"

"Shard trapped you in your mind, please Phinx, let me help you!" Everen pleaded.

"I don't want your help!" Phinx roared, her thunderous voice echoing across her mind.

Before her eyes, Phinx flickered like fire. For a second, it looked like she was two. The second figure had glowing yellow skin, solid bright blue eyes, red hair, and wings made of blue and white fire.

"PHINX!" Everen yelled and leaped for her friend. Her fingertips caught Phinx's wrist, and she concentrated harder than ever before.

When she opened her eyes, she was kneeling beside the Featheren. Phinx shifted and sat up carefully. "Are you okay?" She asked.

Phinx scoffed quietly, "I'm alive." It didn't sound like an affirmative. Everen's heart broke a bit more.

"I'm sorry." She whispered.

Phinx looked away, "It's not your fault." And barely even out loud she added, "It's mine."

Phinx turned and her eyes narrowed on Shard, who was fighting Aldyn, Erica, and Jayden. "Oh, she's mine." She snarled and jumped to her feet.

"Phinx!" Everen called.

"Drop it Everen, save Nathan, I'll deal with Shard."

Shard didn't see Phinx coming as she fought Erica, Aldyn, and Jayden. She managed to catch Erica's leg with her blade and the girl cried out as she fell to the ground. Aldyn stabbed angrily at her, and Shard dodged, slashing Aldyn across the cheek. Aldyn gasped as she stepped back, letting Jayden charge.

Before Jayden could follow through, Phinx landed between them, forcing him off balance and dropping his sword. Jayden yelled at her, but she ignored him, instead unsheathing her claws and lunging for Shard's throat.

Shard grunted in pain when Phinx stabbed her in the shoulder, barely missing her arteries. She retaliated by stabbing her dagger through Phinx's wing, making the Featheren yell in agony.

Everen tore herself away from the fight and focused on Nathan, who was still knocked out from Shard's curse and lying on the ground next to her.

She brushed his hair off his forehead with her fingers and closed her eyes.

Nathan was standing on a small island of light. Darkness surrounded him. He was completely alone and isolated.

"Nathan." Everen breathed, feeling tears gather in her eyes. She walked towards him. He was crying softly, making Everen wonder what was in his nightmare land that she didn't see. She gently hugged him. "I'm here, I'm always here and I always will be." She whispered as she closed her eyes, wondering if he would remember her words when he awoke.

Nathan opened his eyes and met Everen's. "Everen?" He asked.

Everen leaned closer to him. "What?" She answered softly.

He hesitated, then shook his head, "Nothing. We have to deal with Shard." Everen agreed and helped him stand. "What happened?" He asked.

"Shard used some sort of twisted magic to trap us in our nightmares, I pulled the others out, they're fighting her right now." She explained.

Nathan smiled slightly, but it was weak. "Let's take her down."

The two drew their respective weapons, Everen gathered her magic, and he notched an arrow in his bow, pulling it back and sending it flying towards the woman.

The shaft embedded itself in Shard's shoulder and the woman stumbled. Nathan cursed; he'd aimed for her head. He threw his bow down and drew a short sword, joining the others in the mess of a fight, with Everen on his heels.

Somehow, Shard was able to hold her own against them, making Everen realize just how powerful the woman was. She dodged Phinx's claws, Aldyn and Jayden's swords, Nathan's Elven blade, Erica's daggers, and Everen's magic.

"You may have escaped my magic, but your fear is still real. Fear is the killer of strength. Fear is the poisoner of life. It is the greatest weakness, and why I'll always prevail." Shard taunted and Aldyn's grip shook.

"You are powerless here," Aldyn yelled angrily.

"Am I? Then tell me I am wrong. You are consumed with guilt for the countless lives that have been lost around you." Aldyn paled and stepped back. Jayden stepped forward to attack and she turned her malicious glare to him. "You fear losing the ones you care about, you care too much and too deeply; it will ruin you!" Jayden stepped back. Shard turned her gaze to Erica. "You fear being worthless, you know you will never be enough!" Erica's eyes widened and her hands shook. Shard turned to Nathan. "You fear being alone, losing everyone who you hold dear." Shard turned to Everen last. "And you, you are too angry and bitter to let yourself heal."

"You don't know me!" Everen yelled.

"I don't?" Shard questioned, "I know your mother abandoned you and your father because her throne was more important. I know you hated your life on Earth yet were willing to do anything to get back to it. I know you are desperate for answers and terrified to step up, even though you might be the only one strong enough to do it."

"How do you know that?" Everen demanded.

"Magic can reveal much, and I make sure to know my enemies before fighting them," Shard answered.

"We won't let you use magic to hurt anyone else," Nathan said.

"Can you really stop me?" Shard laughed. "You already failed. How many more will die before you accept that?" Phinx saw red and would've charged Shard if Everen hadn't held her back.

"We will not stop until you are beaten," Everen answered coldly. Magic coursed through her veins. She felt the power surging through her.

Everen floated off the ground. Her hair lifted above her head. Gold dust swirled faster and faster around her and her eyes glowed white. "Your reign is over, Shard." Her voice was unnatural and cold. Nathan tried to reach for her, but she rose above his grasp.

Everen spread her arms and the power escaped her. White light blinded them as Shard screamed.

The flash faded. Everyone lay unconscious on the ground. Nathan and Aldyn were the first to stir and stared in shock at Everen.

The Elven girl lay on bare ground with gold dust floating around her. The dust dispersed and Nathan ran to her side, gently shaking her awake. Aldyn helped her to her feet.

"What just," Everen mumbled and looked around, her brow furrowed when she noticed Shard was gone. "What did I do?" She whispered.

"I don't know," Aldyn replied, "But Shard's gone." Everen looked around them and saw the smoke from Phinx's fire fading and creating a faint mist in the morning rays. Around them were the surviving Blackshard warriors, passed out in the dirt.

"What about them?" Nathan asked and Aldyn shrugged.

"Let the Council deal with them, they'll be here in a few hours anyway, thanks to Everen." The half-Pearling shot Everen a toothy grin.

The others groaned and the three helped them to their feet. Once Jayden was awake, Aldyn embraced him tightly. Erica looked around and knelt in the dirt. She lifted the blue book that Shard had earlier and pocketed it in her red cloak.

Shard was gone. They'd survived and stopped the Dragon Hunters. Aldyn set her hand on Everen's shoulder, and the two cousins shared a smile. Everen turned and grinned at Nathan. Jayden's arm rested on Aldyn's shoulder and Erica had a faint smirk on his lips. Phinx stood quietly beside them, the Featheren looked into the sky and Everen followed her lead.

The sun rose, with it a new day and hope for Eldenvine.

Chapter Nineteen: A Mother's Choice.

"We will always remember her." Nathan finished softly, his voice breaking with emotion. Everen couldn't hold back her sobs and her shoulders shook. Aldyn wrapped Everen into a hug and supported the grieving girl. Erica's eyes were glassy, and she wiped them with the back of her hands every few minutes.

Phinx hadn't spoken a word since the battle with Shard. Tears silently fell down her cheeks. Her skin was pale and her eyes sunken and empty. She seemed drained of all life and hope and radiated anguish. Auks had meant everything to Phinx, she was her responsibility, her little sister, her best friend. Phinx couldn't imagine life without her. And now she had to.

They were quiet as Phinx stepped towards her sister. The desperate, denying, emotional wreck of the night before was gone. Only a hollow shell remained of the Featheren warrior. Phinx slowly kneeled to lift her sister's body. Her fingertips brushed Auks' forehead and she closed her sister's stormy grey eyes. She gently set one arm under Auks' neck and the other beneath her knees so she could carry her. Phinx took several steps and then launched herself into the sky with her powerful wings. Within moments the Featheren was gone from sight, hidden in the white clouds.

"I'm so sorry Auks," Everen mumbled she couldn't help but take some blame for the girl's death.

Aldyn stiffened and turned to her cousin. She grabbed Everen on the shoulders tightly.

"You did nothing. Auks made her decision." Aldyn said firmly. She looked at the others and her gaze lingered on Jayden's. "We all made our decisions."

"Where are we going to go next?" Jayden asked and Nathan turned to Everen.

"We don't have to if you don't want to." He said softly.

"I don't. I'm not going after her, she never came for me." Everen's arms were crossed, and she was scowling.

"If you go back to Agatha and go to Earth, you'll never know why she left." He reminded her. Everen hesitated, and her resolve faltered.

"Fine, but she is going to answer for everything," Everen promised angrily.

Nathan nodded, "She will."

"I take it we're going to Elvara?" Erica asked.

Everen nodded, "We're going to Elvara."

Nathan turned. "it's about a day's walk northeast. Once we find a trail, I'll know the way like the back of my hand."

The walk to Elvara was emotionally painful. Everen was seething about her mother, and she was devastated about losing Auks. However, Aldyn and Jayden were good at keeping things lighthearted. They shared stories of the years they spent adventuring and at that moment, Jayden was telling the others about when he and Aldyn stole Cat's Eye's treasure.

"So, Aldyn charged him with a broken sword, and he was so shocked he tripped backward off the dock." He laughed. Aldyn gently elbowed him in the ribs.

"If you hadn't spent so long messing with the ropes, I wouldn't have needed to attack." Aldyn pointed out.

"I almost felt bad for him, except for the whole capturing us part," Jayden added. Nathan and Erica laughed, while Everen managed a smile.

"When Aldyn and I were in Ralaji as kids, we found a group of young Featherens sparring in the mud. Logically, we took bets. I learned two things that day, never bet against Aldyn in a fight, and never join the matches." Erica informed them and Aldyn laughed.

"I think it's obvious to never bet against Aldyn. I've seen her gamble her eyepatch off and win all the money on the table." Nathan informed them.

"I never actually lost my eyepatch," Aldyn interjected.

"You almost lost your sword while gambling in Klondor, multiple times." Jayden reminded her, and she elbowed him again.

"At least I didn't accidentally fall off the plank and almost drown!" Aldyn shot back. Jayden smirked.

"Who said I accidentally fell off the plank?" Jayden asked with a raised eyebrow, "Maybe I wanted you to come rescue me." Aldyn crossed her arms and scowled at him. He laughed.

They crossed most of the way to the capital before they had to set up camp. It had been a long day, and everyone passed out except Aldyn who took the first watch.

Everen's dreams were surprisingly peaceful. She dreamt of Auks. Auks was flying through the clear sunny skies of Ralaji, over the grassy mountains dotted with wildflowers. The Featheren was laughing and diving through the air. Her strawberry-blond hair danced in the wind and her stormy grey eyes were bright with happiness. The image simultaneously broke Everen's heart and made her smile. Auks seemed so carefree and full of life. She felt a stab of guilt. Auks should've been with them, laughing and arguing with Phinx. As she watched, she felt that somehow Auks had sent her the dream so her last memory of her would be happy.

"Goodbye Auks," Everen whispered. She blinked awake with fresh tears on her cheeks.

"What was that Everen?" Aldyn asked from a few feet away.

"Nothing," Everen whispered as she wiped her eyes. She would never forget Auks, the Featheren who had been a friend to everyone.

The five ate a quick breakfast of bread and smoked bacon. Their supplies were running low because the last place they'd restocked was Featherwind. The group was quiet as they made their way through the rest of Elvara. They finally reached the capital just before midday.

The capital of Elvara was called Carikan, and it was built in the forest canopy out of massive platforms and connecting bridges. Everen was grateful that she wasn't scared of heights. The way into the city was through enormous spiral staircases carved into the trees. As Nathan led them up, Everen noticed that Jayden was tightly gripping the balcony. He looked a bit pale, and she wondered if he was scared of heights.

The higher they got, the more Everen's heart raced. She was nervous and angry. In just a bit, she would be meeting her mother for the first time.

"We're here for you," Erica whispered behind her, Everen turned and smiled softly. Erica smiled back. The two of them had become decently close over the last few weeks.

After several minutes of continuous climbing, the five exited out onto a large balcony. Two men in silver armor stood before them. Full quivers hung at their backs, and they held elegant bows. Moss-green cloaks hung off their right shoulders. One had dark skin and silver eyes that looked slightly like Auks.' The other had green eyes and cream-colored skin.

"Hello, Ashbark, Owltree." Nathan greeted, stepping forward.

"Nathan Willowsar, you are with a unique group," Ashbark commented.

"Yes, these are my friends. We have to speak with Her Majesty." Nathan explained.

"Ah, of course. Go on your way." Owltree waved his hand dismissively and Nathan led them on a bridge that connected the balcony to another tree with a larger platform.

The bridge was sturdy and made of wood. Its railings were wrapped in bright green ivy that was currently blooming with white fragrant flowers. They soon reached the second tree platform and saw baskets of fruits, vegetables, flowers, and assorted goods lining the platform. Elves crowded the market, busy buying and selling the goods. Everen noticed that the most common colors were silver, green, and shades of brown and gold. Many Elves also wore armor like Ashbark and Owltree.

"NATHAN!" A voice called and ran up to them. The caller was a woman in her young forties, who wore a long white dress with a dark green cape. Her hair was light blond, streaked with grey, and her face was relieved.

"Mom!" Nathan exclaimed nervously as the woman enveloped him in a tight hug. Nathan was slightly taller than her but not by much.

"I have been so worried about you! It's been weeks since Agatha messaged me! Do you know how terrified I was? You could've at least sent a letter. I called Agatha, and she didn't know what happened! Don't you *ever* do that again!" She yelled, making her son flinch.

"I'm sorry." He apologized.

"Sorry doesn't cut it! Even the *twins* are better than that!" Nathan looked genuinely terrified. Suddenly she hugged him again, "I'm so glad you are okay."

Nathan looked relieved she wasn't going to kill him. "Would you like to meet my friends?" He asked.

"Very much." She answered.

"You already know Aldyn, and this is Everen, Erica, and Jayden." Nathan gestured to each of them.

"Pleased to meet you. I am Sharine Willowsar." She shook hands with each of them. "What are all of you doing in Elvara?"

"We are here to speak with the Queen, It's personal," Everen explained, and Sharine nodded kindly, not prying.

"I will accompany you to the palace gate, I must make sure my son doesn't disappear again." Sharine glared at him, and Nathan cowered.

Nathan expertly led them across several bridges and platforms. Everen gazed around in wonder, the city was beautiful. It was the perfect mix of nature and productivity.

The Elven palace was constructed out of a tree larger than a skyscraper. It was so tall that Everen couldn't see the top. The trunk and branches had been hollowed out to make the levels and magic kept the tree alive. Towers jutted off from the trunk and twisted upwards with roofs made of massive overlapping leaves. Balconies spiraled up the bark and were covered in emerald ivy. Lush mosh streaked the palace walls which were embedded with massive green and gold gems. Everen's jaw dropped. "My mother lives *here?*" She whispered.

Nathan grinned at her reaction, "Emrelvor is over a thousand years old. But rulers have continued to add to it. Queen Jessica, Queen Inaria's grandmother, added the massive gemstones."

Everen nodded mutely and followed him up to the golden doors at the end of the bridge. Six guards stood beside them and held spears. Nathan's mother walked up to the captain and said several words, he nodded and waved his hand. Two Elves opened the golden doors. "Once you meet with the Queen, I expect you to come home." Sharine threatened her son, before stepping back and allowing him to lead the others to go in.

Nathan led the way through the palace towards the throne room. They passed many guards in the Elven armor and men and women in elaborate clothes, who were probably part of the government system. Elvara was a constitutional monarchy with an elaborate senate.

Nathan eventually stopped at an elaborate golden door covered in emeralds. He looked at Everen, "Are you ready?" Everen swallowed. She knew she could turn back, but she didn't want to anymore. She wanted to confront Inaria, and she wanted answers.

Everen steeled her nerves, promising herself that whatever happened next, she would stay strong. "Yes." She answered and her voice didn't waver at all.

Nathan pushed open the golden doors and Everen passed him with clenched fists.

The throne room was the most beautiful part of the palace. It was large and open with sunlight streaming through tall windows. Emeralds and gold were embedded in the walls in natural designs. A long velvet moss-green carpet extended from the door.

The throne was built on a large, raised platform with two dozen guards standing beside it. It was ornately made of gold and styled to look like wood. On it, a small green cushion was mostly covered by the beautiful women who sat on it.

A delicate crown of emerald leaves and golden wires sat upon her amber waves that fell past her shoulders. She had turquoise eyes like a Cat's

Eye's with the same green flecks. She wore copper and gold jewelry and gold leaves hung from her tall pointy ears. Her skin was lightly tanned, and her face was angular. A vibrant green dress hung from her shoulders.

When Everen entered, the ongoing conversation about trade routes was immediately, silenced. "Who are you?" The Queen asked, her voice was kind but full of authority.

"Good afternoon your Majesty." Nathan stepped forward and sent her a grin. "We're sorry to interrupt the meeting but this is important."

"More important than the revelation about the Featherens?" A council member shouted.

Nathan glared at him, "Yes."

The Queen waved her hand, silencing the brewing argument, "Nathan is training for the Queen's Bow, and is one of the top students at Emerald Elite. He has spent the last month on a confidential mission. If he says this is important, it is."

Nathan nodded at her gratefully. "Thank you. We completed our mission and stopped the Dragon Hunters from causing further damage. In our travels, we came across the Featheren survivors and Cat's Eye."

"I had wondered why Queen Athala spoke of a team of children," Inaria commented.

Aldyn stepped beside Nathan, "Your majesty, while we were tracking the Hunters, we came across something serious." She hesitated, unsure how to explain and Everen took that opportunity to speak.

"She came across me. My name is Everen Thatcher, daughter of Henry and Ara Thatcher. I came to Eldenvine with magic and learned my mother was from here."

Inaria got to her feet, she was pale, and her nails were digging into the sides of her throne, but Everen wasn't finished.

"But you already know that. You abandoned your husband and daughter, and now you stand here queen!" Everen yelled, "You are not my mother, you are the woman who left!" Across the room, men and women gasped in shock and horror.

"Everen, please," Inaria said.

"No. You could've come back, you could've explained things, but you didn't." Everen's voice was bitter and cold, she spun on her heels and looked at Nathan and Aldyn. "I'm done." She said before marching out.

Nathan looked at Inaria and flinched, he'd betrayed her immensely by bringing Everen in to humiliate her. "I'm sorry." He whispered, "I thought she'd talk to you."

Inaria shook her head, "No. I'm glad you brought her, but she's right. I did fail."

To the surprise of everyone, Inaria stepped down from her throne. She made her way across the hall and passed by Aldyn, Nathan, Erica, and Jayden.

The Queen opened the golden doors and slammed them behind her, leaving the room in silence.

Everen was leaning against the wall outside the throne room. Her face was flushed, and she clenched her fists. She should've known that Inaria hadn't cared.

"Everen?" A voice called softly, and the Queen stepped through the golden doors, letting them slam behind her.

Everen jerked up and scowled, "What do you want?" She snapped.

"To explain myself." She answered.

"You have two minutes, then I'm leaving." Everen crossed her arms and waited.

Inaria swallowed, "I was banished to Earth by my uncle. There, I met your father. He helped me and we fell in love. When you were born, I was so happy." Everen tapped her fingers against her arm impatiently. "One day, when you were nearing your second birthday, the enchantress who'd banished me appeared. She begged me to return and end my uncle's reign. She could only take me. I had to return to save my people, and I've been trying to find a way back."

"You obviously didn't," Everen commented.

Inaria flinched, "No." She said, "I couldn't go back, the enchantress who knew about the path between worlds was killed shortly after returning me. Anyone else who knew how to help me wasn't powerful enough to do it."

"Eight years! You stayed here for eight years and couldn't find a single way to fix your family?" Everen exploded, "Dad said I shouldn't be angry, but he's wrong! I barely remember you; I was just a little girl!"

Inaria recoiled as though she had been slapped, "Everen, please."

"No. You may be my mother, but you didn't act like it." Everen turned away. "I just want to go home." She whispered.

A tear slipped out of Inaria's closed eyes, "Of course."

Everen glanced at her and felt a shred of guilt, "Did you want me?" She asked quietly.

"More than anything in both of the worlds. I've missed you every day." Inaria whispered.

Everen nodded slowly, "I've been trying to get home since I got here, and I think I know the way. Would you come with me?"

Inaria hesitated, "I want to."

"But your duty is here. I understand." Everen's bitter tone was gone, and all that remained was her exhaustion.

Inaria reached for her daughter, "But maybe, you could bring him here? You both could stay in the palace and Emerald Elite would accept you in a heartbeat. Even if you only wanted to visit, just don't leave."

"I have to talk to Dad, but I think I would like that. I'll talk to Grams and see if that's possible."

"Grams?" Inaria asked.

"Grams is actually a secret Mistry. She met Gramps while exploring Earth. I found out on accident when meeting Agatha." Everen explained.

"It sounds like you've been through a lot," Inaria whispered.

"Yeah," Everen thought for a moment, "We planned to go to Nathan's afterward, you could join us and listen to it all."

"I would like that."

"Everen!" Aldyn's voice called out, and the one-eyed teen ran to her cousin, "Thank Oceana! We were worried you'd left!" Inaria stepped aside as Aldyn wrapped Everen in a tight hug.

"Don't worry. I'm staying." Everen replied.

Nathan grinned at her, "Really?"

Everen nodded and let go of Aldyn, "At least for a little while. I need to work it out."

Erica nodded, "In the meantime, we have to get Nathan home before his mother comes after us." The five laughed at that and Inaria smiled softly.

Nathan knocked on the wooden door of a large house in the treetops. "Welcome to my home."

The door flung open, and five children ran out, three boys and two girls. "Nathan!" One of the girls yelled, she had waist-length golden hair and pale green eyes with sharp features.

"Now we can beat you up for causing us to worry!" One of the boys teased. He was tall and lanky, with blond spiky hair and bright green eyes. One of the other boys, who must have been his twin brother, grabbed Nathan from behind and messed up his hair.

"Lance! Leo!" The third boy scolded. He had wire glasses, grey eyes, and a tall narrow figure. His blond hair was short and pale, and he carried himself with an air of arrogance.

"Yes?" Lance answered innocently.

"That's me," Leo replied cheekily.

"I agree with the Chaos Twins." The second girl interjected. The first girl looked about ten years old, this one looked at least seventeen. Unlike the rest of her family, she wasn't tall, and she was well-built from constantly working out. She had softer features than her siblings and dark hair, which was cut dramatically short and accented her intense silver eyes.

"Hi Gen." He smiled.

"Just be glad I'm not tying you to a tree for staying away so long." She said gruffly. She hesitated for a second, before pulling her younger brother into a hug. "We missed you." She admitted.

After the siblings broke the embrace, Nathan turned back to his friends, "This is my eldest sister, Gendevia."

"Call me Gen unless you want to get stabbed." She suggested.

"My eldest brother, Archer." Archer was the boy who had chastised Lance and Leo. He nodded when his name was spoken.

"You know him because he talks like he ate a dictionary," Lance informed them.

"And you know me, the more handsome twin." Leo introduced himself, winking at Everen.

"Only if you're blind." Lance scoffed, and then lifted Erica's hand to his lips and kissed it. "My name is Lance. Mischief maker extraordinaire and the best of us." Although they were twins, Everen began to notice several major differences between them. Lance's hair was longer, and his eyes were darker while Leo was skinnier and slightly taller.

Gen rolled her eyes, "Ignore the idiots. This is our youngest sister, Liz. Or Lizzian to Mom and Dad." She set her hand on the little girl's shoulder. Liz was shy, but she managed a wave.

"Nathan!" Sharine called, rushing to embrace her son. Her husband followed her and the three hugged.

Nathan's father had brown hair, darker than Nathan's but nowhere near as dark as Gen's. He had blue-grey eyes like Archer's and had the stockier build that appeared in Gen. His skin was a slightly browner tone than his wife and children, and he carried himself with humility and kindness.

"It's good to see you, Oliver," Inaria said, stepping forward. He was one of her trade advisors and the two were good friends.

"Your Majesty, what are you doing here?" Nathan's father asked.

Inaria glanced towards Everen, "That's a long story. Why don't we go inside so we can all hear it together."

"Of course, I'll go prepare some refreshments," Sharine said, opening the door and going inside.

The group made their way to the living room and settled down. Everen took a seat on a couch with Nathan and Aldyn. Jayden joined them and Erica took a chair on the side. The twins sat next to her, cross-legged on the floor.

Oliver and Sharine brought out glasses filled with pink liquid. Everen tried it and noticed it tasted like strawberries.

"Remind me to introduce you to the different drinks and foods we have, mission food is terrible in comparison," Nathan whispered in her ear.

Inaria cleared her throat and the chattering quieted, "I think we would all like to hear what happened."

Aldyn took over, telling the story from the beginning. Erica kept interrupting her to gloss over the more violent and illegal details while Nathan put in his own hilarious comments. Jayden kept correcting them when they got overly dramatic and Everen had fun adding to the chaos.

"Red splattered onto the ground. I couldn't see and blood stained my vision." Aldyn described. Her hand waved around as she spoke dramatically, she was a good storyteller. "The cave was dark," Nathan slapped his hand over her mouth suddenly, so she wouldn't be able to tell Liz about the insane dragonettes.

"I think you had too much to drink." Everen joked, taking away Aldyn's strawberry drink. Jayden snorted and tried to cover it with a cough, while Aldyn glared at him.

After the laughter died down, Aldyn spoke nostalgically. "Remember when we met? I had no idea that we were cousins."

"Yes, I remember your sword to my throat." Everen's tone was dry as she raised her eyebrow and Erica burst out laughing.

"Of course, she did!" The sarcastic and whip-smart girl cackled.

Jayden wrapped his arm over her shoulder and grinned, "That's just Aldyn." She scowled at him and elbowed him sharply in the side, Jayden's grimace sent the others spiraling back into laughter.

"We love her for her threatening nature," Nathan added, grinning at her, and she rolled her eyes and muttered several rude phrases under her breath.

"Yes, we do." Everen agreed, she was genuinely happy. Being in Eldenvine was easy, in an odd way she'd never expected. Her friends were like a family she'd never dreamed of. Her smile faded for a second as she thought about her father. Nothing would be perfectly right without him, she needed him.

She remembered what Agatha and Less had told her, that the path between worlds could only be traveled by one with magic, but she also remembered what her mother had said. Inaria had been banished to Earth and made her way back, without her own magic.

Everen's eyes widened as she realized she was right. She could make her way through the Lost Path, she just had to trust her magic. She could take her father to Eldenvine, and she could reunite her parents.

"Everen, are you alright?" Inaria asked, she'd noticed her daughter's unusual sudden silence and was concerned.

Everen suddenly grinned widely. "I know how to get back to Earth. I'm going to see Dad again."

Chapter Twenty: The Strength of Magic.

Everen stood outside of Agatha's cottage. Fifteen days had passed since Shard's reign of terror ended. In that time, she and Less had read the journals of the old enchantress who had told them the trick to bringing others through the path. Together, the grandmother-granddaughter duo had made their way back to Earth.

It had been a very emotional reunion, and Everen would admit she'd cried a bit. Less had already explained things to him, but she told her father everything else. She told him that she was sorry for running away. She explained that she'd never intended to go to Eldenvine. She told him that she'd found her mother and that their broken family could be fixed. Not all the wounds would heal overnight, Everen still held bitterness for the eight years, but she was working on it. Forgiveness was hard, she knew Aldyn still held anger against Cat's Eye for what had happened to Jayden.

After Everen and Less had explained things to Henry, the three made their way to Eldenvine. Inaria and Henry had talked, and the two decided they would live mostly in Eldenvine with occasional visits to Earth. At the moment, Less was helping Henry move things over from the house on Earth, they would keep it for when they stayed there but otherwise would live in Emrelvor. Everen had been helping earlier, but she knew she needed to talk to Agatha. She had too many unanswered questions, and only Agatha had the answers.

Everen's knuckles rapped against the familiar dark purple door. Agatha opened it and immediately enveloped her in a hug.

"All Eldenvine owes you a debt, you saved many lives." Agatha grinned, her usual stiff mask cracking to show her joy and relief. Everen was glad that she'd been able to help but bitterly wished that it hadn't come at the cost of Auks.

"I know Aldyn already talked to you, so you know what happened," Everen said quietly, and the older woman's hug tightened.

"I know," Agatha whispered.

Everen's voice shook, "Why did she have to die?"

"Because she made a choice." Agatha replied, "Auks saved Phinx knowing it would kill her, she traded their lives." Agatha broke the hug but kept one arm around Everen. She led her inside the cottage and grabbed a mug of warm, purple-colored tea.

Everen sat down on one of the wooden chairs and slowly drank the tea. Agatha got a second mug of tea for herself and sat beside Everen, turning her chair so they were facing each other.

"How are you?" Agatha asked gently.

"Better. Auks' memorial is next month. I'm back with Dad, I have what I wanted. Everything's fixed." Everen's voice should've been elated, but it was tired and dry.

Agatha nodded, "But you're still here. Something is weighing on you." Everen looked away.

"I don't know. Something happened to Phinx, and we haven't heard from her since."

Agatha hesitated, "Phinx, is a special situation. What you observed is a rare condition called Fayra's Touch. All Featherens have a spark of fire inside them, but few can bring it out. Under great emotional strain or physical pain, the fire breaks through. It supercharges her body and allows her to create and control fire and heat. However, the Touch is dependent on her emotions which makes it unreliable and dangerous. Auks' death triggered the awakening, but it could also destroy her." Agatha explained.

"What do you mean?" Everen asked.

"I cannot tell you. The information I have already given you is dangerous. You can share it with your friends and family, but no one else can know." Agatha said.

"Why?"

"In the Sea and Sky war, the Featherens massacred the Pearlings using Fayra's Touch. The carnage was so horrific, it destroyed any chance of reconciliation between the nations. The Pearlings are already furious that the Featherens are alive and in hiding, if they find out about a Fayra Touched Featheren, they will take it as an act of war and will demand her execution."

Everen paled, "I will keep it quiet." She promised.

"Good. Now about your second question, we have learned little about the woman who called herself Shard. We know nothing about who she was before Blackshard, and it will be almost impossible to learn after you defeated her. You already know that she has been secretly murdering dragons and stealing dragon eggs for the last ten years. In the last year, her group had grown, which allowed her to make bigger strikes. She had planned to turn the captured dragonettes into a powerful army that she would use to conquer Eldenvine." Agatha explained, "The only thing we have learned about her personal life is that she has a living child."

"What?" Everen knocked over her mug of hot tea into her lap. "Scales and bones!" she cursed, using Aldyn's favorite phrase as the tea burned her.

Agatha smiled slightly at Aldyn's phrase and handed Everen a napkin. "Yes, Shard had a child, who I doubt will stay missing for long. They will want vengeance for what you did." Her tone was ominous and Everen frowned.

"Is Shard actually dead?"

Agatha hesitated, "I am not sure. I would like to believe your magic destroyed her, but I've lived too long to believe it. She should be, but I can't be certain."

Everen clenched her fist and glared at the wooden table. She hated that woman; Shard had caused Aldyn to lose her family. She had killed dozens of dragons and she had killed Auks.

"If Shard isn't dead, I promise we will bring her in," Everen growled.

"We don't need to worry about her right now. However, I will make sure Hecktra, Sace, and Krissa find out for sure." Agatha promised.

Everen smiled faintly at her mentor, "Thanks."

Agatha smiled. "You are welcome. Over this last month, you have become confident and powerful, I am proud of you."

"Thank you." She whispered, and her smile faded into a thoughtful frown, "How did I even defeat her?"

Agatha's face darkened, "Your magic flowed without your active control, if you were anyone else, I wouldn't believe it. You know that your power is unique. The last one who had your potential was Mistic herself. Magic is like emotions, it can be controlled, but it can also control you. Few magic wielders are at risk of falling to their magic, but your power makes you exceptionally susceptible. You will need to practice and focus to prevent it from ever happening. Less, Hecktra, and I will help you train so you won't have to worry about losing control." Agatha explained. Everen trusted Agatha, but she felt that the older woman wasn't telling her everything, so she made a mental note to research the dangers of powerful magic.

"I should have time to practice in the next few weeks, I'll send you a message."

"Good." Agatha nodded her head. Everen finished her tea and stood up.

"Oh, I almost forgot," Everen said, turning back to Agatha. Everen opened her leather satchel on her waist. "Here." She handed a navy book covered in silver spirals to Agatha.

"What is this?" Agatha asked, holding the book lightly.

"The magic book Shard was using," Everen replied. "She wasn't very experienced and only used it on us once." Agatha's face shifted into a frown as she leafed through the book.

"I will look into it," Agatha said, still frowning.

"Thank you for all your help." Everen replied, "I have to go now, Aldyn is waiting. We have a new friend to meet." Everen smiled mysteriously, and Agatha raised her brow.

"I'll see you again Everen Elvecrown." Everen made a face at the title and Agatha laughed kindly, "Right, Everen Thatcher." Everen smiled, she may be the new heir of Elvara, but at heart, she was her father's daughter and a girl from Earth...

Firex heard a shout from down the hall, and she flew out the window to see the commotion. Her eyes adjusted to the bright sun; a figure was flying lopsided towards the palace. Her eyes focused. She recognized her close friend and cousin Phinx, but something was wrong. Her hair was tangled with twigs and dried blood smeared her cheek and nose. Her once silver breastplate was covered in mud. Her legs were scratched up and laced with blood, as though she had dived through a forest. Phinx's feathers were matted and bent like she had come out of a fight and not bothered to brush them. Firex frowned.

Phinx was holding something in her arms, and when she came closer, Firex gasped and her eyes watered. Firex landed on the mountainside and ran to meet her cousin. She heard the beating of wings behind her and saw Robin land on the ground. His face filled with hope as he ran out to meet Phinx.

"Wait! Robin, wait!" Firex cried, seconds too late. Phinx touched down in front of them, and Robin caught sight of Auks. Her stormy grey eyes were glazed, and an arrow pierced her chest, close to her heart. Firex kneeled beside her cousin and pulled out the arrow, it was covered in dried Fire Bane. She snapped the arrow with her fist, careful not to let the poison touch her skin.

"Auks!" Robin cried in desperation, as Phinx dropped to the ground from exhaustion. Phinx had flown from the southern coast of Elvara to Ralaji without stopping while carrying her dead sister. Robin caught Auks, but her grey wings lifelessly hit the ground. He let out a soft sound, like a sob, only more broken. Robin traced her cheek with a shaking hand, brushing her strawberry blond hair out of her face. He leaned down and gently kissed her forehead. "Please, don't leave me." He whispered.

If Auks hadn't just died, Firex would've immediately demanded Phinx's money, the two had bet an absurd amount of gold on Auks' secret boyfriend, along with Hawk, Kasia, and Wren. Phinx had thought it was Raverick and Firex thought it was Robin. But it was no time for settling bets. Firex helped Phinx move to give him room and Phinx fell against her, sobbing.

Firex heard shouts from the palace and looked up to see Athala fly out of one of the towers. She was followed directly after by her husband Feathron.

Athala dove towards them and stumbled when she saw Auks. Tears fell from her eyes and the strong woman broke as she reached for her daughter.

Feathron landed solemnly beside his grieving wife and gently set his hand on her shoulder. Phinx turned away from her parents and cried into Firex's shoulder. "It was my fault." She whispered.

Firex's blood turned cold at Phinx's words. Phinx continued, "She took that arrow for me, if she hadn't, she'd be alive." Firex's eyes glanced over Auks, and she realized Phinx was right. Small purple veins lit up around Auks' eyes and her pale skin was practically translucent. The poison had been quick, near enough to her heart to not drag out the process. Also, Auks had already been weakened by Fire Bane before, so her body wouldn't have been able to slow the poison.

When Athala had been pregnant, the Queen had been caught in a conflict with Pearling spies. She'd managed to exterminate the invaders, but in the fight, she'd been hit with a laced spear. Featheren healers were able to burn the poison out of her, but not before it had affected Auks. When the princess was born, everyone in Ralaji knew the effect the Fire Bane had wrought. For a Featheren, Auks had been weak, and everyone except her knew it.

Firex wished that she'd trained Auks harder. She wished she had pushed the girl to make up for the lack of physical strength with hard work. There were many things they should've done better, and now Auks suffered for it.

Featherens were trained since infancy to control their claws, but for the first time in years, Firex lost control. She clenched her fists, and her heartbreak and rage unsheathed them. She felt a hand on her shoulder, she looked up to see Robin who was gazing at Auks with an expression of pure agony.

For the first time in her life, she understood him. Robin was unique among Featherens. He was calmer and quieter and rarely got into fights. He and Auks were the closest of best friends, she was his other half. Firex couldn't completely comprehend his pain, but a surge of murderous fury flooded her. Auks had been Firex's younger cousin, basically her baby sister. Someone had stolen her life. Whoever had killed Auks better be dead, or they would wish they were by the time she was through with them.

Firex returned her attention to Phinx, who still leaned against her, and she felt a flash of dread. Auks' death would hit Phinx the hardest, it could even break her. Phinx was known for being stronger than anyone their age, and even stronger than some of the elder warriors, but Firex knew how unstable she could be.

Each Featheren's power came from deep inside them, from their deep, fiery, emotional cores. They had to be stronger than it or risk losing themselves to destruction. In desperate battles, or when they lost close friends, some Featherens would break, sending them down a spiraling path with no return.

Firex silently prayed to Fayra that she wouldn't lose Phinx as well. "Phinx?" She asked quietly. The Featheren raised her gaze to Firex.

Phinx's glassy brown eyes glowed with gold and flickered like flames. Firex's heart broke again, and tears flowed down her cheeks harder. She turned her head away and her shoulders shook. Firex hadn't just lost Auks. She'd lost Phinx as well.

Epilogue: (A Few Days Later - Calestia)

Everen and Aldyn walked along the woodland path into the center of Calestia. It hadn't taken them long to travel from Agatha's thanks to her magic. Towards the center of the land was the capital, Jewelestrica. Everen looked around, Erica had told her Calestia was the most beautiful place on Eldenvine, and she was right. All the trees either blossomed or glowed with emerald leaves. Large red toadstools nestled in the rich moss over golden bark and the sky above was a brighter blue than even over Ralaji.

"I wonder what Cestrys are like," Everen commented, turning to Aldyn, who was walking several steps ahead of her.

"They are known for their lighthearted nature. Many of the Calestic can change their sizes at will, which makes finding them difficult. They are the most peaceful group of people on Eldenvine and have managed to stay out of most of the wars." Aldyn responded with a shrug. "I've only met a few, last time was before Jayden and I were separated."

Everen nodded and focused on the woods again as they continued walking. Vibrant evergreens were spread among the grand oaks that shaded the ground with darker hues. Bright emerald-tinted light came down through the massive leaves and gave the soil an odd glow. Everen had noticed that the trees were almost unnatural in their beauty. Tiny gold speaks drifted in the filtered light around them, drifting away from the cousins' touch.

The two girls came to a tall elaborate gate at the end of the overgrown wide dirt path. It was crafted of golden vines and delicate detailed leaves. As Everen and Aldyn neared the gate, two beautiful dragonesses appeared out of thin air.

"Welcome to Jewelestrica!" A tall silver and rose-colored dragon greeted in a melodic voice. Everen was startled, and Aldyn had instinctively drawn her sword.

The dragoness laughed kindly, a beautiful sound like bells. "Magic makes our words sound in your native tongue."

Everen nodded mutely and Aldyn returned her sword to its sheath. "What brings you here travelers?" The other one asked, her blue scales were like cut gems and they glinted in the late morning sun. Purple splotches like watercolor patterned her scales. Just like her first dragon encounter, Everen was shocked by the two dragons' sheer size, both were almost two stories tall.

"We are here searching for a boy named Maximus," Aldyn answered and Everen noted a hint of anger in her voice. Aldyn's hatred of dragons had shrunk significantly after Shard revealed her involvement in the burning of Cedar, but Aldyn was still tense around the scaled creatures.

"The prince?" The rose silver dragoness raised her brow and shared a look with the blue one.

"I have no idea. He probably looks like me, and he is half-Elve and half-Pearling. I really need to speak to him." Aldyn's tone carried a threat and Everen became nervous, she didn't want to get caught up in the chaos if Aldyn started a fight.

"Of course, you can speak with him." The silver one smiled kindly. "My name is Silver Rose; I am a Stone Strike who was raised in Calestia. Dream Hue and I guard the main entrance of Jewelestrica." Dream Hue raised her wing in greeting, the sunlight caught the scales and they glittered.

Silver Rose looked at Everen's inquisitive expression and smiled. "The Queen bestowed some of her magic on Dream Hue and me. It gives us our unusual beauty, and our ability to speak. She is our queen, very literally." She explained.

"Now shall we lead you to Monartha the Fair? She will know where Maximus is." Dream Hue asked. Everen and Aldyn nodded nervously, and Everen wondered again if they should have brought the others for backup.

At their answer, Sliver Rose placed her talon in the middle of the vines. Suddenly the gate swung open with a blast of wind.

Inside the gates was a land even more stunning than the rest of Calestia. Everen felt her breath go away and heard Aldyn gasp quietly beside her. Inside the golden gates were dozens of arches of flowering vines. The arches formed over a cobblestone path that led into the center of the capital. The sweet smells of a million flowers filled Everen's nose and she was thankful she hadn't inherited her father's sensitivity towards pollen. She looked up and saw many colored glass orbs hanging from trees. Inside them were small swirling lights like a jar of fireflies.

"Wow," Everen whispered.

"Yeah, wow." Aldyn agreed as they followed the two dragonesses. They followed the path for a while until they came to a pavilion that seemed popular because it was surrounded by Cestrys. The pavilion was supported by thin wood pillars with pale pink flower vines growing on them. A crosshatched fence made a low wall between the pillars and a curtain of white and pink flowers drooped over the back. A hedge lay right beyond it with a path going through it.

When they came close to the pavilion Everen got a good look at the beings who surrounded it. The Cestrys had skin that glowed softly and had large butterfly wings that grew out of their backs. The pavilion they were at was surrounded by female Cestrys, who mostly wore elaborate dresses made of flowers, jewels, and beautiful fabrics. Everen also spotted tiny Cestrys flying around them as well, and she remembered that Cestrys could change their size.

"Your Majesty, there are two outsiders who wish to speak with you." Silver Rose announced. The Cestry crowd quieted and parted, revealing a tall Cestry who sat on a golden flower-covered chair in the pavilion. She had raven black hair streaked with vibrant orange that hung to her calves. Her wings were large and resembled a monarch butterfly's and she had glittering orange eyes.

The Queen barely needed a second to make her decision. "Come." She ordered, "We will discuss this matter in the hedges." She stood up and beckoned the girls with a flick of her wrist. The other Cestrys bowed immediately and made their way to disperse.

However, before Aldyn could speak, a gold-feathered Featheren rushed forward. "Your Majesty," She started, sounding panicked. The cousins glanced at each other with identical faces of shock. Although they knew Featherens were alive, the survivors were few and hidden in Ralaji.

"Astia, I will be discussing this matter in private," Monartha said firmly, but the Featheren refused to back down. Everen noticed that every Featheren she had encountered had the same stubborn streak, she wondered if it was characteristic of all Featherens and if it was part of why they had fallen to the Pearlings.

"My Queen we do not know if we can trust them. Please let me accompany you, I will defend you with my life." Astia insisted.

Monartha sighed. "Astia, how many times have we spoken about this? Calestia is a place of peace, not war."

"What is a Featheren doing here?" Everen interjected.

Monartha turned to her with a surprised expression, "For a long time I assumed Astia was the last of her kind, my late husband found her as an infant in the ashes of Ralaji. I adopted her into our magic, using it to save her life and give her unique power. Silver Rose and Dream Hue also received the same treatment, for thousands of years the king or queen of Calestia has had this power." Monartha explained.

"We even have an Elve here; Moonshine is very shy though," Astia added.

"Now, I have something important to discuss. Astia, you are excused." Monartha said sternly. Astia bowed respectfully and walked away, although her tense wings revealed her displeasure. Monartha sighed as she turned back to the cousins with sadness in her eyes.

"I know who you are and why you came." The Queen said, cutting directly to the point.

"How?" Aldyn asked, with a flicker of surprise flashing across her face.

"The ruler of Calestia has a direct link to magic, and over time I have learned to feel and sense things. The second I saw you; I knew your intent, relationships, and reasons for being here." She explained vaguely. Strangely, Aldyn's cheeks pinked at the Queen's words, and Everen wondered what it was about.

After a second, Aldyn asked, "Then you know I want to speak to Maximus. Can you lead us to him?"

Monartha nodded solemnly and signaled for them to follow her as she walked deeper into the massive garden. Aldyn suddenly froze and Everen's heart dropped.

"Are you okay?" She asked quietly, squeezing Aldyn's hand gently.

"I'm," She hesitated, "Just nervous. He's my brother and doesn't even know I exist."

"I'll be right here," Everen reassured her. Aldyn nodded and the two followed Monartha into the hedges.

They soon came to a single-story circular pavilion. It was open air with white pillars that supported a slate-shingled roof. Flowering vines had overgrown the pillars and formed into natural archways. A small cobblestone path came out from the hedges up to the pavilion.

A boy with tousled light brown hair stood on the path. In one hand he held a sword, and he was practicing forms with it. He was good with the blade, but Everen could tell he didn't have the discipline necessary to master it. His strikes were light and dramatic, instead of focused and firm, like Aldyn's.

He wore a loose long-sleeved cream shirt with navy pants. On his feet, he wore short worn leather boots and his hair curled at the nape of his neck.

An empty scabbard hung from his belt that was made of bronze and high-quality leather.

"Max, some people have come to speak with you," Monartha announced softly, her voice had an undertone of sadness that she had previously kept hidden. Everen felt a stab of guilt, knowing her actions would cause a divide between the mother and the boy she'd raised as her own.

"Fine," Max responded and sheathed his sword. He grinned at the three as he walked over to them. When he reached them, he casually crossed his arms and raised an eyebrow. He was a lot taller than Aldyn and his blue eyes glinted with constant mischief. He had a constant grin and freckles across his cheeks. He looked at Everen and Aldyn, seeming faintly surprised like he had been expecting someone else.

Aldyn was pale as she stepped forward, but she somehow stayed strong and met the boy's gaze.

"Who are you?" Maximus asked, frowning slightly with concern.

"I'm your sister."

A Brief Guide To Eldenvine:

Eldenvine is an ancient realm, as such, magic flows throughout it. Pure, raw magic is Gleamaric, which is refined into the seven branches of magic.

Mistic: The magic technique discovered and first practiced by Lady Mistic. Wielders are Mythean females called Mistrys. Mistica is the land of Mistic; however, it was long abandoned after the War of Magic, (two thousand years prior), in which Mistic was outlawed and Mistrys were persecuted. Before they were illegalized, Mistica was governed by the current head Mistry, and her best apprentice, who would inherit the position.

Elderic: The brother magic to Mistic. It was founded by Lady Mistic's brother Alder, after she had already formed her branch. Wielders are Mythean males called Elders. The Elders protect Eldenvine and work to keep order and the laws, from their capital Alderen in Eldersa (Land of Elderic). The Elders are governed by the Elder Ring, a group of sixteen experienced Elders with equal power.

Featheric: Ralaji is the land of Featheric, inhabited by the Featherens, Firens, Northbirds, Boneflyers, and Sky Giants. The Featherens made up the vast majority of the population and they were wiped out in the Great War against the Pearlings, when Ralaji was burned in the Great Fire, on the Night of a Thousand Tears. The last ruler of Ralaji was Deathwing, a woman famous for wearing armor made of rare black metal.

Oceanic: Pearlings, Wavens, Aquanians, and Deep-Sea Dwellers are the wielders of Oceanic. Islaria is the land of Oceanic, which includes the massive Pearling Bay. The Pearlings and Featherens have hated one another for thousands of years, leading to several wars and the eventual extinction of the Featherens. The current rulers of Islaria are Queen Aquanda and her husband Sharkir, they have a son Jazon, and a daughter, Lana.

Dragic: The magic of the dragons. Dragaria is home to the twelve warring tribes, each with its own queen or king. The twelve tribes are Forest Flights, Fire Flights, Crystal Strikes, Stone Strikes, Sun Bringers, Star Bringers, Wave Riders, Dawn Riders, Frost Furies, Wind Furies, Storm Callers, and Shell Walkers. Dragic magic is one of the least used magics due to the constant warfare in its land. Most knowledge on the branch has been destroyed. Each dragon tribe has a leader who takes the throne through single combat.

Calestic: Calestic magic is the magic of the Cestrys who reside in Calestia. They are known for being incredibly beautiful, able to change their size at will, and their unique magic which creates glamours and illusions. Calestic magic is also the most adept at healing and neutralizing poisons. The land is currently ruled by Queen Monartha.

Elvic: Elvic is the magic of the Elves and Nightrians (The Dark Elves). The land of Elvic is Elvara. This magic specializes in the control and manipulation of nature. Enchanters and enchantresses usually collaborate closely with Queen Inaria Elvecrown, who overthrew her uncle, King Sonoson, after her return from exile, eight years prior.

Geography of Eldenvine: Mytharica is the largest landmass and only known continent of Eldenvine. The continent is divided into Wryrom, Elvara, Islaria, Eldersa, Mistica, Calestia, Mythea, and Ralaji. Wryrom is the region of the Dark Woods, a lawless land with no recognized government and a small population. It is full of outlaws, runaways, and wild beasts. Dragaria is a massive island off of Mytharica's western coast and it is considered a death sentence to journey there due to the ongoing war. Klondor is a group of small islands run by merchants, traders, and pirates. Located southeast of Mytharica, it is currently ruled by Cat's Eye the Pirate King. Vlarcia is to the far north of Mytharica and is inhabited by the reclusive Vikings, who pillage ships that travel too near their borders. Mythea is filled with dozens of small villages and kingdoms, including but not limited to, Wolfmoon, Crownthorne, Pine Village, Oak City, Ventusria, Claw Village, and Dawnbreaker. Each small city/kingdom of Mythea is self-governed. Wryrom, Klondor, Mythea, and Vlarcia are all magicless lands, meaning they do not have specific magic connected to them and therefore have much fewer magic wielders.

Acknowledgements:

I started writing this in creative writing class during Covid while I was in the seventh grade. However, the idea was much older than it. When I was little, I loved to create stories in my mind, and I had a crazy imagination. Featherens are based on my childhood dream to fly as a superhero. I was in fourth grade, or even younger, when I came up with the love story between an Elven prince turned pirate and a mermaid-like creature called a Pearling. The entire world grew from there. I'd given up on the story, literally throwing the pages in the back of my closet. I ignored it for years and had practically forgotten it, until that class.

Earlier that year, I had gotten Jade, my precious tortoise, as my pet. I remembered this story and I decided to recycle it, including some aspects of tortoises. I gave it a new life, and dare I say it, a beautiful one. Eldenvine is unique from anything else I have ever written about, it's a mix of classical fantasy, dramatic plot twists, and a taste of my own creative insanity. If the little girl I used to be could see what her idea had grown into, she wouldn't recognize it, but she would love it.

It took me less than a year to finish my first draft, about a year to re-write it, and another year to finish editing it and preparing it for publishing. I spent months working on cover art and procrastinated the actual publishing longer than necessary because I wanted perfection. I know that it will never be perfect, but I don't think any author truly feels their work couldn't be improved in any way. However, I'm content with what I have created, and I'm happy to continue Eldenvine's story with the second book. As I look back on my story, I fondly remember every hour I spent hunched over my computer, burning my eyes. Eldenvine's plot, characters, and mechanics have changed countless times since I started writing, but at the core, it is still a story a little girl imagined and decided to pursue.

Now, I thank everyone who has helped me on the path to finally publishing.

My mom. She listened to me as I ranted on the car ride home from school. I highly doubt she caught everything that was coming out of my mouth, but I am endlessly grateful that she listened. She cared about me, and by extension what I was working on. The encouragement she gave me will forever stay with me.

My dad. Throughout my life, my dad has been the one to give some of the best advice I've ever heard. He's always helped me to fix things, and he's always comforted me when things didn't work out. I think one of the most memorable ways my dad helped me with my book is how he literally saved it when I accidentally broke my flash drive. He gave me the biggest hug ever and asked our neighbor for help. He was very good with engineering and had the power tools to literally rebuild the flash drive. (Thank you so much, Mr. Nathan!) My flash drive was saved, along with the only copy of my book.

Afterward, Dad taught me how to use One Drive, so I would never have that happen again. My dad is always there for me no matter what.

My brother, Eli. Whenever my writing drained me out or I was stressed, my brother would get me to watch Clone Wars with him. I love watching shows with him because we always end up laughing as we yell at the characters on the screen. He's the best little brother in the whole world and the best person to geek out about Greek mythology, Star Wars, DC, or Marvel with.

My sister, Evalina. I'm so grateful for my little sister. Although we get on each other's nerves, we stick together like glue. She loves reading almost as much as I do, and I love sharing my favorite books with her. I remember her hugs, smiles, and kindness that she seemed to radiate. Thank you Leens for keeping me going!

All of my friends, there are so many of you, and if I tried to write a paragraph for everyone, it would be longer than the actual book. Thank you for everything, feedback, hugs, giving me the rest of your coffee/protein drink (Caylin!), obsessive shippers, and a disturbing amount of simping over Aldyn... (You know who you are). To Lacey and Amber, I remember our Nachos and Chacos Creative Writing Club back in seventh grade, where were shared ideas and encouraged each other. To Jess, my best friend to Mars and back, since the SIXTH GRADE! We wrote our books together, (And I won that bet.) To Grace, it's honestly shocking how quickly we clicked, you're my taekwondo bestie (Thanks for cheering me on at the black-belt test!) and my honorary sister, we've adopted each other at this point. To Aislyn, I couldn't have ever gotten this far without you beside me since toddlerhood. You have been and always will be my Aisy, my bestie, the Mother Goose. Thank you, Ais, love you.

Shoutouts: Aunt Cheryl and Uncle Dan, thank you Aunt Cheryl for reading and giving me editing advice! Sam's mom, Laura Peterson a fellow writer who helped me a lot with finalizing this! Random people who read my book over my shoulder, your actions made me laugh so hard. All of my AMAZING extended family, I love you Grammy, Big Papa, Mimi, Papa, Auntie Bet, Uncle Tom, and all my other awesome aunts, uncles, cousins, and others. My incredible teachers at Bear Creek, who put up with my silliness (You all helped shape me into the young woman of God I am today, thank you for everything). To Yueyang (Volleyball besties forever!) and Mia (The Queen of Sarcasm). To Matilda, Isabel, Katelyn, Cami, Lanea, and Emily. To Inara, my Apprentice. To Madeline, Eldenvine's #1 fangirl. To Marie, Sadie, Sam, Caylin, Olivia, and Izzy. (And to everyone else who has EVER been a friend to me, you aren't forgotten!) To Ayana, Sarah, Alexcia, Kaylee, Ashani, Viba, Ethan, Pierson, Josh, Jacob, Thomas, Instructor Nicholas, and everyone else at taekwondo, you all are my second family and I love you. To Matthew Aussem, Aldyn's biggest fan, and my brother in Christ (Ha! I didn't forget you!). To Ms. Freitas the librarian, for talking with me, laughing with me, and always having a smile. To all the librarians, authors, and teachers everywhere, becoming an author starts with being a reader, and you are the people who make readers, thank you.

Thank you, reader! You saw this book's potential and picked it up, I'm so grateful to you and I hope you've loved the journey.

Made in United States
Troutdale, OR
06/13/2024